Critical acclaim for Ed McBain

The Frumious Bandersnatch

'The showbiz world is not McBain's usual territory, but he's as comfortable here as in his detectives' shabby squad room. The verbal badinage is sharp, clever and – like the mechanics of Carella's investigation – always true to life' *Daily Mirror*

'An engrossing plot that will take the readers on a thrill ride through trouble. The name McBain guarantees a good read'
Good Book Guide

'Ed McBain is still as sharp as a tack. This is an up-to-the-minute, witty and clever deconstruction of today's shallow pop world' *Irish Independent*

Fat Ollie's Book

'One of the best fictional characters around . . . it's Fat Ollie who steals the show' *Daily Mirror*

'The fact that his novels, like this one, are intricately plotted and beautifully structured demonstrate his mastery of the crime form . . . That a book so late in a series can be so light and lively is a tribute to McBain's skills. He has always admired "pros" such as Wodehouse. *Fat Ollie's Book* demonstrates, once again, that he is himself a consummate professional'
Peter Guttridge, *Observer* Review

'The outcome is clever, but the greatest pleasure is the skill of the narrative' *Scotsman*

Ed McBain is one of the most illustrious names in crime fiction. In 1998, he was the first non-British author to be awarded the Crime Writers' Association/Cartier Diamond Dagger Award and he is also holder of the Mystery Writers of America's coveted Grand Master Award. *The Frumious Bandersnatch* is his latest novel in Orion paperback, and his latest novel in hardback, *Hark!*, is also available from Orion. Visit his website at www.edmcbain.com.

BY ED McBAIN

The 87th Precinct novels

Cop Hater • The Mugger • The Pusher • The Con Man
Killer's Choice • Killer's Payoff • Killer's Wedge • Lady Killer
'Til Death • King's Ransom • Give the Boys a Great Big Hand
The Heckler • See Them Die • Lady, Lady, I Did It!
The Empty Hours • Like Love • Ten Plus One
Ax • He Who Hesitates • Doll • Eighty Million Eyes • Fuzz
Shotgun • Jigsaw • Hail, Hail, the Gang's All Here
Sadie When She Died • Let's Hear It for the Deaf Man
Hail to the Chief • Bread • Blood Relatives • So Long As You
Both Shall Live • Long Time, No See • Calypso • Ghosts • Heat
Ice • Lightning • Eight Black Horses • Poison • Tricks • Lullaby
Vespers • Widows • Kiss • Mischief • And All Through the House
Romance • Nocturne • The Big Bad City • The Last Dance
Money Money Money • Fat Ollie's Book
The Frumious Bandersnatch • Hark!

The Matthew Hope novels

Goldilocks • Rumpelstiltskin • Beauty & the Beast
Jack & the Beanstalk • Snow White and Rose Red • Cinderella
Puss in Boots • The House That Jack Built • Three Blind Mice
Mary, Mary • There Was a Little Girl • Gladly the Cross-Eyed Bear
The Last Best Hope

Other novels

The Sentries • Where There's Smoke • Doors • Guns
Another Part of the City • Downtown • Driving Lessons
Candyland • The Moment She Was Gone

THE FRUMIOUS BANDERSNATCH

An 87th Precinct novel

Ed McBain

ORION

An Orion paperback

First published in Great Britain in 2004
by Orion
This paperback edition published in 2004
by Orion Books Ltd,
Orion House, 5 Upper St Martin's Lane,
London WC2H 9EA

A CIP catalogue record for this book is available
from the British Library.

Printed in Great Britain by
Clays Ltd, St Ives plc

Well, here's a big surprise!
This, too,
is for my wife,
Dragica Dimitrijevic-Hunter

The city in these pages is imaginary.
The people, the places are all fictitious.
Only the police routine is based on
established investigatory technique.

THE FRUMIOUS
BANDERSNATCH

1.

SHE CAME CRUISING downriver like the city personified, all bright lights and big bad music, banners and flags flying from bowsprits and railings, a hundred and sixty-three feet of sleek power and elegant design. It was costing Barney Loomis $6,000 to charter the yacht and its staff of twenty. The additional cost of catering food and drink for a hundred and twelve music-industry movers and shakers was close to $12,000. Add the cost of the ten-piece orchestra, and a 15% service charge, and the 8.25% city tax, and Loomis figured the launch of *Bandersnatch* would cost Bison Records something like twenty-five grand overall. But it would be worth ten times that amount if the CD jumped to the top of the charts.

The boat, or the ship, or the vessel, or whatever the people at Celebrity Yacht Cruises had called it when Loomis was negotiating for the bash, had picked up the assorted glittery guests at Pier 27 West, just off the new marina complex in the renovated Overlook Zone of the city. The boat, or the ship —

Loomis liked to think of it as a launch.

'We'll charter a *launch* for the launch!' he'd told Tamar, and she'd clapped her hands in excitement — well, hell, she was still only twenty, she reacted like a teenager more often than not.

The official *launch,* then, of the new album had started at six P.M. with cocktails on the bridge deck of the *launch* — he *loved* that pun — where bistro tables were festooned with roses that picked up the red of the mask the beast was wearing on the album cover, and where the mahogany-topped bar seemed haphazardly strewn with giveaway CDs and tapes. The covers on each version of the album showed Tamar as skimpily dressed as she was in the video that had aired simultaneously last night on MTV, VH1, BET, and WU2. Wearing a shredded white tunic that seemed to have been torn forcefully from her legs, she struggled in the clutches of a muscular black dancer wearing an oversized red mask that made him look like some sort of fire-breathing mythical beast – the Bandersnatch of the title song – who brought her close to his gaping jaws, while she tried to fend him off, creamy white breasts tumbling virtually free of her equally tattered top.

'Like in *King Kong*,' Loomis had told her.

'Like in King *who?*' she'd asked, never having seen either of the movies – well, she *was* only twenty.

A mahogany stairway swept the assembled guests down to the main deck salon where the passed hors d'oeuvres included raw oysters (even though this was already the fourth day of May, which was not an 'R' month when oysters were supposed to be safe, according to the 'Oysters "R" in Season' legend), and chanterelle-and-lobster risotto cakes with white truffle crème fraîche and chives, and salmon tartare on scallion potato chips. For dinner, there was first a mesclun salad with walnuts, Stilton, and cranberries, and then a choice of either grilled tarragon chicken or seared mustard salmon, both served with steamed asparagus. For dessert, the chef had prepared chocolate pâté with vanilla bean sauce and raspberries. Merlot and Chardonnay were served with the meal. A champagne toast was planned for later this evening, after Tamar sang the title song of the new album.

Barney Loomis was a big man, and he didn't get that way by accident. His plate was heaping full, and he demolished his dinner with obvious gusto now, listening to the chatter all around him, alert to every signal beamed from this influential crowd. For a record company mogul – he tended to think of himself as a mogul – he was dressed somewhat conservatively, wearing a mocha-colored cashmere sports coat over slacks a shade darker, a beige sports shirt open at the throat, a gold necklace showing. His hair was black and worn in a sort of shaggy-dog style, his eyes brown. He fancied a spade beard the same color as his hair but strewn with a few white whiskers that gave it a distinguished professorial look, he thought.

As the launch cruised up the River Dix, passing under the bridges that connected Isola with Calm's Point and Majesta, gliding past Cavanaugh Island and the exclusive Cavanaugh Club, and coming back inbound on the deep water range to head downtown again on the River Harb, a disc jockey began spinning songs from Tamar Valparaiso's debut album, and the talk was of nothing but *Bander-snatch* and the spectacular television video that would cause the single to leap onto the charts – Loomis hoped, he hoped. The stars and the moon were bright overhead.

The music swelled.

Several brave souls ventured out onto the dance floor.

TONIGHT WAS OLLIE'S first date with Patricia Gomez.

Man, she looked like a million bucks.

He had first admired her feminine pulchritude in uniform, the blue tailor-mades showing off her perky figure to great advantage, ah yes. But in uniform, she wore highly polished flat black rubber-soled shoes. And in uniform, her long black hair was pulled up and tucked under her cap, and she wore no lipstick or eye shadow, and she carried a nine-millimeter Glock on her right hip.

But tonight . . .

On this balmy, breezy, first Saturday night in May . . .

Patricia Gomez was wearing a tight-fitting red dress cut high on the thigh and low on the neck. And tonight, Patricia Gomez was wearing her raven hair falling to the shoulders, punctuated by dime-sized circles of red ear-rings on either side of her beautiful face. And tonight, Patricia Gomez was wearing glossy red lipstick as bright as the dress, and midnight-blue eye shadow that made her look slinky and sexy and Spanish, like some señorita coming down a long wrought-iron staircase in a movie with banditos and good guys. And tonight, Patricia Gomez was barelegged in strappy red satin sandals that made her seem even taller than her five-feet-seven, which Ollie had already informed her was a perfect height for a woman.

Best of all, Patricia Gomez was in his arms, and they were dancing.

Detective/First Grade Oliver Wendell Weeks was a damn fine dancer, if he said so himself.

The place he had chosen for their inaugural outing was a spot called Billy Barnacles, which was perched on the edge of the River Harb, on the city's Upper North Side. The place served great sea food — he had asked her two nights ago if she liked sea food — and it had the advantage of a live band and a parquet dance floor under the stars and directly on the river's edge. The band called itself The River Rats . . .

Ollie wondered what their name was when they were playing someplace less proximate, ah yes, to the river, but they'd been playing here forever, and in fact Arnie Cooper, the leader, was Billy Cooper's brother, who *owned* Billy Barnacles, but that was another story.

The band played all kinds of music, all of it danceable.

Dixieland from the twenties, swing from the thirties and forties, doo-wop from the fifties, rock from the sixties all the way to the present, even a rap song or two to satisfy the handful of Negro customers who wandered in from Diamondback further uptown. Ollie did not mind dancing on the same floor as 'people of color,' as they sometimes preferred calling themselves, so long as they behaved themselves. The trouble with most Negroes — and Ollie preferred calling them this because he knew the outmoded label pissed them off — was that they seldom knew how to behave themselves. He considered this a crying shame, which was why he tried to take as many of them off the street as he possibly could.

But this was a Saturday night, and not a time to be ruminating about the difficulties of the job in a city as large and as diversified, ah yes, as this one. He considered it a comment upon his social aptitude that he had never once discussed police work all through dinner, and was not now discussing it as he and Patricia glided nimbly across the floor to a spirited version of 'When the Saints Go Marching In,' another of the tunes in The River Rats' repertoire.

To watch Ollie prance around the dance floor was tantamount to watching the hippos in *Fantasia* performing to 'Dance of the Hours,' except that Ollie wasn't wearing a tutu. He was wearing instead a dark blue tropical-weight suit he had purchased at L&G, which was short for Lewis and Gregory, two brothers — literally and figuratively — whose shop Ollie frequented on Chase Street in the Eight-Eight Precinct, where both he and Patricia worked. Ollie suspected that half the clothing at L&G had fallen off the back of a truck, which meant it had been stolen. But 'Don't Ask, Don't Tell' was a very good policy to follow when you were looking for designer-label garments at discount prices. The suit made Ollie look a lot thinner than he actually was, which meant he looked like an armored weapons carrier instead of a tank, not to mix metaphors with hippos, oh no, m'little chickadees. Ollie was also wearing a white shirt and a red tie, which made him look patriotic in the blue suit, and which also picked up Patricia's dominant color scheme, the tie, that is.

For a fat man . . .

Ollie knew that there were some people in this city who called him 'Fat Ollie,' but never to his face, which he considered a measure of respect. Besides, he would break their heads. He himself never thought of himself as being 'fat,' per se. Large, yes. Big, yes.

For a big, large man, then, especially one who was gamboling about the dance floor the way he was, Ollie sweated very little. He figured this had something to do with glands. Everything in life had something to do with glands.

He twirled and whirled Patricia.

The number was reaching a climax.

Ollie pulled Patricia in as close as his belly would allow.

'A HIT VIDEO is all about screwing,' Todd Jefferson was telling Loomis. 'The guys out there want to whack they castles on Britney's bellybutton, the teenybopper girls want to wrap they little boobs around Usher's dick. It's as simple as that.'

Loomis tended to agree with him, but he wished he was talking about Tamar Valparaiso instead of Britney Spears. As for Usher, he didn't give a rat's ass about him *or* his dick.

'Hit videos are all about guys and girls in they under-wears,' Jefferson said. 'White guys like to see leggy black girls in they sheer panties. Black dudes like to see titty white girls in they skimpy bras. All this black-white shit really grabs 'em.'

Todd Jefferson was a black man himself, with a black wife, but he was purported to have a white mistress. Loomis figured he knew whereof he spoke.

'Take J. Lo,' Jefferson said. 'She worked both sides of the street. In the movies, she was screwing white guys, in real life she was screwing ole P. Diddy. Your little girl could take a few lessons from her.'

Loomis knew he was talking about Tamar.

Little girl.

34-C cup.

Some little girl.

'Her being Hispanic and all.'

Loomis knew this was only half-correct. Tamar's father was Mexican, hence the soulful brown eyes, but her mother was of Russian descent, hence the blond hair with a little help from Miss Clairol. Her South-of-the-Border heritage pretty much guaranteed the loyalty of the Hispanic market. It was the crossover crowd they were going for with *Bandersnatch*. Bring in all those little Anglos who belonged heart and soul to Britney. If they failed to do that . . .

'Not too many singers can do what J. Lo did, you know,' Jefferson said. 'Only other artists done it before her was Boyz II Men.'

Loomis didn't know what the hell he was talking about. Did he mean screwing white men in movies? Screwing a black man in real life?

'Three number-one hits in the Billboard Hot 100 for five weeks or more,' Jefferson said, nodding. 'J. Lo did it with "Ain't It Funny." She's the lady your little girl has to beat, man.'

'We're hoping for a number-one single with the title song on *Snatch*,' Loomis said.

'By the way,' Jefferson asked, 'is that related to her pussy in some way? The title of the album?'

'No,' Loomis said. 'What makes you think . . . ?'

''Cause it sounds somewhat pornographic, you know? Bandersnatch? Sounds like the girl has a whole rock group going down on her pussy. *Band,* you know? *Snatch,* you know? Bandersnatch. You know whut I'm saying?'

'No, it's not intended that way.'

'That's not necessarily *bad,* mind you,' Jefferson said. 'That kind of association. It relates back to what I was saying before. About videos being all about screwing. Does your little girl screw somebody on this video?'

It dismayed Loomis to learn that Jefferson hadn't even *looked* at the fucking thing yet. CEO of WU2, the fourth-largest video TV station in the country, he hadn't even *glanced* at the new video.

'Yes,' Loomis said, 'she screws the frumious Bandersnatch.'

'Uh-huh,' Jefferson said.

'This big black dude wearing a monster mask,' Loomis said.

'Is that what Bandersnatch means? Big black dude? Cause *I'm* a big black dude, man, and nobody ever called me no Bandersnatch before. Nor any *other* kind of snatch.'

'No, it has nothing to do with being black.'

'Then what *does* it have to do with?' Jefferson asked. ''Cause I have to tell you, man, the word "Bandersnatch" is bewildering to me.'

'Actually, it's a word Lewis Carroll invented.'

'Who's that? Bison's Artistic Director?'

Bison was the name of Loomis' label. His Artistic Director was a man named Carl Galloway, whom Loomis had hired away from Universal/Motown, where he'd been Manager of Artist-Development. Jefferson should have known that. CEO of WU2, Loomis thought again, doesn't know Lewis Carroll was an English writer and not Bison's fuckin *Artistic* Director. Shit, man!

'Lewis Carroll wrote *Alice in Wonderland,*' Loomis said.

'Ah. Nice. I liked that movie,' Jefferson said. 'Disney, right?'

'Not the movie,' Loomis said. 'The book. The one that had "The Jabberwock" in it.'

Jefferson looked at him blankly.

Loomis began quoting.

'Beware the Jabberwock, my son!

'The jaws that bite, the claws that catch!

'Beware the Jubjub bird, and shun

'The frumious Bandersnatch!'

'Frumious, huh?' Jefferson said. '*Still* sounds pornographic to me.'

'THERE IS SOMETHING totally obscene about chocolate,' Patricia was telling him.

She was dipping into the double chocolate soufflé she had ordered. Ollie was on his second wedge of strawberry shortcake. The band was playing a tune Patricia recognized from Christina Aguilera's first album. It was called 'When You Put Your Hands On Me,' and it was all about this girl who gets all oozy when this guy touches her. It was a very hot song that sounded as if Christina had written it herself from her own personal experience, but she probably hadn't. There was a time — before Patricia joined the force — when she wished she could be a rock singer like Christina Aguilera. Every young Hispanic girl in the city wished she could be a rock singer like either Jennifer Lopez or Christina Aguilera. There was only one trouble;

9

Patricia had a lousy voice. Even her mother said she had a lousy voice.

'My sister went to Australia last year on one of these tours,' Patricia said. 'And . . . I forget which town it was . . .'

'You have a sister?' Ollie said.

'I have *two* sisters, actually. And a brother, too. My older sister went to Australia with her husband, and I think it was Adelaide where . . .'

'Is that your sister's name?'

'No, that's the name of the town. At least, I *think* that was the name of the town. Where she had this great chocolate dessert. They have this shop sells chocolate desserts there, you know? And it's called "The Chocolate Slut." Isn't that a terrific name?'

'Great,' Ollie said. 'The Chocolate Slut. Perfect. What *is* your sister's name?'

'The one who went to Australia?'

'Well, yes. Well, both of them, actually.'

'She's called Isabella. The other one, my younger . . .'

'Come *on*,' Ollie said, and almost dropped a piece of cake off his fork.

'What?' Patricia asked, puzzled.

'That's *my* sister's name!'

'Get out of here!'

'I mean it. Well, not Isabell-*a,* but it's Isabelle. Yes.'

'How about that?' Patricia said, grinning.

'What's the other one's name?'

'Why? Do you have two sisters, too?'

'No, just the one. But I'm curious.'

'Enriqueta. It means "Henrietta."'

'Do you know what Patricia means?'

'Well . . . Patricia, I guess. I think it's the same in Spanish as in English.'

'*I* know what it means,' Ollie said, and grinned knowingly.

'How do you know what . . . ?'

'I looked it up.'

'Get out!'

'It means "one of noble descent." It's from the Latin.'

'No kidding?'

'That's what the book said.'

'Gee,' Patricia said.

'I think it suits you,' Ollie said. 'Would you care for another soufflé?'

IF THE THREE people on the boat had been hired by Central Casting, they'd have been labeled The Hunk, The Pretty One, and The Nerd.

The Hunk was driving the boat.

His name was Avery Hanes.

Tall and somber looking, with curly black hair and dark brown eyes, he was muscularly built – not because he'd ever done time but simply because he worked out regularly. Like the other two, Avery was wearing black jeans, a black sweatshirt, and black running shoes. Later tonight, he would put on one of the masks. But for now he was enjoying the mild May breezes that blew in off the stern of the boat, riffling his hair, touching his face like a kiss. Avery had once worked for the telephone company and then had sold electronics at The Wiz. Then he'd got the job at Lorelei Records on St. John's Av. The gig tonight was sort of related.

The Pretty One was Avery's girlfriend.

Some five-feet-six-inches tall, twenty-four years old, redheaded and green-eyed and freckled and lithe and lean and wearing for the job tonight the same black jeans and Reeboks and black sweatshirt without a bra. Her name was Kellie Morgan, and she was here because this had to look like a nice little boating party cruising up the river and not some people intent on mischief. She was here because a pretty face in the crowd had a way of stilling the most dire fears. She was here because her boyfriend Avery had told her this would be a piece of cake that would be over and done with by Tuesday night at this time, and there was nothing to worry about because it was all planned to the minute and no one would get hurt and there'd be a quarter of a million bucks for the three of them to split when all was said and done.

The Nerd had straggly blond hair and intense blue eyes and contact lenses over those eyes. He looked like a man who might be an accountant for a small private firm, while actually he was an ex-con who'd been paroled only five and a bit more months ago after having done time for 1st Degree Robbery, a Class-B felony punishable by a prison term not to exceed twenty-five years. That didn't mean Calvin Robert Wilkins wasn't smart; it merely meant he'd been caught. He wasn't as smart as Avery, but then again he didn't have to be. He'd got along just fine until the bad break that night of the bank heist when he got a flat tire during the getaway. He'd tried to ride out the flat, but the tire fell all to pieces and shreds, and suddenly he was riding on the rim with sparks flying and the fuzz gaining, and before you knew it his luck ran out completely and there he was upstate, wearing a number. He'd been paroled from Miramar shortly before Thanksgiving. Until just before Christmas, he'd been working as a dishwasher in a deli on Carpenter Avenue. Then he'd found the job at Lorelei Records, which was where he'd met Avery.

The boat they were on was a Rinker 27-footer powered with a 320-hp Bravo Two that could juice up to almost forty-three miles per at top speed. There was an aft cabin with an oversized mattress, and the dinette seating in the lounge could convert to a double berth, but they didn't expect to be sleeping on the boat.

If everything went as planned tonight, by this time Tuesday, they'd all be sleeping in their own little beddie-byes.

If everything went as planned.

TOM WHITTAKER was program director for radio station WHAM. He was telling Harry Di Fidelio — Bison's Vice President of Radio Marketing — that the question his station recently had to ask themselves was whether they should skew their targets younger or still go for the mother/daughter double play.

'It wasn't an easy decision to make,' Whittaker said. 'With all these new uptempo releases, we all at once had a responsive audience for teen-based pop and hip-hop acts.'

'So which way are you going?' Di Fidelio asked.

'Well, we'll continue to beam primarily to our twenty-five to thirty-four base. But what we've done over the past few months is expand our focus to the eighteen to twenty-four demographic. We're trying to get away from that image of a thirty-something station. We want our listeners to think of us as dynamic and youthful instead.'

'That makes sense,' Di Fidelio said, and then got down to what Bison was paying him for. 'We think Tamar will have a broad base among the thirty-somethings as *well* as the younger group. Her appeal is what you might call universal.'

'Oh, hey, she's terrific,' Whittaker said, gobbling down his second helping of chocolate pâté with vanilla bean sauce and raspberries. 'What I'm trying to say, though, Barry . . . may I call you Barry?'

13

'Harry. Actually, it's Harry.'

'Harry, right, what I'm trying to say, Harry, is that it was merely a matter of re-examining our goals. A lot of Top 40 stations try too hard to pitch their product to both the kiddies and their parents, and the result is mass confusion. At Radio 180, we *augmented* our focus rather than radically change it, and we actually improved our ratings with demos who wanted to feel younger or who just wanted to listen with their kids.'

'"Bandersnatch" should appeal to both,' Di Fidelio said.

'Oh, hey, she's terrific. I feel sure she'll get hundreds of plays on our station.'

If much of what Whittaker was saying sounded like total horseshit, that's because much of it *was* total horseshit. Whittaker knew, and Di Fidelio knew, and – with the exception of the crew and the caterers and the black dancer who'd be playing the role of the Bandersnatch when Tamar performed the song later tonight – everyone on this showboat vessel knew that most Top 40 and rock radio stations today got paid by the record manufacturers, and in some instances by the performing artists themselves, to play their songs on the air.

Moreover, this practice of Pay-for-Play, as it was called, was entirely legal provided the station mentioned on air that payment had been made. Usually, the deejay merely said, 'This record was brought to you by Bison Records.' Whittaker knew, and Di Fidelio knew that the music industry was a twelve-billion-dollar-a-year business. They further knew that only three broadcasters controlled more than half of the top hundred radio markets in the U.S. There were 10,000 – count 'em, Maude – 10,000 commercial radio stations in the land, and record companies depended on about a thousand of the largest ones to create

14

hits and sell records. Each of those thousand stations added approximately three new songs to its playlist every week.

Enter the independent record promoter.

Hired by the record company, the indie got paid each time there was an 'add' to the playlist of a Top 40 or rock station. Average price for an add was a thousand bucks, but the fee could go as high as five or ten thousand depending on the number of listeners a station had. All in all, the indies earned about three million bucks a week for their services.

That was a lot of fried corn husks, honey.

Whittaker knew, and Di Fidelio knew, and everyone connected with either Bison Records or WHAM – 'Radio 180 on your dial!' – that a record promoter named Arturo Garcia, who worked for the indie firm of Instant Prompt, Inc., had made a deal with WHAM that guaranteed the station $300,000 in annual promotional payments provided its list of clients regularly made the station's playlist. Morever, in certain special circumstances . . .

Consider, for example, the case of Tamar Valparaiso's debut album, *Bandersnatch.* What with Carroll's original rhyming (which would certainly sound like hip-hop doggerel to many teenagers), and what with Tamar's poundingly simple five-note melody (that would most certainly sound sexually-driven to many teenagers), the title-song single seemed poised, please dear God, to do what Alicia Keys' *Songs in A Minor* had done in its first week, more than 235,000 copies for a debut album, #1 on both the Billboard Top 200 Album Chart and the R&B Album Chart, please dear God, let it happen!

But just in case God wasn't listening, and just in case all that legal payola didn't do the trick, IPI (ever mindful of its guiding slogan, 'The Tin Is in the Spin') was paying WHAM – and each of forty other top stations around the country – a $5,000 bonus for fifty plays in the first week of 'Bandersnatch's' release. That came to a hundred bucks a spin, and that was a whole lot of tin, man.

To put it mildly, much was riding on the success of that album.

Meanwhile, in the main stateroom of the *River Princess*, Tamar Valparaiso was getting into her scanty costume.

EVER SINCE 9/11, and especially since the FBI began issuing vague warnings of terrorist attacks hither and yon but nowhere in particular, the Police Department had been on high alert for any possible threats to the city's bridges. There were 143 men and 4 women in the Harbor Patrol Unit, which operated a municipal navy of twenty vessels, ranging in size from twenty to fifty-two feet. The workhorse of the HPU was the new thirty-six-foot launch, which could travel up to thirty-eight miles an hour – more than twice the speed of the older vessels in the fleet. The Police Department had recently purchased four of these boats at a cost of $370,000 per. To the relief of taxpayers everywhere in the city, the boats were expected to last twenty years.

Not too long ago, Sergeant Andrew McIntosh would have been wearing the same orange life vest over his blue uniform, but there wouldn't have been a Ruger Mini-14 semiautomatic rifle lying across the dash. You broke those out only when you were going on a drug raid. Those and the twelve-gauge shotguns. Nowadays, with lunatics running loose all over the world, the heavy weapons were *de rigueur* for the course, as they said in old Glasgow, Scotland, from which fine city McIntosh's grandmother had migrated.

McIntosh was fifty-two years old, and he'd been driving boats for the HPU for twenty-two years now, before which he'd operated a charter fishing boat in Calm's Point. Back then, watching the police boats pulling into the marina, he'd wondered what the hell he was doing ferrying drunken fishermen all over the Sound. He finally asked himself, Why not give it a shot? Took the Police Department exam the very next week, asked for assignment to the Harbor Patrol the minute he got out of the Academy.

Back then, the Police Department was still calling itself the Isola PD, even though precincts were located in all five sections of the city. Eventually, Calm's Point, Majesta, Riverhead, and Bethtown rose up in protest, demanding equal rights or some such. The department, figuring it would cover all the bases and not cause any more riots than were absolutely necessary, began calling itself 'Municipal PD,' and then 'Metro PD,' and then 'MPD' for short. Some of the older hands, however — McIntosh included — felt they had changed the name only because the acronym 'IPD' for Isola Police Department was being translated by the ordinary citizenry to mean 'I Peed,' a not entirely flattering descriptive image for stalwarts of the law rushing to the rescue.

There was nothing suspicious about the twenty-seven footer moving slowly toward the Hamilton Bridge, except that she was cruising along with just her running lights on. No lights in the cabin or anywhere else on the boat. Well, that wasn't *too* unusual, McIntosh supposed, but even so, in these difficult times he didn't want to be blamed later on if some crazy bastard ran a boat full of explosives into one of the bridge's pylons. So he hit a switch on the dash, and a red light began blinking and rotating on the prow of the launch, and he signaled to Officer Betty Knowles to throw a light onto the smaller boat ahead.

Aboard the Rinker, Avery Hanes whispered, 'Let me handle this.'

Well, hell, he was the smart one.

'**WHY DO I** have to be black?' Jonah was asking her.

Tamar didn't know what to answer the poor man.

Because the good Lord intended you to be that way?

She hated deep philosophical questions.

Like when a reporter from *Billboard* magazine asked her what she thought of Mick Jagger, and she'd had to admit she didn't know who Mick Jagger was. When the reporter explained that he was a seminal rock singer, she didn't mention that she didn't know what 'seminal' meant. Instead, she told them she didn't consider herself a rock singer, and besides she was very young. So, of course they asked what kind of singer she considered herself to be, and she'd had to admit she thought of her kind of music as mainstream pop. But a question like Jonah's absolutely floored her. She'd never suspected till this very moment that he was so deep.

What she was hoping was that nobody would be disappointed because she and Jonah wouldn't be duplicating all the bells and whistles on the video, but of course how could they do that on a little boat in the middle of the river? Tonight, she'd be lip-synching, which was okay because everyone in the crowd was very hip, she guessed, and surely nobody expected her to really *perform* the entire video, did they? Shit, it had cost hundreds of thousands of dollars to shoot the thing with all the special effects and everything, so how could anyone expect a *duplication* of all that on this dinky little boat here, even though Barney kept calling it a 'launch.' She certainly hoped nobody had such wild expectations in mind, which was a good title for a song and maybe for her next album, 'Wild Expectations.' She certainly hoped they would appreciate her just lip-synching while she dry-humped Jonah.

Jonah was as gay as a bowl of daisies.

This was okay because he only came across that way when you were talking to him. Lisping and all, and sort of limp-wristed, a total caricature of a fag.

'Why do I have to be black?'

And a little limp flick of the wrist.

Cause you unfortunate, *amigo,* Tamar should have said.

Jonah hadn't done any talking on the video, and he certainly wouldn't be doing any talking tonight, either. Even Tamar herself wouldn't be talking until after the record played and they danced to it. Then she'd do the interview with Channel Four, and whatever other interviews she had to do with all the press people out there, and then they'd call it a night and hope for the best.

The video had premiered last night on all four music channels during their prime-time debut spots —

'I meant why does the *beast* have to be black?' Jonah asked.

Another philosophical question.

He was sharing the main stateroom as a dressing room with her, but that was okay because he was gay, and she didn't mind if he saw her naked boobs. She was half-naked in the costume, anyway, which she guessed was the whole point of the video, to expose herself as much as possible without getting arrested. She had to admit that she somewhat enjoyed all that screaming and yelling whenever she made a personal appearance, part of which she knew was for her voice — she really felt she did have a very good mainstream pop style and a very good vibrato besides — but part of which was for the way she shook her considerable booty, *muchachos.*

'So?' Jonah asked.

One hand on his hip.

Pouting little look on his face.

He was perhaps six-feet-two-inches tall, with a dancer's firm abs, and strong biceps and forearms from lifting girls considerably heftier than Tamar, thighs like oaks, an altogether wonderful specimen of a man, but oh what a waste! He had good fine facial features, too, a pity they'd been covered by all those masks he had to wear on the video, and would be covered by masks tonight as well – not the same masks, of course. They'd used maybe ten or twelve different masks during the shoot, so that it looked like the Bandersnatch was changing form each time he – or *it*, more precisely – violated her or tried to violate her, rape or attempted rape as the case may have been, who knew? All these videos were supposed to be somewhat mysterious and murky, like adolescence itself, thank God *that* was behind her.

She was glad her video wasn't about a black guy going to jail while his chick moped around looking mournful and forlorn. She was glad it wasn't about a drive-by shooting, either, which a lot of the rap groups thought was entertainment. One of the Bison veeps had wanted the title song on the debut album to be something called 'Raw Girls,' and he'd suggested that they shoot the accompanying video in a high-school locker room, with all these young chicks, white, black, Latino, coming in and stripping down to their underwear as they got ready for a soccer game. Tamar had gone directly to Barney Loomis to tell him she wouldn't do any video that looked like a G-rated version of *Debbie Does Dallas,* and she wouldn't sing any song called 'Raw Girls,' either.

Tamar knew exactly what she wanted to be.

Tamar knew exactly where she was going.

*

'**SORRY TO BOTHER YOU,** sir,' McIntosh said. 'Everything okay here?'

Standing on the bow of the police launch, Officer Knowles was playing the boat's spotlight around the chest of the man at the wheel of the Rinker. Something they taught you when you began training for the HPU. Unless the suspect was a known perp, you kept the light out of his eyes. Courtesy, Service, Dedication. That's what the decal on the side doors of all the police cars in the city said. That's what it said on the side of Harbor Charlie's cabin, too. Courtesy. Meant you kept the light out of a person's eyes, unless he was a perp.

Avery Hanes was about to become a perp in an hour or so, but Officer Knowles didn't know that yet, and neither did Sergeant McIntosh, at the wheel of the police launch, or Officer Brady, standing in the stern with his hand resting casually on the butt of the Glock holstered on his hip, just in case this guy driving the Rinker turned out to be some Al Qaeda nut determined to blow up either himself or something else, or else some drug runner or something. These days, you never could tell.

'Everything's fine, Sergeant,' Avery said, because he was the smart one, and he'd seen the stripes on McIntosh's uniform sleeve.

'Saw you runnin' with all your lights off,' McIntosh said.

The launch was idling alongside the Rinker, which had come to a dead stop on the water.

'Ooops. Thought I had them on,' Avery said, and flicked the dashboard switch that turned the running lights on and off, clicking it several times to make sure, and then turning to look at McIntosh with a slightly puzzled shrug.

'I meant in the cabin,' McIntosh said.

'I'll turn them on if you like,' Avery said. 'Such a nice night and all, so many stars, thought we'd take advantage. They shine so much brighter without any lights.'

'Where you bound?' McIntosh asked.

'Back to the marina.'

'Where's that?'

'Capshaw Boats. Fairfield and the water.'

'Off Pier Seven, would that be?'

'Yes, sir.'

'Who've you got aboard, Captain?'

'My girlfriend and my best man. We're getting married in June, wanted to check out the River Club.'

'Nice venue,' McIntosh said.

'Yes, sir, it sure is. Might be too expensive for us, though.'

'Well, sorry to've bothered you,' McIntosh said. 'Enjoy the rest of the evening.'

'Thank you, sir. Did you want me to put on those cabin lights?'

'No need.'

Knowles turned off the spot. The waters went instantly black. McIntosh eased the throttle forward, and the police launch pulled away from the Rinker. On the stern, Officer Brady took his hand off the Glock's butt.

J. P. HIGGINS was holding forth on the various types of videos on the air these days. He was Bison's Executive VP in charge of Video Production, and he was obviously impressing the foreign affiliates who'd been invited to tonight's launch party. The man from Prague didn't understand English as well as Bison's people from London (well, of course not) and Milan, or Paris and Frankfurt, but he was nonetheless hanging on every word because he hoped to learn how to promote the 'Bandersnatch' video

22

in his own country, now that the flood waters had subsided, and once the video and the album were released there. One drawback was that Tamar Valparaiso was virtually unknown in the Czech Republic. Well, she was virtually unknown here as well. But that was why Bison had spent a pot full of money on the video, not to mention all the publicity and promotion preceding tonight's launch party when – in exactly one hour by the Czech's imitation Rolex watch – Tamar Valparaiso herself would be performing with the very same dancer who'd accompanied her on the video.

There was a palpable air of expectation.

Something big was going to happen tonight.

Just how big, none of the assembled guests could ever possibly imagine.

Higgins was a man in his early forties, and he liked to think he'd learned all there was to know about video production by the time he was thirty. Convincing the foreigners gathered around him was a simple task. He concentrated instead on trying to sell his savvy to a young black girl wearing what appeared to be nothing but three chain links and a diamond earring, sitting on a hassock alongside their man from London.

'Your cheapest video to shoot is what I call your "Pool Party" video,' Higgins said, trying to catch the black girl's eye, but she seemed absorbed in her chocolate pâté, which was the exact color of her barely covered breasts, topped with a pair of red raspberries – the dessert, not her breasts. 'One of the execs at any label is sure to have a house with a swimming pool. You go to that house, you set up your cameras around the pool, you decorate the premises with girls in bikinis and guys in thongs, and then shoot your artist against a backdrop of all these half-naked young people writhing in time to the music. You

23

don't have to worry too much about lighting because you're shooting in broad daylight. Only thing you have to worry about is airplanes flying overhead. But that's the same as on any daytime shoot.'

Higgins didn't know what it was he'd said that suddenly captured the black girl's attention. Maybe she was interested in auditioning for the role of one of those half-naked young people writhing. She was half-naked herself right now, albeit not writhing. Higgins plunged on regardless.

'Your second cheapest video is what I call the "Disco Party" video, which is a variation on the poolside theme. You rent a disco for the night, you pack it with those same young people from the swimming pool, except the guys are in tight jeans and tank tops and the girls are in halter tops and hip huggers that show their bellybuttons. You use the club's own strobe lighting except for your star, who's performing in their midst and needs special lighting to show her own bellybutton or however much else of herself you'd like her to show,' he said, and turned his steely blue-eyed gaze full force on the black girl, who licked chocolate pâté from her fork, and smiled at him. 'You've got to remember,' he said directly to her, 'that there's absolutely nowhere your artist can go after she's stark naked.'

Everyone laughed. The man from London had a sort of horsy laugh. The man from Paris sounded like he was choking on a Gauloise. Higgins figured he was both amusing and instructing these two stereotypes. Encouraged, he continued with his thesis, which he would try to get published in *The New Yorker* magazine one day.

'A little more expensive is what I call your "Back to the Hood" video. This only works with black or Latino artists,' he said, and winked at the black girl, 'since your white performers don't come fum no hood, sistuh,' and winked again. The black girl winked back. Higgins figured he was home free. 'This is a video you shoot outdoors, with your male or female artist roaming the old neighborhood and feeling sentimental about it. You see shots of old black guys playing cards on an upturned garbage can, you see shots of little girls jumping rope and teenage dudes shooting baskets in the school yard, you see shots of what look like dope buys going down, this is like a documentary that says, "Look where I came from, boys and girls, and now I'm a big rock star, ain't that something?" And your artist is roaming through all this like a hidden camera, with a soulful look on her face, singing her little heart out while she remembers what it was like to be a kid in this hood.'

The black girl was nodding dreamily now, remembering what it was like to be a kid in the shitty hood where she herself was born, but look at her tonight, man, here on a million-dollar yacht, wearing chains and a diamond and flirting with a veep from a big-time label, oh lordy!

'The song doesn't have to have anything at all to do with the hood or memories of the hood. The song can have a lyric any twelve-year-old can remember in six seconds flat, "I'll love you till the day I die," something like that, "I'll love you till the day I die, I'll love you till the day I die, I'll love you till the day I die-ai-ai," like that. Nothing at all to do with growing up poor, the growing-up-poor is only the sub-plot. What the video does is tell all those kids out there who bought the album that here in this America – or for that matter any of *your* countries, too, my friends – anywhere in the entire free *world,* for that matter, you can grow up to be a diva who will love someone till the day she die-ai-ai-s.'

Higgins smiled. They all smiled with him.

The black girl wasn't too sure Higgins wasn't dissing

the sort of hood she grew up in, but she smiled, too, what the hell, and grabbed a glass of white wine from a waiter passing a tray.

'Your next cheapest video is what I call "Smoke and Mirrors," it's all bullshit flashing lights and blinking neon. Looks like a million bucks, but doesn't cost a nickel. Well, it costs a lot more than the other three, but that's only in the construction. The shooting is cheap. Just your set and your artists on the set. This is the kind of set you use when your song is about absolutely nothing. In fact, not anybody out there can understand the words to the song. Nobody. Not a single living soul. I'm not talking rap. You can usually understand the words in a rap song. I'm talking about a song that has lyrics nobody on earth can understand, no matter how often you listen to the song. This is a song that kids keep listening to over and over again, trying to dope out what the hell the lyrics mean. This is a song that's usually a big hit overseas, because you don't have to understand it in Germany or Italy, it's the same as if you're hearing it in America, where nobody can understand it, either, because it's designed to be unintelligible. Are you beginning to get my drift?'

The guy from London was beginning to get Higgins' drift. Higgins was leading up to talking about 'Bandersnatch.' The man from London nodded sagely, like a member of Parliament who'd just been advised that his Prime Minister had the goods on Osama bin Laden.

'Your next-to-the-most-expensive video is your "Story" video. This can be a video that actually *follows* the story of the lyrics in any given song, illustrating the song, so to speak, putting it into pictures for the twelve-year-olds out there, or it can be a video that tells a story entirely *different* from the one the lyrics are telling. Usually, the Story video is directed by some guy who has dreams of doing a feature film for Miramax. He is more interested in the *video* itself than he is in the *song* the video is supposed to be selling. In many respects, it's like your "Back to the Hood" video. Your artist can be singing, "I'll love you till the day I die-ai-ai," and the picture on the screen will be showing a car crashing through the guard rail on the Calm's Point Bridge and hurtling to the dark swirling mysterious waters below. The "Story" video is full of artsy-fartsy shots and dissolves and fades you learn in Directing 101 in film school. There are women with horns and pointy red breasts . . .'

Higgins glanced at the black girl again.

'. . . or guys who suddenly sprout huge wings and fly off into a sky torn apart by thunder clouds. You're sometimes watching two or three stories at the same time, either having to do with the song, or having nothing at all to do with it. The idea is to make the video look like a hi-tech movie so that the kids will run out to buy the album, thinking maybe it, too, gee whiz, is like a high-tech movie. Razzle-dazzle. It's all razzle-dazzle, thank you, Kander and Ebb. Which brings me to the most expensive video of all, and that is the "Production Number" video, and that is what the "Bandersnatch" video is.'

Finalmente, the guy from Milan thought.

'Leave me dispense with generalities,' Higgins said, 'and invite you directly into my boudoir,' and here his gaze brushed the black girl's long and shiny legs, and her pert and perky tits, and then her overblown lips and her loam-colored eyes, asking his question to those eyes, asking it with a small inquisitive lifting of his brows, and getting his answer with a slight imperceptible nod, Yes, the girl in the chains was saying, oh yes, yes, yes.

'"Bandersnatch,"' Higgins said, 'although I feel certain

Lewis Carroll didn't intend it this way, is the story of an attempted rape, the story of a thwarted rape, the story of a victim triumphant. Most importantly, it is in *fact* a story — a *genuine* story and not one of those invented film-school stories that have nothing to do with the song they're selling. "Bandersnatch" is the story of a girl who is warned of the beast out there on those mean streets, but who goes out to find that beast, anyway, and to slay it, my friends, to kill it dead, to emerge victorious, "O Frabjous day! Calloo! Callay!" Yes, you're right if you're thinking this is the story of "Beauty and the Beast," told in nonsense syllables that captivate and mystify, part hard driving rock, part rap, so that we go after and deliver to both audiences. You may well ask — especially our friend from Britain here, who may be more familiar with the poem than some of you others . . .'

'I'm familiar with the poem,' the black girl said.

Higgins looked at her.

'In fact, I know it by heart,' she said.

'Then you may be wondering how . . .'

'I am indeed wondering,' she said.

' . . . how the *boy* in the poem . . .'

'"Beware the Jabberwock, my *son*,"' she said, stressing the word.

'Exactly,' Higgins said.

'"Come to my arms, my beamish *boy*,"' the man from London said.

'Exactly right,' Higgins said. 'How does this boy become a girl, become a rape victim, become in fact Tamar Valparaiso?'

'My magazine is wondering the same thing,' the black girl said.

'Which magazine is that?' Higgins asked.

'Rolling Stone.'

Ooops, Higgins thought.

SHE HAD CUT her hair short for the video.

It was growing back now, but if the album was a hit and Tamar had to go on tour with it, she'd have it trimmed back to the length it was two months ago, when they shot the video at what used to be a bakery but what was now the Sands Spit Studios across the River Dix, which in fact they'd passed not half an hour ago. The *River Princess* had already come around the tip of the island and was now heading downtown, cruising the waters between the two states, moving at a leisurely pace toward the bridge.

On the video, the short hair made her look like a blond Prince Valiant. Or more like a Peter Pan, she guessed. No question there was a girl in that tattered tunic at the end of the song, though, the beast clawing and biting at the garment till it came away in shreds under his talons and teeth, no question about that at all. They'd even had to edit out a thirty-second shot where her left nipple distinctly showed, and another longer sequence where too much cheek and almost some pussy were revealed when Jonah lifted her; you couldn't risk offending all those soccer Moms out there, as if they didn't have pussies and nipples of their own.

Started her quest in what looked like a sturdy-enough white thigh-length tunic, sandals strapped to the calf, subtly heeled to give the leg its essential curve . . .

He took his vorpal sword in hand:
Long time the manxome foe he sought —
So rested he by the Tumtum tree,
And stood awhile in thought.
And, as in uffish thought he stood . . .

That was when Jonah burst upon the scene wearing the first of his masks. That was when the innocent boy in the song began morphing into a female rape victim as more and more of Tamar's body was revealed in the shredding garment. There was a lot of meaning to this song. This song spoke to gender problems and crises of identification. This song spoke to adolescent boys and girls in turmoil. This was a very deep song.

She was worried that some of its depth and meaning might be lost in the live performance tonight. It had taken hours and hours of shooting time to capture the dual morphing effect. Tamar's transformation from adolescent boy to vulnerable maiden to ferocious defender of her virginity had required repeated costume changes to achieve the effect of a gradually more girl-revealing garment, the rape becoming in effect a subtle striptease. Nor had it been simple to morph Jonah from a merely *somewhat* threatening creature (albeit with eyes of flame) that came whiffling through the tulgey wood in a blue mask, burbling as it came, into the raging monster in a red mask, slain and bleeding at the end of the battle. How on earth would they convey all that tonight? Eyes of flame? Wouldn't it have been simpler and better merely to show the video? But it had previewed last night on all four music channels and tonight Barney wanted something to top that. Something like Tamar Valparaiso, live and in person!

And scared to death.

IT WAS ALREADY nine-thirty, and Honey Blair hadn't yet shown up. Binkie Horowitz had busted his ass setting up the Channel Four interview, but now he was beginning to wonder if the PD for the Eleven O'Clock News had changed his mind. Or else sent Honey somewhere else where hotter news was breaking. Binkie couldn't imagine what might be hotter than Tamar Valparaiso performing the new Hit Number One Song from her Platinum Album (aluvai and from your lips to God's ear!) live and in person, right here on this little old yacht, but then again he never knew what the hell went on in the heads of program directors.

As VP in charge of Promotion at Bison Records, he'd been working the PDs at radio stations all over the country for the past two months now, courting them the way he would a young girl (some of them were, in fact, young girls), making them familiar with the tricky lyrics of 'Bandersnatch,' playing the single for them over and over again, hoping they would come to like the song well enough to add it to their rotation. Binkie was shooting for plays on both Top-40 Teen and Top-40 Adult stations, hoping to catch the pubes and their soccer Moms as well. Your dead zone on radio was from seven to eleven P.M., a time slot the big-money advertisers shunned. That's where the Teen-Appeal records usually landed, square in the middle of Death Valley. In radio, your big bucks were in the eighteen- to twenty-four-year-old market. Binkie secretly suspected that Tamar's appeal would be to the teenybopper crowd, but nobody argued with Barney Loomis, and besides, there was plenty of time to go after the younger crowd later on.

For now, what he was looking for was some ninety to a hundred weekly spins on each of Clear Channel's twelve hundred stations. Used to be a record could take off with as few as forty, fifty spins a week, without going into power rotation at any of the stations. Nowadays, if you did a sampling of top hits around the country, you came up with 83 spins in Bakersfield, 86 spins in Des

Moines, 95 in San Antone, as many as 115 spins in Vegas, and so on. Moreover, the biggest stations tended to utilize high spins early on in a record's life. They'd play a song for a week or so and then conduct random telephone surveys, calling listeners and playing a snippet of the tune for them, asking if they recognized it. If they got a positive reaction, they added the song to their rotation. Binkie's job, though, was to get the damn song played in the first place.

He knew that Bison had to sell 500,000 copies of Tamar's single before they could turn a profit. In their wildest hopes, the 'Bandersnatch' single would hit the Top 10 before the album was even shipped. But not too many records achieved that goal. Of the close to 6,500 albums shipped by the major labels the year before, less than two percent of them turned a profit. A lot of time and energy and talent and money – *especially* money – was riding on Tamar Valparaiso's first outing. So where the hell was Honey Blair?

Higgins sidled up beside him, leaned into him.

'Where's the blond cooze?' he whispered.

'She'll be here, don't worry,' Binkie said.

But he *was* worried.

IN THE MAIN stateroom of the *River Princess,* Tamar was starting to get nervous herself. Too many things were bothering her. Would the dance floor be too small or too slippery for her and Jonah to perform the strenuous dance routines that simulated a young girl struggling in the clutches of an animal intent on raping her? Would the audience be sitting too close for Jonah's mask changes to be effective? They'd morphed twelve masks for the video, but tonight they'd be depending solely on a few masks and some dramatic light changes to enhance the effect of increasing menace. Would her tunic, admittedly skimpy to begin with, but certainly intact and pristine, break away strategically when and where it was supposed to, gradually revealing her long shapely legs and firm boobs, but not too much more than that, not with Channel Four's cameras taping her performance.

So many things could go wrong.

Would she be able to hear the lyrics clearly enough through the pickup tucked in her hair? Were the Channel Four sound people any good, and where the hell were they, anyway? She'd hate to be rapping 'One-two, one-two, and through and through, the vorpal blade went snicker-snack!' and instead have the sound from the video telling the cameras and later tonight the world, ''Twas brillig, and the slithy toves did gyre and gimble in the wabe.' Well, she'd got her start in karaoke clubs, she supposed she could lip-synch her way through tonight, which would be sort of karaoke in reverse, she supposed.

But what if somebody had spilled a drink or something squishy and sloppy on the floor? All Jonah had to do was lose his footing and his grip on her — his grip on *himself,* for that matter — for this whole thing to go out the window in three seconds flat, Tamar Valparaiso and the rapacious beast doing a comic pratfall in front of millions of viewers when they aired the tape on the Eleven O'Clock News. Goodbye dreams of rock stardom, goodbye little Russia-Mexicana-American girl making it huge in the big bad city and the wide wicked world.

'How do I look?' she asked Jonah.

'Hot,' he said, the friggin faggot.

Tamar's father used to go to church in Mexico every Sunday morning and pray for something to eat the next day. Tamar's mother was born in a Communist country and didn't know from religion or from praying.

Tamar wasn't praying now, either.

But she was wishing with all her might that after tonight she would be the biggest fucking diva who ever came down the pike. 'So don't let anything go wrong,' she whispered to Whomever. Tamar's ambition was to bury J. Lo, bury Britney, bury Brandy, bury Shakira, bury Ashanti, bury Pink, bury Sheryl Crow and Christina Aguilera and Michelle Branch, bury each and every one of them, bury them all.

Was that such a crime?

THE SUBJECT MATTER had finally got around to ambition and crime.

Ollie and Patricia were sitting out on the restaurant's wide verandah, looking out over the River Harb and the twinkling lights of the next state. Further uptown, they could see the warmer, somehow cozier lights of the exclusive community, Smoke Rise, and yet further uptown the lights of the Hamilton Bridge spanning the river, a yacht coming under the bridge now, all aglow with lights itself, and moving steadily downstream. Patricia was drinking a crème de menthe on the rocks. Ollie was drinking a Courvoisier straight up.

'My ambition is to become first a detective . . .' Patricia was saying.

'Ah yes,' Ollie said.

'. . . and next a detective on the Rape Squad.'

'Why the Rape Squad?'

'Because I think that's the worst crime there is.'

'I tend to agree,' Ollie said, although he didn't know whether he actually agreed or not.

Actually, he probably thought killing little girls was a worse crime. But when a woman who looked as beautiful as Patricia did in the moonlight reflected from the water told you she thought rape was the worst crime there was, then it seemed appropriate to agree with her, ah yes.

'Why is that?' Patricia asked.

Not that she doubted him. But he'd seen so much, and knew so much . . .

'Because it isn't fair,' Ollie said.

'Who says it has to be fair?' Patricia asked, and smiled, and said, 'My mother used to tell me that whenever I complained about anything. But you're right. Rape isn't fair. If men had to worry about rape all the time, the crime would carry the death penalty.'

'Do you worry about rape all the time?'

'Not since I became a cop. Not since they let me pack a gun.'

'Are you packing now?' he asked.

'Always,' she said, and tapped her handbag with one painted fingernail. 'Even when I go to bed, Josie is right there on the night table beside me. But before? When I was a kid . . .'

'Josie?'

'The piece. I call her Josie. Doesn't yours have a name?'

'No.'

'Let's name it.'

'Why?'

'Because it's a trusted friend.'

Ollie wondered if the conversation was taking a sexual turn. He knew some guys who named their cocks. Women, too. Gave names to their boyfriends' cocks. Louie. Or Harry. Or Pee Wee in some cases. He didn't think that's where Patricia was going here, but you never knew. He'd held her awfully close on the dance floor.

'I wouldn't know where to begin,' he said. 'Besides, I don't think of it as a trusted friend.'

'Have you ever had to use it?'

'Oh sure.'

'Ever kill a man?'

He hesitated.

'Yes? No?'

'A woman,' he said.

Patricia looked at him.

'She was coming at me with a shotgun. Stoned out of her mind. I shot her once in the thigh, she kept coming. An inch closer, she'd have blown my head off. I dropped her.'

'Wow,' Patricia said.

'Yeah.'

'The same piece you carry now?'

'No. This was when I was a patrolman. It was a thirty-eight back then.'

'What do you carry now?'

'A Glock nine.'

'Me, too.'

'Heavy for a woman.'

'Regulation.'

'Josie, huh?'

'Is what I call her.'

'So what should I call mine?'

'You think of a name.'

'Nah, come on.'

'Go ahead.'

'I'm not good at this.'

'How do you know? Give it a try.'

Ollie furrowed his brow.

'What's your best friend's name?' she asked.

'I don't have a best friend,' he said.

'Well . . . any friend,' she said.

'I don't have any friends,' Ollie said.

Patricia looked at him again.

'Then how about someone you really trust?'

Ollie thought about this for several moments.

Back inside the restaurant, the band began playing again.

'Steve,' he said at last.

'So name it Steve.'

'I don't think so,' he said.

'Why not?'

'I don't know. I guess it wouldn't be professional. Naming a weapon.'

'Do you think I'm unprofessional?'

'Hey, no, I think you're very professional. You're a good cop, and I think you're going to make a very good detective.'

'You think so?'

'I really do. The Rape Squad'll be lucky to have you.'

'What I was saying about rape before . . .'

'Yes, tell me. Would you like another one of those?'

'Are you going to have one?'

'If you are.'

'I think I'd like one, yes.'

'Good, me, too,' Ollie said, and signaled to the waiter.

'What I was saying is that in this city, rape was a constant concern of mine. Because, you know, well, I was growing up to be fairly attractive . . .'

'Beautiful, in fact,' Ollie said.

'I wasn't fishing for a compliment.'

'But you are beautiful, Patricia.'

'Well, thanks, but what . . .'

'A cream dee mint,' Ollie said to the waiter, 'and another of these cognacs.'

'Yes, sir,' the waiter said, and walked off.

'What I was trying to say,' Patricia said, 'is, for example, as a young girl in this city, I *never* felt safe, never.

For example, we're enjoying a few drinks together here, and I feel perfectly safe with you . . .'

'Well, thank you,' Ollie said, 'ah yes, m'dear. And I feel perfectly safe with you, too.'

Patricia laughed.

'But when I was in my twenties, I'd be out with some guy . . . well, even lately, for that matter, before I became a cop. I mean this isn't something that just goes away, it's a constant with a woman. I'd be having a drink with some guy . . .'

'How old are you, anyway?' Ollie asked.

'Oh, gee, you're not supposed to ask that.'

'Why not? I'm thirty-eight,' he said.

'I was thirty in February.'

'February what?' he asked, and took out his notebook.

'You gonna write it down?' she said, surprised.

'Sure.'

'Why?'

'So I can buy you a present. Provided it ain't too close to Valentine's Day.'

'No, it's February twenty-seventh.'

'Good. So then I can get you *two* presents,' he said.

'Nobody ever gave me a Valentine's Day present,' Patricia said.

'Well, you wait and see,' he said, and scribbled her name and the date of her birthday in his book.

'Crème de menthe for the lady,' the waiter said, 'and a Courvoisier for the gentleman.'

'Thank you,' Ollie said.

'My pleasure, sir,' the waiter said, and smiled, and walked off again.

'Cheers,' Ollie said.

'Cheers,' she said.

They both drank.

'Gee, I *still* feel safe,' Ollie said.

'Me, too,' she said, and grinned. 'But what I was saying, Oll, is that before I became a cop, I'd be having a drink with some guy who took me out, or even just standing with some guy who was chatting me up in a bar, and I'd all at once be on my guard. Like don't drink too much, Patricia, watch out, Patricia, this guy may be the son of a bitch who'll rape you, excuse my French, Oll. Or coming home late at night on the subway, cold sober, I'd always be afraid some two-hundred-pound guy was going to pounce on me and beat me up and rape me. I'm five-seven . . .'

'I know,' Ollie said, and smiled. 'That's a good height.'

'Thank you. And I weigh a hundred and twenty pounds. What chance would I have against some guy's been lifting weights in the prison gym? That's why I'm glad Josie's in my bag. Anybody gets wise with me, he's got to deal not only with me but with Josie, too.'

'I'd sure hate to meet you in a dark alley,' Ollie said.

'You would? I take that as a compliment, Oll.'

'You know something?'

'What?'

'Nobody ever called me "Oll" before. I mean before tonight. I mean before you did.'

'Really?'

'Really.'

'Well . . . is that all right? I mean . . . "Oll" sounds so natural. I mean . . . it seems to fit you.'

'Oll,' he said, trying it.

'Oll,' she said, and shrugged tentatively.

'Here's to it,' he said, and raised his glass. 'Oll.'

'Here's to it,' she said, and clinked her glass against his.

The band was playing 'Tenderly.'

'Wanna dance again?' Patricia asked.

'Yes, I would,' Ollie said.

'You're a good dancer, Oll,' she said.

'Oll,' he said, testing the name again, tasting it like wine.

'Is it okay?' she asked.

'Yes, it's just fine, Patricia,' he said, and led her inside and onto the dance floor.

CHANNEL FOUR'S OWN private motor launch pulled up alongside just as the *River Princess* slowed her speed and lowered the loading platform and ladder on her port side. Somewhat a celebrity in her own right, more for her spectacular legs than for her news coverage, Honey Blair drew a sizable crowd of somewhat-celebrities themselves to that side of the boat, where — followed by her crew of three — she climbed to the main deck, an abundance of leg and thigh showing in the short leather mini she was wearing. Honey was accustomed to dressing somewhat skimpily for her roving reporter assignments on the Eleven O'Clock News, a penchant that made her one of the station's favorites. Tonight, to complement the short blue leather mini, she was wearing calf-high navy leather boots with not-quite stiletto heels, and an ice-blue, long-sleeved, clingy silk blouse, its pearl buttons unbuttoned to show just the faintest shadowed beginnings of her cleavage. Honey normally looked cool and swift and sexy. But in tonight's crowd, she resembled somebody's maiden aunt from Frozen Stalks, Idaho.

Tamar Valparaiso was scheduled to be taped at ten P.M., which would give Honey time enough to get back to the studio, do some quick editing, and get the piece on the air by eleven-twenty, after they'd covered all the local fires, murders, political scandals, and a weensy bit of international news so that the channel wouldn't seem like just another hick television station here in one of America's biggest cities. Honey's taped segment would be followed by Jim Garrison doing the day's sports, which meant that a lot of male viewers in their thirties, a large part of Tamar's target audience, would be watching her do 'Bandersnatch' for two or three minutes, after which Honey would interview her, all panting and sweaty — Tamar, not Honey — for another minute or so. That was a hell of a big bite of television time, and don't think Binkie Horowitz and everyone else at Bison didn't realize it.

It was one thing to have the video premiere on all four music channels yesterday. It was another to get coverage like this on one of the big three networks, during the Eleven O'Clock News, no less, following the Saturday night movie. Binkie had every right to feel proud of himself for landing the spot.

Now that Honey was here, Binkie's job was to make sure she was a) comfortable and b) well prepared for the short interview that would follow Tamar's performance. Honey was meticulous about not drinking on the job, so while her crew set up their cameras alongside the polished dance floor where Tamar and her partner would be performing, Binkie plied Honey with rich dessert and hot tea while filling her in on Tamar's background, such as it was.

'She comes from karaoke,' he said, 'can you imagine? Used to perform in clubs in southwest Texas, her father's Mexican, you know, her mother's Russian. Nice little background story there, by the way, how they met. He's a vacuum cleaner salesman, her mother's a beautician, this is a real American success story, immigrants coming here from different parts of the world, raising an all-American girl who's poised on the edge of stardom — do I detect a skeptical look on your face?'

Honey raised her shoulders and her eyebrows.

'My dear woman,' Binkie said, 'Tamar Valparaiso is like nothing you have ever seen before, just you wait. She is new, she is original, dare I say she is seminal? She already had vibrato when she was eight, she has a five-octave range, and she can sight-read any piece of music you put in front of her, including opera. She's not only going to be the biggest diva to explode on the CHR-pop scene in decades, she's also going to be a big movie . . .'

'What's CHR-pop?' Honey asked.

'Contemporary Hit Radio,' Binkie said by rote.

'You don't want me to use that word on the air, do you?' Honey asked.

'What word is that?' Binkie asked. 'Radio?'

'Diva.'

'Why not?'

'It's derogatory. It's customarily used to describe a temperamental opera singer.'

'Not in rock music, it's not.'

'You really want me to call your girl a *diva?*'

'That's what she's gonna be after tonight,' Binkie said. 'Once "Bandersnatch" hits the charts . . .'

'Why'd she choose a Lewis Carroll poem?'

'Ask her, why don't you?'

'I will. Is she smart?'

'Smarter than most of them,' he said, which said it all.

Honey looked at her watch.

'Where's the Ladies'?' she asked. 'I want to touch up my makeup.'

It was twenty minutes to ten.

BECAUSE PATRICIA had been leaving directly from work earlier tonight, she'd changed in the precinct swing room and met Ollie at the restaurant. Now, at a quarter to ten that Saturday, she sat beside Ollie on the front seat of his Chevy Impala, driving uptown on the River Harb Highway, watching the lights of a yacht that had stopped dead out there on the water, and was now apparently riding her anchor. Music from a station that played what it called 'Smoothjazz' flooded the automobile.

'By the way,' Ollie said, 'have you thought of a song you want me to learn for you?'

'I've been trying to think of one all week,' Patricia said.

'Have you come up with anything?'

'Yes. "Spanish Eyes."'

'I don't think I know that one.'

'Not the one the Backstreet Boys did on *Millennium*,' Patricia said. 'The one I'm talking about is an older one. It was a hit when my mother was a teenager.'

'The Backstreet Boys, huh?' Ollie said.

He had no idea who she meant.

'Even they're on the way out,' Patricia said. 'In fact, who knows how long 'NSync's gonna last. These boy bands come and go, you know.'

'Oh, I know,' Ollie said.

'But I'm talking about the *old* "Spanish Eyes,"' she said, and sang the first line for him. '"Blue Spanish eyes . . . teardrops are falling from your Spanish eyes . . ." That one.'

'I'll ask Helen.'

'Who's Helen?'

'My piano teacher. Helen Hobson. Any song I tell her I want to learn, she finds the sheet music for me. I'll ask her to get "Spanish Eyes."'

'But not the one the Backstreet Boys did.'

'Who did the other one? The one you want me to learn?'

'Al Martino. He recorded it in 1966, I wasn't even born

43

yet, my mother was still a teenager. She still plays it day and night, that's how I happen to know it.'

'Al Martino, huh?' Ollie said.

He'd never heard of him, either.

'Yeah, he was a big recording star. Well, I think he's still around, in fact.'

'1966, that's a long time ago,' Ollie said. 'I hope she can still find the sheet music. Lots of these people who were big hits in the fifties and sixties, they just disappear, you know.'

'But lots of them are still around,' Patricia said.

'Oh sure.'

'And better than ever.'

'Oh, I know.'

'The older they get, the better they get. Look at Tony Bennett.'

'You want me to learn a Tony Bennett song for you?'

'No, I want you to learn "Spanish Eyes." Just for me. So you can play it for me when you come up the house.'

'You got a piano?'

'Oh sure. My brother plays piano.'

'I'll be happy to learn "Spanish Eyes" for you.'

'You promise?'

'I promise.'

'You'll like it. It's a very lovely love song.'

'I like lovely love songs,' Ollie said.

'It's the next exit, you know,' she said.

'Pardon?'

'You get off at the next exit.'

'Oh. Right, right.'

The next exit was Hampton Boulevard, and Hampton Boulevard was one of the worst sections in Riverhead. The population on Hamp Bull, as it was familiarly called, was largely Puerto Rican and Dominican; the local cops joked that around here *English* was the second language. The Hamp Bull Precinct was nicknamed The Dead Zone, and for good reason; it was worth your life to walk around here after dark, even if you were a policeman. Drug-infested and crime-ridden, the ten square blocks encompassed by the precinct were at the very top of the Commissioner's list of Red Alert Areas. Ollie swung the car off at the exit sign, and drove up the ramp.

He said nothing for several moments.

At last, he said, 'So this is where you live, huh?'

'1113 Purcell,' she said, and nodded.

'How long you been living here?'

'I was born here.'

'Your folks, too?'

'No, my parents were born in Puerto Rico. Mayagüez. You make the next left.'

Ollie nodded.

Young men were standing on every street corner.

'My brother and my sisters were born here, though,' Patricia said.

'1113, you said?'

'The project up ahead.'

'Got it.'

He pulled the Impala next to the curb. Some young guys wearing gang bandannas were playing basketball under the lights in the playground. They turned to watch as Ollie came around to let Patricia out on the curb side. In a seemingly casual move, he unbuttoned his jacket and flipped it open to show the holstered Glock. Patricia caught this, but said nothing. She watched as he locked the car.

'No wonder you worried about getting raped all the time,' he said.

'Kept me on my toes, that's for sure,' Patricia said, and

smiled. 'But I've got Josie now,' she said, and patted the tote bag hanging at her side.

'Can I give you some advice?' Ollie asked. 'Man to man?'

'Man to man, sure,' she said.

'There used to be a time when the shield and the gun meant something. You flashed the tin, you pulled the gun, it meant something. Which building?' he asked, and offered his arm.

'You gonna walk me home?' she asked, looking surprised. 'Gee.'

'If I lived here,' Ollie said, 'I'd even walk *myself* home.'

Patricia laughed.

'I'm used to it,' she said.

'That's because you still think the shield and the gun mean something. They don't, Patricia. You flash the buzzer nowadays, it's an invitation for some punk to shoot you. You pull your Glock, that's only telling some punk to show you his bigger AK-47. We're outnumbered and outgunned, Patricia, and there's too much money to be made in dope. So don't count on Josie, *ever*, and don't count on your shield, either.'

'What should I count on, Oll?'

'This,' he said, and tapped his temple with the forefinger of his right hand. 'We're smarter than any of them. That's all you have to remember.'

'But throw back your jacket and show the weapon, anyway, right?' she said knowingly.

'With some of them, it still works,' he said.

'Admit it,' she said.

'Okay, it still works sometimes.'

'Who's Steve?' she asked.

'I don't know. Who's Steve?'

They were walking up the concrete path to her red-

46

brick building. Some teenage boys and girls were sitting on the stoop, under a lamp swarming with the first insects of the season. One of the boys seemed about to say something, either to Patricia about her splendid tits or Ollie about his splendid girth, but he spotted the Glock and cooled it. Ollie gave him a look that said *Wise decision, lad,* and walked Patricia into the hallway. In this city, especially on Hamp Bull, too many bad things happened in hallways.

The tiled walls were covered with graffiti.

So were the elevator doors.

'Would you like to come up for a while?' she asked.

'Thanks, no, it's late,' he said.

'I had a wonderful time,' she said.

'So did I, Patricia.'

She looked into his eyes. Her face seemed suddenly forlorn.

'Will I ever see you again?' she asked.

'What do you mean?' he said, genuinely surprised. 'Why not?'

'Well,' she said, and shrugged, and then opened her hands wide to indicate the building and the hallway and the graffiti. 'This,' she said.

'Where you live is where you live,' he said, and shrugged.

The elevator door slid open.

The elevator was empty.

Ollie put his foot against the door to hold it.

'Well, thanks again,' Patricia said, and took his hand, and then reached up to kiss him on the cheek, surprising him again.

'Listen, what are you doing Tuesday night?' he asked.

'Nothing,' she said.

'Wanna go see a movie?'

47

'Sure.' She was still holding his hand. 'Will you know "Spanish Eyes" by then?'

'I don't think so. I won't be able to ask Helen for the sheet music till Monday. My piano teacher. That's when I have my piano lesson. Monday nights.'

'Remember, it's the Al Martino one.'

'I'll remember. Patricia . . . ?'

'Yes?'

'I really did have a very nice time tonight.'

'I did, too.'

'So I'll see you Tuesday, okay? Are you working Tuesday?'

'Yes. The day shift.'

'Me, too. So maybe we could go straight from the precinct . . .'

'That sounds good . . .'

'Grab something to eat . . .'

'Okay. But nothing fancy like tonight.'

'No, just a hamburger or something.'

'Okay.'

'And then go to the movies afterward.'

'That sounds good, Oll.'

'We'll talk before then, find a movie we'd both like to see.'

'Not a cop movie,' she said.

'Definitely not a cop movie.'

They were still holding hands.

'Well . . .' he said. 'Goodnight, Patricia.'

'Goodnight, Oll.'

She dropped his hand, and stepped into the elevator. He watched as she pressed the button for her floor, waved as the elevator door closed on her. He listened for a moment as the elevator started up the shaft.

Smiling, he walked out of the building and down the

steps past the teenage kids, and then up the path to where he'd parked the car.

His jacket was still thrown back to show the Glock.

'THIS IS HONEY BLAIR for Channel Four News, coming to you live from the ballroom deck of the *River Princess*, somewhere in the middle of the River Harb. In about a minute and a half, we'll be privileged to see and hear Tamar Valparaiso, the rock world's new singing sensation, performing live and in person the title song from her debut album, *Bandersnatch*. For those of you who may be wondering what on earth a bandersnatch might be, the word derives from Lewis Carroll's poem "Jabberwocky," which some of you may recall from your childhood reading of *Through the Looking-Glass*. Remember sweet little Alice in Wonderland? Well, from what I understand . . . hold it, I'm getting a signal here . . .'

Honey looked off camera, striking the familiar 'Legs Slightly Apart' pose that had gained her millions of devoted viewers, mostly male, assuming as well the some-what bewildered expression that made her appear like an innocent trapped in the wilds of TV-Land, a moue that seemed particularly appropriate to the song she was intro-ducing.

'They're telling me we've got forty seconds,' she told the microphone and the millions of people who would later be watching the Eleven O'Clock News. 'I was saying that Tamar's rendering of "Bandersnatch" – if you re-member the poem – has nothing to do with childhood fun and games. In fact, what this emerging diva boldly addresses here is the attempted rape of an innocent . . . ten seconds, they're telling me, you can already see the lights beginning to change behind me, in eight, seven, six, five seconds . . . ladies and gentlemen, here's Tamar Valparaiso with *"Bandersnatch"!*'

On the video, the song was introduced with a repetitive bass note strummed on a synthesizer, no melody as yet, just a resounding B-flat note repeated against an animated yellow sky with pastel-colored clouds and whimsical budding flowers and fanciful floating insects, a children's garden of delights, with the only sound that of the insects' whirring wings and the resonant synthesizer bass note.

Here on the ballroom deck of the *River Princess,* the speakers picked up the same repeated note from the video, yes, but of course there wasn't any animated garden. Instead there was only a playful display of lights suggesting the innocence of childhood, and suddenly, in a pale saffron spot that bathed Tamar in its ivory-yellow glow (on the video, she materialized in a field of blooming white flowers) she appeared now from nowhere, it seemed, wearing a short creamy-white tunic, palms flat on her thighs. On both the video and here in this simpler performance aboard the launch, she looked directly out at the audience, raised her hands in open-fingered surprise, grinned in delight at the magnificence of this sparkling new fairyland-day, and began singing a melody she herself had written, a tune that played around a blues figure, hinting at misery to come, but which – unlike real blues – stayed rooted in the key of B-flat for the first stanza.

'''Twas brillig, and the slithy toves
 'Did gyre and gimble in the wabe:
 'All mimsy were the borogoves,
 'And the mome raths outgrabe . . .'

AVERY HANES was anticipating a swim platform running athwart the boat on the stern, with a narrow vertical ladder going up to the lower deck. Instead — and he considered this a stroke of absolute good fortune — a loading platform was in place on the boat's port side, and a proper ladder with side rails and steps, instead of rungs, was pointed up at a forty-five-degree angle toward the boat's second level where, he knew, cocktails had been served earlier tonight. The action now was on the lower deck, the ballroom level, the main deck salon where dinner and dessert had been served to a hundred and twelve guests who now sat watching Tamar Valparaiso performing on the parquet dance floor, all unaware. It would have been riskier to board the yacht on that main deck, bursting into the midst of the party, so to speak, although surely this was what they intended to do, anyway. But it would be far better to board on the second level, so handily made accessible by whichever Gods were in charge tonight, and work their way down by stealth to where they eventually wanted to be.

'The masks,' Avery told Kellie, and she went below to fetch them as he eased the Rinker in alongside the loading platform and cut the engines to idle speed.

BETWEEN STANZAS one and two, there was a four-measure interlude in the unrelated key of G, punctuated by drum beats and slashing, off-beat, E-minor power-chords on electric guitars. The drum beats grew louder and more insistent as the synth picked up the B-flat note again, more ominous-sounding now, and Tamar's almost-blues melody reached out with the words of the second stanza, her voice tremulous, her brown eyes wide and darting uneasily, the lights behind her becoming dark and swirling as if in anticipation of a sudden storm.

'Beware the Jabberwock, my son!
'The jaws that bite, the claws that catch!

'Beware the Jubjub bird, and shun
'The frumious Bandersnatch!'

BISON RECORDS had used twelve different rubber masks during the shooting of the video, changing colors, shapes, and sizes to achieve the morphing effect they were looking for, the transmogrification of an insistent date-rape hazard into a crazed and violent beast intent on rape and possibly murder.

There were only three masks aboard the Rinker tonight, and they would not be used for effect, merely for disguise.

Avery handed one of them to Kellie.

He himself pulled another one over his head and face.

Cal Wilkins put on the last one.

Kellie took the wheel of the boat.

Both men lifted AK-47s from the deck, came through the gate on the transom entry, and stepped onto the loading platform.

In the ballroom, Tamar Valparaiso was about to soar into the third stanza of 'Bandersnatch.'

IT WAS STRANGE how all tension left her the moment she began performing. She knew she had them, each and every one of them, could tell by the pin-dropping silence out there that they were hanging on every word she sang. She was hanging onto each word herself, for that matter, caught in the suspense of the moment she alone had created, waiting for whatever was going to happen next, just like when she was a kid listening to stories her mother told her, and then what, Mama, and then what?

There was the insistent B-flat note again, pulsing from the speakers left and right. She imagined that sound magnified a thousandfold, visualized herself singing on the stage of a vast arena, hundreds of thousands of fans cheering and whistling as she stamped around the stage in her flirty little tunic, wanting more of her, ever more of her, screaming for more of her.

Behind the screen on her left, she could see Jonah looking all muscular and masculine and macho in the clay-colored mask he wore for his entrance, waiting to come on, just waiting to burst onto that dance floor and tear off all her clothes.

'He took his vorpal sword in hand:
'Long time the manxome foe he sought –
'So rested he by the Tumtum tree,
'And stood awhile in thought . . .'

AS THEY CLIMBED the ladder to the second deck, Avery glanced upward to the sun deck and the pilot house above, where he could see two uniformed figures busily performing nautical tasks, half-turned away from where he and Cal tried to flatten themselves against the side of the yacht so that no one listening to the big performance in the ballroom would catch sight of them in their rubber masks. They reached the second deck of the launch undetected, paused for an instant, but only an instant, to listen to the music coming from the main deck . . .

'So rested he by the Tumtum tree,
'And stood awhile in thought . . .'

. . . and then, AK-47s in hand, moved into the lounge.

The space was empty now, bottles gleaming behind the bar, bar stools bolted to the carpeted deck. Abruptly, the singing from the deck below ended. Now there was only a steady beat that sounded to Avery's garage-band ears like a quarter note, a quarter-note rest, then two more quarter notes as they started for the wide mahogany staircase that led down to where Jonah, in a mask quite unlike the ones they were wearing, burst onto the dance floor.

THIS PART OF 'Bandersnatch' was straight hip-hop, harsh and relentless, the repeated quarter notes in the background serving as a sort of submerged pulse that seemed slower than the Lewis Carroll lines, making the talk seem crammed over it, word after word crowding into the stanza, but always covertly in time.

'And, as in uffish thought he stood,
'The Jabberwock, with eyes of flame,
'Came whiffling through the tulgey wood,
'And burbled as it came!'

And here indeed did Jonah come whiffling from behind that tulgey screen erected at one side of the dance floor, wearing the grotesque clay-colored mask, red pin-spots knifing the air to catch the eye sockets as if they were belching flame or spouting blood, burbling as he came.

And now they danced.

Oh, how they danced!

On the video, Tamar and the beast danced for three solid minutes while he tried but failed to defile her. Here on this small parquet floor, they danced an abbreviated version, to be sure, but none the less violent for its brevity. Silently they struggled, the insistent beat in four behind them, Jonah at first insinuating himself upon her in oily intimidation, muscles gleaming, confident of his advances and his allure, Tamar surprised and timorous, but suddenly intuiting intent and beginning to back away from him, which signaled the first blinding light change and —

The audience gasped.

Where an instant earlier there had been a neutral gray

mask covering Jonah's face, almost benign in appearance, a slight smile on the mouth . . . well, perhaps he *was* behaving like an overly ardent suitor, perhaps he *had* drunk a wee bit too much, but this playful creature certainly wasn't anyone a girl in a creamy-white tunic need worry about, was he? Not on a lovely day like today, when the borogoves were all mimsy and the mome raths were outgrabing all over the place.

But now, in the blinding flash of an instant, that nice little fraternity brother who just a heartbeat ago had been beseeching a kiss or negotiating a copped feel was suddenly wearing a tarnished copper mask, and his genial smile had been replaced by something more closely resembling a smirk or a snarl, as if the little girl singing her heart out here had somehow offended him by spurning his advances.

And to show how annoyed he was, to demonstrate clearly and without ambiguity exactly how much he'd been insulted by her having denied his heartfelt compliments and sincere gropings, to indicate without a modicum of doubt precisely how mightily pissed off he was, with one vicious swipe of his right hand — which all at once looked rather like a claw — he slashed out at the skirt of her tunic, opening a slit from her waist to her thigh, down the lefthand side of the garment.

Tamar backed away.

He came at her again, this time clawing at the garment's bodice, leaving in tatters a goodly portion of the fabric over her right breast. The pulsing beat behind them, insistent, a rap riff without words, a rap stroll without talk, he began stalking her now, closing and retreating, swiping and withdrawing, each new slash of either claw ripping more and more of her tunic away. Viciously, he slashed at her again — and missed! Seizing her advantage, Tamar shoved out at him, knocking him more completely off balance. He fell to the floor, and lay there as if dead, his hands and arms covering his head and his face. Tamar circled him cautiously . . . the quarter note, the quarter-note rest . . . and drew a sharp breath, breasts heaving on the quarter note again, again.

Silence.

She moved closer to him.

Bent over him.

A sudden blinding flash of light transformed the copper mask to one of sheer crimson and the creature on the floor became a fully realized raging beast that sprang to its feet and attacked again without warning.

There was no question in this last minute or so of the dance that Tamar was struggling for her life. With each slash of the beast's claws, as more and more of her garment was torn away to reveal the flesh beneath, she appeared to grow weaker and weaker until at last the beast seemed to become a dozen or more beasts, and the assault became not some college-boy adventure in the back seat of Daddy's Ford but a realized gang-rape in the middle of a dark municipal park.

Tamar reached out and up for something.

Both hands closed around something.

She struggled from her knees to her feet.

The beast circled warily, ready to charge her again.

Her eyes turned fully upon him, a laser beam caught in a hot follow spot.

And she rapped out the words in exultant victory.

'One, two! One, two! And through and through

'The vorpal blade went snicker-snack!

'He left it dead, and with its head

'He went galumphing back.'

The rap ended.

The beast in its enraged red mask lay dead on the floor at Tamar's feet.

Now there was only the B-flat note again, that single repeated bass note, and Tamar fluidly moving the tune into the bluesy figure of its opening melody.

'And hast thou slain the Jabberwock?

'Come to my arms, my beamish boy!

'O Frabjous day! Calloo! Callay!

'He chortled in his joy.'

Tamar's eyes shone, her voice rang out. She was home, baby, she was home.

''Twas brillig, and the slithy toves

'Did gyre and gimble in the wabe:

'All mimsy were the . . .'

'Don't nobody fucking *move!*'

Saddam Hussein and Yasir Arafat were coming down the wide mahogany staircase.

2.

TALL AND LEAN and with the easy stride of an athlete —
which he most certainly wasn't — Steve Carella came into
the squadroom at twenty minutes to twelve that Saturday
night, fresh as a daisy, and ready to go to work.

'It's for you,' Andy Parker said, and handed him the
phone.

Actually, it wasn't for Carella.

It was for whichever detective happened to be on duty at
the Eight-Seven at this hour of the night. But the Graveyard Shift was just beginning to meander in, and Parker
was never too eager to catch a new case, so he considered
himself officially relieved, and passed the call on to Carella,
who was a bit bewildered by the precise timing.

'Carella,' he said into the phone.

'Hello, Carella,' a gruff, smoke-tarnished voice said.
'This is Captain Jimson, Harbor Patrol.'

A jumper, Carella thought at once. Someone's taken a
dive off the Hamilton Bridge.

'Yes, sir?' he said.

'I just had a call from one of my people out on the water,
a Sergeant McIntosh, aboard one of our thirty-six footers.
At around ten-thirty, he responded to a distress call from
the skipper of a cruise yacht called the *River Princess* . . . are
you with me, Coppola?'

'It's Carella, sir.'

'Sorry. The *River Princess,* some kind of party for a rock
singer.'

'Yes, sir?'

'Two armed masked men boarded the boat around ten-fifteen and kidnapped her.'

Oh boy, Carella thought.

'You're the local onshore precinct. Coast Guard has a DPB waiting to take you out there from Pier 39 . . .'

'Yes, sir,' Carella said.

He didn't know what a DPB was.

'. . . that's on the river and Twelfth. How long will it take you to get crosstown?'

Carella glanced at the precinct wall map.

'Give me fifteen minutes, sir,' he said.

'The man you're meeting is a lieutenant j.g. named Carlyle Apted.'

'Yes, sir. Sir, would you know who the singer . . . ?'

But the captain had already hung up, and Cotton Hawes was just walking into the squadroom.

'Cotton,' he said, 'don't get comfortable. We're up.'

COTTON HAWES felt right at home on the Coast Guard's little thirty-eight-foot DPB. This was the kind of boat he'd commanded during *his* little war. Everybody in America had his own little war, and everybody in that war did his own little thing. Carella had trudged through mud as a grunt in the infantry. Hawes had stood on the bridge of a boat not unlike this one, grinning into flying bullets, spray and spume. Everybody in America who'd ever fought or merely served in any of the country's innumerable little wars would never forget his own particular war, although sometimes he would like to. But there would always be more little wars and even some big ones, and therefore many more opportunities to remember. Or perhaps forget.

Cotton Hawes stood on the bridge of the cutter alongside Lieutenant Carlyle Apted, a man in his late twenties, he guessed, who had been summoned to the scene the moment Sergeant McIntosh realized he was dealing with a kidnapping here.

'Guess he figured this would get Federal sooner or later,' Apted said.

Then what are *we* doing here? Carella wondered. Let the Feebs have it now, and welcome to it.

'What you're on now,' Apted told Hawes, perhaps suspecting that Carella didn't really care to know, 'is a Deployable Pursuit Boat, what we call a DPB. She's a thirty-eight footer, designed to give the Coast Guard a new capability in the war against drugs.'

Another little war, Carella thought.

'What it is, you see, most of your illegal narcotics are smuggled in on these "go-fasts," we call 'em. They're these small, high-speed boats that can carry up to two thousand keys of cocaine. But they can't outrun our DPBs. Means we can intercept and board and make a sizable dent in the traffic.'

Carella hated boats. He hated anything that moved on water. Especially DPBs, which seemed to move faster than any damn thing he'd ever seen on water. When he used to bathe his infant twins – lo, those many years ago – even the floating rubber duck in the bathtub made him seasick. Well, perhaps that was an exaggeration. But he *was* feeling a bit queasy now, and he was also fearful that all that dark greasy water splashing over the bow might be polluted. His face wet, his hair flying in the wind, he wondered what a nice boy like himself was doing on a swiftly moving vehicle in the middle of a deep river on a shift that had just barely begun.

Tonight, Carella felt – and therefore looked – more like a beloved professor of economics at a municipal college than a detective. Hatless, dark-haired and brown-eyed, the eyes slanting downward to give his face a somewhat Oriental appearance, he was wearing an orange-colored life vest over dark brown slacks and matching loafers and socks, a blue button-down shirt, a brown tie, and a tweed jacket that was, in truth, a bit too heavy for the mild weather and a bit too shabby for the sort of party that had been interrupted out there on the *River Princess*. He was frowning. Well, he was more than frowning. In fact, he looked as if he might throw up. Unamused, he stood on the deck of a tossing peanut-shell vessel, braving the raging briny while two old sea-faring types chatted it up and grinned into the wind.

Hawes, on the other hand, was in his element.

Dressed somewhat casually, even for the midnight-to-eight A.M. shift, he was wearing his life vest over blue jeans, a crew neck green sweater, a zippered brown leather jacket, and ankle-high brown boots. He had not expected to be pulled out onto the River Harb tonight – in fact, he'd been planning to do a field follow-up on some bikers he suspected were involved in a liquor store holdup, and he figured the protective coloration might help him. Actually, though, his costume would have fit in beautifully at Tamar Valparaiso's launch party, where many of the music industry's moguls were similarly dressed.

'Ever hear of this girl before?' Apted asked him.

He had given up on Carella as a lost-cause landlubber.

'What's her name?' Hawes asked.

'Tamar Valentino,' Apted said.

'No. Is she famous or something?'

'Not to me,' Apted said.

'Me, neither,' Hawes said. 'Steve!' he yelled over the roar of the wind. 'You ever hear of a singer named Tamar Valentino?'

'No!' Carella yelled back. 'Who is she?'

'The one who got snatched,' Apted said.

'If she got snatched, she must be somebody,' Hawes said reasonably.

Carella was wondering if the FBI had already been notified.

'**I HAVE TO** tell you the truth,' Sergeant McIntosh said, 'I been with the Harbor Patrol Unit for twenty-two years now, this is the first time I ever caught a kidnapping.'

'We don't catch many of them onshore, either,' Hawes said.

'I know, anything we catch — other than immediately addressable — we're supposed to notify the onshore locals. But ain't a kidnapping federal stuff?'

'It could become,' Carella said.

'I mean, wouldn't this be considered "Special Maritime and Territorial" jurisdiction?'

'I really don't know,' Carella said.

'I know the Great Lakes are covered,' McIntosh said, 'and the St. Lawrence River, and prob'ly the Mississippi and the Hudson . . .'

'I couldn't tell you.'

'Anyway, what I did was raise the Coast Guard, who I figured would know.'

'Did they?'

'No.'

'The way I figure it,' Carella said, 'there's a state line down the middle of the river, and if the boat crossed that, then the Feds come in automatically.'

'Sometimes they come in if the case is really high profile,' Hawes said. 'Like if this rock singer is somebody really important.'

'Who is she, anyway?' McIntosh asked.

'Somebody named Tamar Valentino,' Hawes said.

'Never heard of her.'

'Me, neither.'

'So scratch the FBI.'

'Unless the boat crossed that state line,' Carella said.

'Excuse me, gentlemen,' a man in a white uniform said, breaking into the little intimate law enforcement circle. 'I'm Charles Reeves, Captain of the *River Princess.* I'm sorry to interrupt, but we've got a hundred and twelve guests aboard this vessel and we've been sitting here dead in the water ever since the incident occurred, waiting for some sort of clear indication that we can begin moving her back to port. Is there anyone here who can . . . ?'

'You can move her,' Carella said.

'You are, sir?'

'Detective Stephen Louis Carella. Eighty-seventh Squad.'

'And you are authorized to . . . ?'

'It's our case, yes,' Carella said, and thought, So far. 'This is my partner. Detective Cotton Hawes.'

'Then I'll get the engines started,' Reeves said dubiously.

'Yes, that'll be fine,' Hawes said.

'We should be docking in about half an hour,' Reeves said. 'Will you be finished here by then?'

'Finished?'

'What I'm asking is will I be able to disembark the passengers? The yacht was only leased for the night, you know, not the entire month of May.'

Carella looked at him.

'I mean, we all have jobs to do,' Reeves said. 'I've never had anything like this happen before on any vessel I've commanded. Never.'

'It'll be all right, sir,' Carella said. 'Why don't you go get your engines started?'

Reeves hesitated a moment longer, as if there were something more he wished to say. Then he merely nodded and went off toward the pilot house.

'You don't plan to talk to all hundred and *twelve* of these people, do you?' McIntosh asked.

Carella was wondering the same thing.

EVERYBODY wanted to go home.

What had started out as a nice party on a nice boat on a nice river had turned into some kind of Fellini nightmare with people in masks running around doing violence to the same pretty young girl.

Nobody seemed to agree on exactly quite what had happened.

Given that eye witnesses were notoriously unreliable, this bunch seemed to be more untrustworthy than most. Perhaps they'd been plied with too much alcohol before the occurrence (though the promised champagne toast had to be forsaken, given the unforeseen circumstances) or perhaps the lighting had been too dim or the power of suggestion too strong. Tamar and the young black dancer had, after all, been engaged in some pretty realistic although terpsichorean violence, and all at once two *other* black guys . . .

The witnesses were all convinced the kidnappers were black . . .

. . . came marching down the grand stairway there, brandishing machine guns, and yelling for nobody to fucking move.

Even Jonah Wills, Tamar's dance partner, was convinced the two guys who'd kidnapped her were black. Perhaps this was because they were both entirely dressed in black: black denims and black sweatshirts and black running shoes and black leather gloves. Their AK-47s were black, too, which might have contributed to the overall impression of black power. Then, too, Jonah himself was black – although this wasn't an accurate description of his color, which was more closely related to the mahogany of the stair rail than the color of anthracite, say, or obsidian – and his presence on the dance floor, muscles rippling and gleaming, wearing a mask quite different from the Hussein and Arafat masks the intruders were wearing, might also have contributed to the consensus of opinion that there were now *three* black men molesting this poor blond white girl wearing hardly anything at all.

Or perhaps the words 'Don't nobody fucking move!' hadn't sounded ofay enough to this largely white crowd, although in truth the black-to-white ratio here tonight was larger than you'd find at similar glittery events hither and yon throughout this fair city. Then again, this was the music industry here.

Even so, everybody wanted to go home.

Having inherited this cockamamie case from Parker – who was already nursing his third beer in a bar around the corner from his apartment, and chatting up a blonde he didn't realize was a hooker – Carella and Hawes were reluctant to let anyone go just yet, not until they had a clearer picture of just what the hell had happened here. They were mindful of the fact that the FBI might be coming in behind them, and they didn't want to hear the usual crap the Feebs laid down about 'inefficient and insufficient investigation at the local level.' So they went through the facts – or the perceived facts – again and again until they were able to piece together a more or less scenario-by-committee, not unlike many of the movies one saw these days, where a hundred and twelve writers shared screen credit, except that it was by now almost two in the morning.

The party guests unanimously understood that the black guy in the mask that kept changing color and shape throughout the course of the song was supposed to be some kind of mythological beast, some kind of *Bandersnatch,* in fact, since that was the name of the song, though the man *did* warn his son to beware the Jabberwock, my son, didn't he? So maybe the beast was a *Jabberwock* or even a *Jubjub* bird. What*ever* the damn thing was, it was something to be *shunned,* man, as subsequent events were all too soon to demonstrate.

Most of the guests agreed, too, that the police should have been called while Tamar's partner was throwing her all over the dance floor and tearing her already flimsy nightgown, or whatever it was, to tattered ribbons, never a cop around when you needed one. Neo-realism was one thing, but here was this big muscular guy tossing around this little thing who couldn't weigh more than a hundred and ten pounds, if that, in an utterly convincing attempt to rape her. It didn't help that she was blond and he was black, the stereotype reinforced. What he was doing to her on that dance floor was intolerable.

So it was with considerable relief that the audience, black and white alike, saw Tamar wrap her tiny defenseless little hands around thin air, saw her grasp whatever imaginary something she was grasping (a vorpal sword, as it turned out), and rise up against this vicious *animal,* was what he was! who was determined to violate and despoil this flower of virgin maidenhood. 'One two! One two!' they all agreed, 'and through and through, the vorpal blade went snicker-snack! He left it dead,' they further agreed, 'and with its head, he went galumphing back.'

The witnesses they questioned all seemed somewhat puzzled as to *who* exactly the 'he' in the lyrics was since Tamar was very much a 'she,' especially now that she was standing there tall and proud but bedraggled in her tattered underwear, or whatever it was, with half her admirable attributes hanging out for all and sundry to see. (This was a point that would spark considerable debate in the days to come, but Carella and Hawes didn't yet know the kind of notoriety this case would inspire; for now, they were just two working stiffs doing their jobs, and trying to protect their asses from Federal flack down the line.) In any case, just as Tamar's father, or whoever he was, her guardian perhaps, finished congratulating her on having slain the Jabberwock (instead of the Bandersnatch, by the way, after whom the song was named) and just as everything was back to normal again, with all the creatures gyring and gimbling and all the mome raths . . .

Just then, these two big black guys came barreling down the stairway with automatic weapons in their hands. One of them had his right hand on the mahogany banister, his left hand pointing the barrel of the gun up at the overhead. The other man had his weapon sort of cradled in his arms, his right finger curled around the trigger. Both of them came gliding down the steps almost as gracefully as the black rapist had glided through the song, one of them yelling, 'Don't nobody fucking move!,' which effectively stopped *Tamar* dead in her tracks – but not the words to the song.

Until that moment, many people in the audience hadn't realized she was lip-synching. But now the words kept blaring from the speakers on either side of the dance floor . . .

'. . . borogroves
'And the mome raths outgrabe . . .'

. . . even though Tamar's mouth wasn't moving anymore. She was just standing stock still, staring wide-eyed at these two masked apparitions who came rushing toward her with seemingly malicious intent. She wondered for a moment – as in fact did the audience – if this wasn't somehow part of the act. Had Barney Loomis hired a supplementary dance team to add additional spice to the evening? But just then Jonah, the beast lying dead at her feet, popped up from the floor in response to the growled 'Don't nobody fucking move!' Hunched in a dancer's crouch, arms widespread for balance, still wearing the hideous crimson-colored mask he'd worn in the finale, he must have seemed enormously threatening to the two men who were now not two feet away from where Tamar still stood in dumbfounded shock.

The left-handed one (the witnesses all agreed that Saddam Hussein had carried the weapon in his left hand throughout) reacted at once, swinging the gun at Jonah's head. Designed for the Soviet Army following World War II, the AK-47 was a sturdily built, well-designed gun with a pistol grip as well as a rifle stock. It was the stock that caught Jonah under the chin, sending him falling backward and onto the floor, where once again he lay prostrate as if dead – but this time a thin line of blood began seeping from under his mask.

The two men and Tamar stood frozen in surreal proximity, she in ivory-white tatters, they in inky black costumes and Middle Eastern masks, Mr. Hussein and Mr. Arafat. Nobody in the audience moved. The witnesses all agreed on this; there was only a stunned silence. The sole sound or motion was on the dance floor itself, where Tamar suddenly tried to break free of the little knot of three, only to be yanked back at once and slapped very hard by Hussein, the left-handed one. She reeled from the blow. The other one, the taller of the two . . .

The witnesses agreed that Yasir Arafat was about six-feet-two-inches tall, and his left-handed accomplice,

Saddam Hussein, was some two or three inches shorter than that, a bit under six feet perhaps, both of them very muscularly built, which perhaps accounted for the first impression of a dance team coming down the steps . . .

The taller of the two suddenly clamped a wet rag over Tamar's face, and she fell against him limply. He threw her over his shoulder. The left-handed one shouted, 'You move, she dies!' and they backed away up the steps, their guns trained on the still-speechless audience.

That was about it.

BARNEY LOOMIS, CEO of Bison Records, was furious. Or perhaps frumious. Or perhaps both.

'That son of a bitch *slapped* her!' he shouted into Carella's face. He smelled of seared mustard salmon, which was the entrée he'd had for dinner. He also smelled of a men's cologne named 'Acrid' which a lot of men in the music industry favored because it had the silhouette of a Luger pistol on its label. 'She's a fragile person,' Loomis shouted, 'a child practically! This is a child kidnapping, she's a child, she just celebrated her twentieth birthday in January! I want her *back* here! That man was a maniac, you could see he was deranged, first he hit Jonah with the gun . . .'

'I think I'm still bleeding,' Jonah said.

He had taken off the monster mask, and it was plain to see he wasn't still bleeding, but he kept exploring his jaw line tentatively, his eyes still wide in fright. Carella hoped he wasn't going to faint.

'You're not bleeding,' Loomis told him. 'Go put on some clothes, go get dressed for Chrissake! How many kidnappings have you investigated this year?' he asked Carella.

'None,' Carella said. 'This year? None.'

'How about last year? How about the past five, ten years? How many friggin kidnappings have you ever handled in your entire life as a cop?'

'One,' Carella answered. 'In my entire life as a cop,' he added.

Loomis blinked at him.

'Well, at least you're honest,' he said.

'At least that,' Carella agreed. 'But you don't have to worry. I'm sure the FBI will . . .'

'Whoever,' Loomis said. 'All I want is Tamar back. And *fast!*'

'All *I* want,' a woman's voice said, 'is to get my tape on the air. And *fast!*'

They all turned.

Carella recognized the woman at once. He had met her in the Grover Park Zoo this past Christmas when she was covering the 'Lions Attack Woman' story. He had spoken to her on the phone only recently, soliciting a possible job at Channel Four for his wife, Teddy.

'Hello, Honey,' he said and extended his hand. 'Nice to see you again.'

'I taped the whole thing, you know,' she said. 'In case anyone's interested.'

'*Interested?*' Carella said. 'When can we . . . ?'

'Back off,' Honey said. 'Nobody sees it till Channel Four airs it.'

'Good!' Loomis said at once. 'Let the whole damn city see what happened here tonight. Let the whole *world* see it! That maniac hitting her!'

'No one's broadcasting any evidence tape until I clear it with my superiors,' Carella said.

'Evidence tape? What?'

'I'll subpoena it, Honey.'

'Ashcroft notwithstanding, I thought this was still a

free country.'

'A girl's been kidnapped here, Miss,' Hawes told her.

She turned to look at him.

'This is my partner, Cotton Hawes,' Carella said. 'Cotton, this is Honey Blair of Channel Four News.'

'I watch you all the time,' Hawes said, and nodded.

Honey looked him over. She was seeing a tall, wide-shouldered man with blue eyes and flaming red hair except for a white streak some two inches wide over his left temple.

Hawes was seeing a blonde some five-feet-seven-inches tall, wearing a blue leather mini and an ice-blue, long-sleeved blouse and calf-high navy leather boots and looking infinitely more beautiful than she ever had on television.

Honey Blair and Cotton Hawes had met.

'Red, tell your partner here . . .' Honey started.

'It's Cotton,' he said softly, and looked into her eyes.

'Cotton, please tell your partner,' she said, returning his gaze, 'that I'm sitting on the biggest scoop I've ever had in my life, a live tape of a kidnapping in progress, and if he doesn't let me go in the next five minutes, Channel Four will bring suit against the city,' she said, and smiled sweetly.

'We'll slap a court order on the tape,' Carella said.

'I don't care what you do after we air it.'

'I'll seize it as evidence right this minute.'

'My crew won't let you have it.'

'Then I'll arrest them as accessories to the crime of kidnapping.'

'As *what*? You'll *what*?'

'For withholding vital evidence,' Hawes explained.

Honey gave him a curt, dismissive look.

'Am I still bleeding?' Jonah asked.

71

'Will you go put on some clothes?' Loomis said.

'How'd I look on camera?' Jonah asked Honey.

'Gorgeous, darling.'

Jonah beamed and went off toward the changing room. The natives were beginning to get extremely restless, milling and seething and whiffling all around the ball-room deck as McIntosh and his crew continued taking names, addresses, and telephone numbers.

'So who *will* be handling this?' Loomis asked Carella. 'You or the FBI?'

'For now, it's us,' Carella said. 'We caught it, we'll fin-ish up here, and then go do the paperwork. I'll talk to my lieutenant as soon as we get back to the squadroom, see what he advises. I'm sure this'll go to them, don't worry. Meanwhile, we'll want to contact the girl's parents. Do you know where we can . . . ?'

'Forget it,' Loomis said, 'they're divorced. Her father's living in Mexico with his second wife, her mother's in Europe someplace.'

'Are they people of means, would you know?'

'He used to sell vacuum cleaners, Christ knows what he's doing now. Her mother's a hairdresser. I'm sure nei-ther of them is wealthy.'

'Then why would anyone want to kidnap her?' Hawes asked.

'Maybe because Tamar Valparaiso . . .'

Valparaiso, Carella thought. *Not* Valentino.

'. . . is under contract to Bison Records,' Loomis said, and nodded in sudden understanding. 'Of course,' he said. 'That's got to be it. I'm CEO and sole shareholder in the company. They're going to ask *me* for the goddamn money.'

'Then you better sit by the phone,' Hawes suggested.

*

BY FOUR A.M., McIntosh and his HPU team had gathered all the vitals from the passengers, crew, and caterers, had passed the list onto the detectives from the Eight-Seven, and had gone tootling off on their thirty-six footer into an early morning mist. The Mobile Crime Unit had arrived some two hours earlier and were examining the primary access routes. Half a dozen male and female technicians were still dusting and vacuuming the salon stairway and the small dance floor where most of the action had taken place. Another three were doing the same thing outside on the loading platform and boarding ladder, concentrating especially on latent footprints. And yet another three were searching for evidence on the second-level cocktail lounge, where it was presumed the perps had entered before moving down to the lower deck.

Disembarked and disoriented after their nocturnal ordeal, the weary voyagers dispersed in various directions, Captain Reeves – as befitted his role as commander – being the last to leave his vessel.

('Captain *Peeved,*' Hawes called him behind his back but within earshot of Honey Blair, who, he noticed with satisfaction, acknowledged the sarcastic sobriquet with a reluctant smile of approval.)

The fog gathering around them, the detectives and the television people walked together in silence to where they'd parked in the AUTHORIZED PERSONNEL zone dockside. Carella had indeed seized the tape as evidence. Honey was indeed intending to bring suit against the city. Hawes did not think this was such a good start for a relationship.

Honey and her crew climbed into the Channel Four van; the two detectives got into their unmarked Chevy sedan. The streets were empty at this early hour of the morning. Carella and Hawes made it back to the squad-room in less than ten minutes.

There was still a lot of work to do before the shift ended.

'**YOU SHOULDN'T HAVE** hit her so hard,' Avery was telling Cal.

'Come on, it was only a slap,' Cal said.

'You knocked her down. That was more than a slap.'

'She was making a run for it.'

Tamar Valparaiso was still unconscious and draped alongside Kellie Morgan on the back seat of the Ford Explorer, her head on Kellie's shoulder, her hands and feet bound, a blindfold over her eyes.

Kellie, to tell the truth, was sort of overwhelmed to be in such close proximity to someone she perceived to be a rock star even though she'd only seen her perform once at a club over in the next state, and that was at least nine months ago, before Tamar had got her recording contract.

They had left the Rinker at the Fairfield Street dock, all the way downtown in the Old Quarter of the city, taking with them only any personal items, and the masks, and the weapons, transferring all and sundry into the Ford. Avery was now driving. Cal was sitting beside him. They were moving slowly through the fog and the deserted streets, observing the speed limit, stopping at any red traffic light or full stop sign, but not traveling so slowly as to attract police attention. That was the last thing they needed at this stage of the game.

The tendrils of the fog embraced the car as if to crush it. Fog frightened Kellie. You never knew what might come at you out of a fog.

'When they pay the ransom,' Avery said, still on the case, 'we're supposed . . .'

'*If* they pay the ransom,' Cal corrected.

'They'll pay it, don't worry. But then we're supposed to return her safe and sound. If we send her back with her face all bruised . . .'

'Ain't no bruises on her face,' Cal said.

'Girl's face is her fortune,' Kellie said from the back seat.

'Ours, too,' Avery reminded her.

'Tits ain't so bad, neither,' Cal said and grinned.

'Hey, cool that shit,' Kellie said.

'The way you hit her,' Avery said, refusing to let go, 'her face is gonna swell up like a balloon.'

'Black and blue already,' Kellie said, looking over at Tamar and nodding.

'How's she doing otherwise?' Avery asked.

'Still out like a light,' Kellie said. 'We got a blanket or something? She's half-naked here.'

'That ain't our fault,' Cal said. 'She stripped her own self buck ass naked. They can't blame us for that.'

'They can blame you for swatting her,' Avery insisted.

'How'd you like my swatting the monster, huh?' Cal asked, grinning, turning to look at Avery. 'Or didn't you like that, either? Him crouched and ready to spring for our throats, how come *you* didn't swat him, Ave? You were standing right there in front of him. How come *you* didn't take a swing?'

'Because we agreed no violence.'

'That was our agreement, yes,' Kellie said.

'You go in with 47s,' Cal said, 'you got to expect violence.'

'Not if we agreed beforehand.'

'That was before I knew anybody was gonna go for my throat.'

'I don't think he was about to go for you,' Avery said

reasonably. 'He was just assessing the situation. He heard you yelling, he naturally wondered what was going on, him being on the floor and all, where he couldn't see. So he lifted himself up to take a look. You shouldn't've hit him and you *certainly* shouldn't've hit the girl. I don't want you hitting her again, Cal, you hear me?'

'Tell him,' Kellie said.

The car went silent.

The fog embraced it.

'Any questions?' Avery asked.

'Yeah. How do you get out of this chickenshit outfit?' Cal said, and laughed at his own witticism.

Nobody laughed with him.

IN THIS CITY, the facades of the buildings conceal a multitude of endeavors, many of them criminal. Whore houses flourish on any avenue or side street, blatantly advertising themselves in the trendiest magazines as massage parlors, offering up to the tired businessman or the restless college kid a variety of pleasures to satisfy the most obsessive connoisseur. Here in this carnal candyland, the night stalker can find whatever he desires, at whatever price. Nor is this American flesh bazaar limited to the big bad city alone. Travel to the so-called heartland. Open the yellow pages of the local telephone directory, or surf the Internet in your hotel room. It is there. It is everywhere. It is available.

Many of the hidden warrens in this and other American cities now house drug pads to shame the ancient opium dens of China. Where not too many years ago, you could smoke a crack pipe in one of these places for a mere five bucks, this cheap cocaine derivative has now mysteriously fallen out of favor, to be replaced by heroin as the drug of choice, an ascendancy that no doubt thrills the poppy growers in Afghanistan now that they've been liberated by American soldiers. A sharp loaded with a heroin hit now cost almost three times as much as a puff of crack used to cost. You lay on a narrow cot, and an attendant wrapped a rubber tube around your arm and serviced you. It was like getting blown by a Korean whore in a similar shabby little apartment two blocks away, only better.

Early Sunday morning, far from the sordid city scene, in a gray-shingled beach house on a fog-shrouded beach in Russell County, miles from where the abduction on the River Harb had taken place, Tamar Valparaiso was just regaining consciousness.

3.

SOMETHING was covering her eyes.

She could not open her eyes because whatever it was — a cloth blindfold, duct tape, whatever — was so tight. Her first instinct was to reach up with her right hand to pull it free, whatever it was, but she discovered at once that her hands were bound behind her back. Her next instinct was to scream, but there was a gag in her mouth, as tight as the blindfold over her eyes. Run, she thought, run!, and tried to get to her feet, but her ankles were bound, too. She struggled for a moment, angrily, panicking in her helplessness, kicking out at nothing, and then lying still and silent, breathing hard, trying to figure out what was happening to her here.

All at once, she remembered.

Two men coming down the steps just as she was finishing the number. One of them hitting her. The other one clamping a sweet-smelling rag over her nose.

She lay still in the darkness.

Remembering.

She knew even before she began exploring with her legs, reaching out with her legs and her sandaled feet to touch the boundaries of the space she was in, knew somehow even before her feet touched the confining, defining walls, that she was in a closet. Lying on the hard wooden floor of a closet, her shallow breathing seeming to echo back at her in a small airless cubicle.

She almost panicked again.

She kicked out at the walls, tried to scream again,

almost choked, tried to cough out the gag, tried to force her eyes open, her lids fluttering helplessly against the blindfold. She tried to calm herself. Sucked in great gulps of air through her nose. Lay still and silent for several moments, regaining her cool, telling herself to relax, be still.

She eased herself up into a sitting position, her back to what she supposed was the rear wall of the closet. Exploring with her feet, she located what she guessed was a hinge, the thin sole of her slightly heeled sandal catching on something that jutted from the otherwise flat surface, yes, it had to be a hinge, yes, she was indeed facing the closet door.

Bracing both feet hard against the floor, she inched her back slowly up the rear wall of the closet, banging her head on what was obviously a recessed horizontal shelf, but easing her way up and around it, and struggling to her feet at last. Her hands tied behind her back, her feet bound, essentially blind and mute, she used her head and her shoulder to explore the hinged side of the door, locating another hinge higher up. Using her nose as a pointer, she zeroed in on a small protruding knob at the top of the hinge.

The blindfold ended just above her cheekbone. She pressed the side of her face against the hinge, and tried to hook the edge of the blindfold over the knob. She was about to give up, when – on the eighth or ninth attempt – she finally snagged it. Yanking downward with a sharp jerk of her head, she pulled the blindfold loose, and opened her eyes.

A thin ribbon of light limned the lower edge of the closet door.

She waited for her eyes to adjust.

Duct tape.

It was duct tape.

The same thing that bound her ankles, and undoubtedly her hands, which she could not see.

She searched the closet floor and the shelf at eye level for any sharp object that might help her free her hands or her feet.

There was nothing.

She tried to hook the gag over the same hinge that had served her with the blindfold. But because it was a rag twisted an inch or so inside her mouth, and tied tightly at the back of her head, there was no slack to it at all, and she could not free it.

She did not know what to do next.

CARELLA wanted to know what they were supposed to do next.

He had waited till a respectable seven A.M. before phoning Lieutenant Byrnes, and now the two men were discussing whether or not they should drag the FBI into this.

'For all I know, Loomis has already called them,' Carella said.

'Who's Loomis?' Byrnes asked.

In the background, Carella could hear a television set going. He imagined his boss at breakfast, sitting at his kitchen table over bacon and eggs, watching television as he ate. Byrnes was a compact man in his fifties, white-haired and blunt-featured. He had no particular fondness for the FBI.

'Barney Loomis,' Carella said. 'He's the CEO of Bison Records. He thinks the perps are going to ask him for the ransom.'

'Oh? How come?'

'Her parents are divorced, one in Mexico, the other in

Europe. Also, neither of them has any money.'

'State line been crossed here?' Byrnes asked.

'We don't know where the boat went after the snatch. Could've gone across the river, sure, docked someplace there. In which case, yes, a state line's been crossed.'

'You say this girl's a celebrity?'

'Personally, I never heard of her, Pete. According to Loomis, she's the hottest thing around. But he owns the label, so what do you expect him to say?'

'You think he may have already called the Feds?'

'I have no idea. He wants that girl back.'

'What'd you say her name was?'

'Tamar Valparaiso.'

'Cause here she is now,' Byrnes said, and got up to raise the volume on the television set. 'Can you hear this?' he asked Carella.

'I can hear it,' Carella said, and nodded grimly.

'. . . from a luxury yacht in the River Harb last night,' a television newscaster was saying. 'According to U.S. Coast Guard reports . . .'

'How'd they'd get in this?' Byrnes said into the phone.

'Harbor Patrol called them.'

'. . . two armed and masked men boarded the *River Princess* at about ten-fifteen, seizing the talented young singer as she was performing her debut album, *Bandersnatch,* for a hundred or more invited guests . . .'

'What channel is that?' Carella asked.

'Five,' Byrnes said.

'Four's gonna sue the city.'

'. . . Barney Loomis, who says Bison has not yet received a ransom demand. In Riverhead this morning . . .'

'That's it,' Byrnes said, and lowered the volume. 'Sue the city? Why?'

'Cause I confiscated a tape of the kidnapping.'

'Ooops.'

'It was evidence. So what do we do here, Pete? Pursue this or phone the FBI?'

'Let me talk to the Commish. I'll tell you the truth, I don't know. What I *don't* want is for the Feds to use us as errand boys. That's the last thing I want. Nobody called from them yet, huh?'

'Not yet.'

'Let me see what the Commish advises. I know he won't want heat later on, anybody saying we dropped the ball prematurely. You're about out of there, anyway, aren't you?'

Carella looked up at the clock.

'Half an hour,' he said.

'Get some sleep, you may have to come back in. I don't know how this is gonna fall, Steve, we'll have to play it as it lays. Call me later, okay?'

'You coming in today?'

'No, it's supposed to be my day off. Call me at home.'

'There's the other line,' Carella said.

'I'll wait. Maybe it's the Feds.'

Carella put Byrnes on HOLD, stabbed at a button on the base of his phone.

'Carella,' he said.

'Carella, this is Sandy McIntosh, HPU. You got a minute?'

'Yeah, hang on.' He switched over to Byrnes again. 'It's the Harbor Patrol. Am I on the job, or what?'

'Stay with it for now,' Byrnes said. 'Call me later.'

Carella switched to the other line again.

'Okay, Sandy, I'm back,' he said.

'This may be nothing at all,' McIntosh said, 'or maybe you can use it. Around nine-fifteen, nine-thirty last night . . .'

IT WAS NOT often that this precinct caught something as big as a celebrity kidnapping – if, in fact, Tamar Valparaiso *was* a celebrity and not some figment of a record label's imagination.

Neither Bert Kling nor Meyer Meyer had ever heard of her. Perhaps this was not too surprising in Meyer's case. His kids listened to rock, but he was tone deaf when it came to anything more recent than the Beatles. Kling, on the other hand, was familiar with all the new groups, and even listened to rap on occasion. He had never heard of Tamar Valparaiso, even though her face and her story were splashed all over that morning's tabloids.

The two men signed in at seven-forty-five, were briefed by Carella and Hawes – who were exhausted after a long night on the water – and then headed out at eight-thirty, to pick up where the departing team had left off.

Sandy McIntosh had reported stopping a twenty-seven-foot Rinker at around nine-fifteen, nine-thirty last night, heading inbound toward Capshaw Boats, its home marina, at Fairfield and the river, just off Pier Seven. Three passengers aboard. Two men and a woman. Name on the boat's transom was *Hurley Girl*. Serial number stenciled on each of her sides was XL721G. Capshaw Boats was where Meyer and Kling were headed on this misty Sunday morning.

Today was the fourth of May.

Meyer had celebrated his wife's birthday the night before, ordering champagne for everyone in the small French restaurant where they'd dined – not an enormously big deal in that there'd been only half a dozen other patrons. He'd sure as hell impressed Sarah, though. Sarah Lipkin when he met her all those years ago. 'Nobody's lips kin like Sarah's lips kin' was what the fraternity banter maintained, a premise Meyer was eager to test. Married all these years now, never tired of her lips. Married all these years now, he could still impress her with six bottles of champagne. Veuve Cliquot, though, don't forget.

Clear-eyed this morning, despite the full bottle of bubbly he and Sarah had shared last night, he was at the wheel of the police sedan, wondering out loud if the Feds would be coming in on this one.

'Thing I don't like about working with them,' he said, 'is they have this superior . . .'

'Way I understand it, it's a dead cinch they'll come in,' Kling said.

'Then why are *we* shlepping all the way downtown?'

'Way the Loot wants it. Guess he'd like a heads up, case there's static later on.'

'*What's* her name again?' Meyer asked.

'Tamar Valparaiso.'

'Never heard of her.'

This was the third time he'd said this.

'Me, neither,' Kling said.

Third time for him, too.

The two made a good pair.

Both men were some six feet tall, but Meyer presented a burlier look, perhaps because he was entirely bald, perhaps because he was possessed of a steady, patient demeanor that made him seem somewhat plodding in contrast to Kling's more open, enthusiastic country-boy style. Born and bred in this city, Kling nonetheless looked like he'd been found in a basket in a corn field. He was the perfect Good Cop to Meyer's Bad Cop, although often they switched roles for the fun of it, blond, hazel-eyed, fuzzy-cheeked Kling suddenly snarling like a pit bull, steely blue-eyed big bald Meyer purring like a pussy cat.

The man who owned Capshaw Boats and its adjoining marina was a one-eyed former Navy SEAL who called himself Popeye, not to anyone's great surprise. He had opened the marina at a little before six this morning . . .

'Lots of skippers like to get out on the water before all the river traffic begins. That's a nice calm time of day, you know,' he said, 'that time just before sunrise. It's called morngloam, not many people know that.'

Meyer certainly didn't know it.

Neither did Kling.

'I think it's a Scottish word,' Popeye said. 'Morngloam. The opposite of it is evengloam. That's the time just before sunset. Evengloam. I think it comes from the word "gloaming." I think that's a Scottish word. The derivation, I mean. I think it's Scottish.'

'Tell you what we're looking for,' Kling said. 'Harbor Patrol stopped a boat from your marina last night . . .'

'Oh?' Popeye said, his one good eye widening in surprise.

'Name's *Hurley Girl,* serial number's . . .'

'Oh, sure, the Rinker. She was already back in this morning, when I got here.'

'Whose boat is she?' Meyer asked.

'Mine. Well, Capshaw's. I rent her out.'

'Then she doesn't belong to one of your customers, is that it?'

'No, she's mine. I just told you. She's a rental boat. I sell boats, and I store boats, and I service boats, but I also rent them.'

'Who'd you rent this one to? Would you remember?'

'Oh, sure. Nice young feller. I've got his name inside.'

'Can you let us know who he was?' Kling asked.

'Oh, sure. Just let me finish here a minute, okay?'

He was washing down one of the boats. Soaping it,

hosing it. Meyer watched him with interest. Kling looked upriver where early morning traffic was already moving steadily across the bridge to the next state.

'When you say she came back in . . .' Meyer said.

'She was tied up at the dock when I got in this morning.'

'When did she go out?'

'Evengloam last night. Nice time of day.'

'You rented her out last night at sundown . . .'

'Just before sundown. Twilight. Evengloam.'

'When was she due back in?'

'Well, she was a twenty-four-hour rental. Actually, she wasn't due back till this evening sometime. I was surprised to find her here this morning.'

'We'd like that name, if you can get it for us,' Kling said.

'Oh, sure,' Popeye said, and turned off the hose. 'Come on in.'

They followed him inside. The office was hung with lobster pots and fishing nets. Through the windows facing the river, Meyer and Kling could see racks and racks of stacked boats. Popeye went behind the counter, vanished from sight for a moment as he knelt beneath it. He emerged again, plunked a long narrow black book onto the counter top, and began riffling through its pages.

'Name was Andy Hardy,' he told them.

'Andy Hardy, huh?' Meyer said.

'There it is, right there,' Popeye said, and turned the registry log so they could see the name.

'That's Mickey Rooney,' Meyer said. 'A character he played in the movies. Andy Hardy.'

'You know, you're right,' Popeye said, opening his one good eye wide in surprise.

'Never occurred to you, huh?' Kling said. 'While this guy was renting the boat?'

'Well, the name did sound familiar, but we get a lot of people in here, you know. Sometimes too *many* damn people, you ask me.'

'How'd he pay for the rental?'

'Credit card.'

'Showed you a credit card with the name Andy Hardy on it?'

'Andy Hardy was what it said. Same as on his driver's license. Picture matched his face, too. You rent a boat, it's the same as when you rent a car, you know. You're responsible for it. There's more boating accidents, ratio of boats to cars, than there are automobile accidents, you know. Anything happens to the boat — theft, fire, accident — I've got the man's credit card.'

'And you got Andy Hardy's credit card for the little *Hurley Girl* out there, is that it?'

'You betcha,' Popeye said.

'Think we can get a line on Mr. Hardy?' Kling asked Meyer.

'Fat Chance Department,' Meyer said.

'I saw his driver's license, too, I just told you,' Popeye said. 'He seemed legit to me.'

'Maybe he is,' Kling said. 'We'll hit the computers when we get back to the office.'

'We'll want our people to look over that boat, too,' Meyer said.

He was already on his cell phone.

'Why?' Popeye asked.

'It may have been used in a crime,' Kling said.

Meyer was dialing a number he knew by heart.

'How'd this Andy Hardy get here?' Kling asked.

'What do you mean?'

'Did he walk up? Drive up in his own car? Arrive in a taxi? How'd he get here?'

'In a black Ford Explorer. Two other people with him. They waited in the van while he filled out the rental papers.'

'Can I take a look at those papers?' Kling asked.

'Sure,' Popeye said, and went digging under the counter again. Meyer was just telling the Mobile Crime Unit where to find them.

'Man and a woman, right?' Kling said. 'These two other people with him?'

'How'd you know that?' Popeye asked.

'Happen to see the license plate number?'

'Didn't look. Here you go,' Popeye said, and put the rental folder for the Rinker on the counter top. Kling leafed through it. Andy Hardy, sure enough. Gave an address in Connecticut.

'Was the driver's license issued in Connecticut?' Kling asked.

'Yep.'

'This address match the one on the license?'

'Yep. That's why I asked to see it.'

Meyer pressed the END button on his cell phone, looked over at the papers Kling had spread on the counter top.

'They're on the way,' he said.

'Did they leave the van here when they went out on the boat?' Kling asked.

'Unloaded it and left it, yes.'

'Unloaded it?'

'Took a carton from it.'

'What kind of carton?' Meyer asked.

'This cardboard carton. Not very big.' He showed the size with his hands.

'Think the masks might've been in it?' Meyer asked.

'You talking to me?' Popeye said.

'My partner.'

'Could be,' Kling said. 'Any writing on the carton?'

'Didn't see any.'

'And you say they left the van here?'

'In the parking lot, yes.'

'Was it gone this morning?'

'Didn't notice.'

'When you came in, I mean.'

'Didn't notice,' Popeye said again.

They were trying to pinpoint the exact time the suspects might have dropped off the boat and departed in the van.

'Do renters usually return boats in the middle of the night?' Kling asked.

'No, when their time's up, usually. The rental period.'

'Are all your rentals for twenty-four hours?'

'No, we sometimes rent for a week. Sometimes longer.'

'But this one was for twenty-four hours.'

'Yes.'

'Evengloam to evengloam,' Meyer said.

'Supposed to be.'

'But Hardy brought it back early.'

'Yes.'

'Anybody here to receive a boat in the middle of the night?'

'We've got a night watchman, but he doesn't check boats in, nothing like that.'

'So they just leave them at the dock, is that it?' Kling said.

'With nobody here to check them in,' Meyer said.

'We don't have too many people bringing boats back before they're due,' Popeye said.

'But Andy Hardy did.'

'What'd this guy *do,* anyway?' Popeye asked.

'Maybe nothing,' Kling said. 'Is your watchman here now?'

'Left when I opened up this morning.'

'How do we find him?'

'Let me get you his address,' Popeye said, and went over to a desk under a calendar of a girl wearing a sailor hat and hardly anything else.

'Phone number, too, please,' Meyer said.

THREE DETECTIVES from the MCU arrived at Capshaw Boats at twenty to eleven that morning. Meyer and Kling were waiting dockside for them. They hadn't yet boarded the *Hurley Girl* because they didn't know how many, if any, rampant prints the perps may have left aboard her, and they didn't want to mess up anything for the technicians. The chief tech, a Detective/First named Carlie . . .

'For Charles,' he explained.

. . . Epworth listened attentively while Kling told him that a Harbor Patrol Unit vessel had stopped two males and a female on the boat right here an hour or so before the abduction last . . .

'*What's* her name again?' Epworth asked. 'The vic?'

'Tamar Valparaiso.'

'Never heard of her,' he said. 'Is she supposed to be famous or something?'

'Supposed to be,' Meyer said.

'Never heard of her,' Epworth said again.

'Anyway, it was only the two males who boarded the *River Princess,* is the name of the launch she was taken from. So we figure the female stayed behind on the boat here, at the wheel. And maybe she left some latents. On

90

the wheel, is what I'm saying. The two males were wearing gloves, but they were up to no good. So maybe the female was more relaxed and got careless.'

'Okay,' Epworth said.

'Is just a suggestion,' Kling said.

'Wearing gloves when they boarded the launch, you mean, right?'

'Yeah, right, when they did the deed.'

'But maybe they took them off when they were on their way home, is another possibility,' Epworth said.

'Opportunities are running rife,' Meyer said.

'Might turn out to be my lucky day,' Epworth said, grinning. 'What'd you say that launch was called?'

'The *River Princess*.'

'I think I saw a file on her back at the office.'

'Anybody get anything yet?'

'I don't know. It was on another desk.'

''Cause this case is getting a lot of play, you know.'

'What do you mean?'

'The papers, the media.'

'You gonna need us here?' Kling said.

'Leave me your card. I'll get back one way or another.'

'We won't be back in the office for a few hours,' Kling said. 'Possible witness we've got to see.'

'To what? The snatch?'

'We've got a hundred and twelve of them.'

'Bold mother-fuckers, weren't they?'

'Depends how you define it.'

'I didn't say "brave," I said "bold."'

'That they were. So when do you think you'll be done here?'

Epworth looked at his watch.

'One, two o'clock, in there,' he said. 'Depends on how clean she is.'

'We should be back home by then.'

'I'll find you, don't worry,' Epworth said. 'Are the Feds in this yet?'

'Not yet,' Kling said.

'But you said it's getting a lot of play, right?'

'Right.'

'They'll come sniffing, you can bet on it,' Epworth said, and opened the gate on the *Hurley Girl*'s transom entry, and signaled to his crew. 'Anybody been aboard her yet?' he asked.

'Just the possible perps,' Meyer said.

'Makes it easy then, don't it?' Epworth said, and grinned.

CARELLA was sound asleep when Lieutenant Byrnes called him at twelve-thirty that Sunday. He waited a respectable four rings before remembering that this was Fanny's day off and Teddy was taking the twins to the park, and then hastily yanked the receiver from its cradle.

'Carella,' he said.

'Steve, it's Pete.'

'Yes, Pete.'

'I spoke to the Commish. First off, you'd better get that tape back to Honey Blaine . . .'

'Blair.'

'Whoever, before the city lands a very big law suit. Channel Four has already contacted the Mayor, who is not particularly known for courageous stands, anyway, and he got on his lawyerly high horse and lectured the Commish about illegal search and seizure and all that bullshit . . .'

'Yeah,' Carella said wearily.

'So you'd better . . . where is it, anyway, that tape?'

'In my bottom desk drawer.'

'I'll call in, have a uniform run it over to the . . .'

'No, the drawer's locked. I've got the key here.'

'This Blaine woman . . .'

'Blair.'

'. . . is sitting down there in the Channel Four offices with a battery of network lawyers, waiting for us to deliver that tape. We've got till three o'clock. Otherwise, they file. Can you get the tape over there by then?'

'Yes. But I still think it's evidence.'

'The network thinks it's a scoop worth forty million dollars . . .'

'More than I make in a week,' Carella said.

'. . . which is what they'll sue for if they don't get that tape by three o'clock. Can you run down to the squad-room? Messenger the tape over?'

'Sure,' Carella said, and yawned. 'What time is it?'

'Twelve-thirty-five.'

'Shall I wake Cotton? Are we still on this case, or what?'

'Far as I know. Nobody's heard a peep from the Feds, so I guess it's still ours. Ain't we lucky?'

'Oh my yes.'

'I guess this singer isn't very important, huh? Did Meyer and Bert get anything on the boat?'

'I've been asleep, Pete.'

'Right, I'm sorry. Stick with it, the four of you. Call Loomis, see if there's been a ransom demand yet. If this is really ours . . .'

'You just said it was, Pete.'

'Well, it is.'

'But you sound dubious.'

'I'm just surprised. I thought the Feds would've come knocking by now. Anyway, call Loomis. Is his office open today?'

'I have no idea.'

'You said he thought the perps might ask him for the money.'

'That's what he told me, yes.'

'So how will they know where to reach him? Did you get his home number?'

'Yes, Pete.'

'Do you think *they* have his home number?'

'I doubt it.'

'So they'll call at his office tomorrow, right? So let's get our Tech Unit to set up some stuff for us. We won't need a court order for a Tap and Trap, Loomis is a friendly, it's his own phone. But you'll need one for a Trap and Trace, maybe more than one. Try to get the equipment set up today, ready for when they call tomorrow, if they call.'

'I'll get on it right away.'

'I hate kidnappings,' Byrnes said, and sighed.

Both men fell silent.

'I sure would like a look at that tape,' Carella said.

'I have a feeling you'll be seeing it on television. Over and over again. But you've got till three o'clock. Play it before you take it back. Who's to know?'

'Is that an order?'

'It's a suggestion,' Byrnes said.

THE WATCHMAN'S name was Abner Carmody.

He was asleep when Detectives Meyer and Kling knocked on his door at one that afternoon. He complained that he hadn't got to bed till eight this morning, time he got home from the marina and all, and he usually slept till three or four, had a late lunch (or early dinner, depending how you looked at it), and went to work again at six, putting in a twelve-hour day (or night, depending how you looked at it), from six P.M. to six A.M.

'"A man works from sun to sun,"' he quoted out of the

94

blue, '"but a woman's work is never done." So why are you waking me up?'

Carmody was in his sixties someplace, the detectives guessed, wearing striped pajamas and eyeglasses he'd put on when he came to answer the door. He hadn't invited the detectives in yet. They didn't care to go in, either. The man wasn't a suspect, there was nothing they wanted to see in his apartment.

'Sometime last night, maybe eleven-thirty, twelve o'clock,' Meyer prompted. 'Twenty-seven-foot Rinker came in, passengers tied her up and drove off in a black Ford Explorer. Happen to see them?'

'What's this about?'

'Maybe nothing.'

'So why're you waking me up the crack of dawn, it's nothing?'

'We can come back later, if you like,' Kling said. With a warrant, he almost added, but didn't.

'Well, I'm up now,' Carmody said.

'Did you see the boat come in?'

'No, I must've been making rounds, other end of the marina. But I saw them carrying the box to the van, and driving off in it.'

'What box, sir?'

'This carton, maybe yay big,' he said, using his hands. 'Two by two, three by three, no bigger'n that.'

'Heavy box? Did it seem to be heavy?'

'Not especially. Woman was carrying it. Couldn't have been too heavy, could it?'

'The masks,' Meyer said.

Kling nodded.

'What'd they look like?' he asked.

'Was only one of them. Just a plain cardboard box. Brown, you know. What they call corrugated.'

'I mean the people who got in the van. Did you happen to get a look?'

'Oh, yeah, the van was parked right under one of the sodium lights.'

'Two men and a woman, were they?' Kling asked.

'Yessir, two men and a woman. All of them wearing black all over – jeans, sweatshirts, jogging shoes. One of the men had curly black hair, the other one straight blond hair. The girl was a redhead.'

'How old would you say?'

'The girl? Early twenties.'

'And the men?'

'I'd say late twenties, early thirties.'

'I don't suppose you happened to notice the license plate on that van, did you?' Kling asked.

Carmody looked offended.

'I'm a watchman,' he said. 'That's my job. To watch.'

And reeled off what he'd seen on that plate, letter for letter, numeral for numeral.

A PATROLMAN with his back to them was sleeping on a cot in the swing room when Carella and Hawes came in to play the Channel Four tape. The television set down here in the basement of the old building was a relic of the eighties, with a screen much smaller than either of the men had at home, but it had a VCR attachment, and it would serve the purpose. They kept the volume low, so as not to awaken the sleeping patrolman.

Watching the tape was an odd experience.

They had heard this crime reported a hundred different ways by a hundred and twelve different people, so in a sense it was familiar to them. In a sense, they were seeing it all over again. But they were also seeing it for the very first time, objectively, no one telling them whether the men were short or tall or wearing black or blue or green, no one describing the action in often erroneous detail. There it was for them to see and to hear. It was rather like witnessing an actual address to the nation, rather than watching a bunch of talking heads commenting on it minutes later.

Hawes and Carella immediately agreed that the girl was a star.

Hawes voiced it first.

'She's good,' he said.

But they weren't talent scouts.

Nonetheless, she *was* good.

'*Very* good,' Carella agreed.

They were watching the part of the tape where Tamar Valparaiso was standing in uffish thought under the Tum-tum tree, all unaware that she was about to be attacked. There he came now, big and muscular, the Bandersnatch, or the Jabberwock, or whoever her father had just warned her about a couple of seconds ago, suddenly leaping from behind a screen on the left side of the dance floor, looking menacing as hell in a scary clay-colored mask, the kind of guy neither of the detectives would choose to run into in a dark alley.

The ensuing rape, the attempted rape, was all too realistic.

Neither Carella nor Hawes had ever witnessed a rape in progress, but they had heard the testimony of far too many vics, and they knew damn well what the crime was all about. The dancer playing the rapist – there was no way this video could be considered anything but a choreo-graphed visualization of a rape – seemed to understand completely that rape had nothing to do with sex (however sexy Tamar looked as her clothes kept shredding away) but instead had only to do with power. This creature, this thing, this animal seemed resolute in his rage to over-whelm this young girl half his size and weight, determined to prove by sheer force of strength that he was the superior being here, he was in control, he was the master, he would dominate, he would conquer, he would enter and invade and eventually humiliate and disgrace and demean and dishonor and utterly destroy. That was the whole thing about rape. It wasn't about getting laid. It was about showing just who owned who, babe.

They almost felt like intervening.

Jumping up and yelling, 'Police! Stop!'

Probably wake up the sleeping uniform.

But the tape was that real and that frightening.

Then, of course, it all came out all right. Unlike rapes in real life, this one had a happy ending. The girl reached up for some imaginary kind of weapon and slashed out at her assailant . . .

'One, two! One, two! And through and through

'The vorpal blade went snicker-snack!

'He left it dead, and with its head

'He went galumphing back.'

Helpless female becomes powerful male in order to defeat another powerful male. Where was the message there?

The rap ended.

The beast in its enraged crimson mask lay dead on the floor at Tamar's feet.

Now there was only the B-flat note again, that single repeated bass note, and Tamar fluidly moving the tune into the bluesy figure of its opening melody.

'And hast thou slain the Jabberwock?

'Come to my arms, my beamish boy!

'O frabjous day! Callooh! Callay!

'He chortled in his joy.'

Tamar's eyes shone, her voice rang out. She was home, baby, she was home.

'She's terrific,' Hawes said.

'A star,' Carella agreed.

"Twas brillig, and the slithy toves

'Did gyre and gimble in the wabe:

'All mimsy were the . . .'

'Don't nobody fucking *move!*'

'Here they come,' Hawes said, and leaned forward.

And here they came.

The detectives watched the screen intently.

This was a professional tape, recorded by skilled technicians. This wasn't something some passing motorist had shot from his car window because he'd happened to notice it occurring as he drove by. Nor was this something recorded on a bank or a supermarket camera, all fuzzy and grainy and virtually worthless for identification purposes. This was clear and sharp and focused and detailed and in full living color. This was the chronicle of a crime in progress and it would stand up in any court in the land.

You could not see the men's faces because of the masks, Saddam Hussein and Yasir Arafat, two gents intent on a little mischief. They were wearing black long-sleeved sweatshirts and black leather gloves. Black denim trousers. Black socks. Black running shoes.

'Reeboks,' Hawes said.

He had just made out the label.

Carella nodded.

Weapons were AK-47s, no question about it.

The shorter of the two was left-handed. Saddam Hussein. At least, he was carrying the rifle in his left hand. Pointing it up at the ceiling, like the real Hussein about to fire at the sky. Right hand on the mahogany banister.

'Ouch!' Hawes said when Hussein slammed the black

dancer with the stock of the rifle.

They kept watching.

'Son of a bitch,' Hawes said, when Hussein slapped Tamar.

The other one, the taller one, Yasir Arafat, clapped a wet rag over her face.

'You move, she dies!' Hussein yelled.

'He sound black to you?' Carella asked.

'I don't know. Kind of muffled under that mask.'

'Witnesses all seemed to think they were black. I'm not getting that, are you?'

'Let's take another look,' Hawes said, and got up to rewind the tape.

'What's going on?' the sleeping patrolman asked, raising his head.

'Nothing, man, cool it,' Hawes said.

'I was up all fuckin night,' the patrolman said, and rolled over on the cot again.

They played the tape two more times.

They both felt they were missing something.

But they didn't know what.

4.

THE FIRST THING Kellie saw when she took the padlock off the closet door, and then opened the door itself, was a pair of big brown eyes glaring out at her. She slammed the door shut at once.

'Oh, shit!' she said, and fumbled the padlock into the hasp, and snapped it shut again. 'Ave,' she yelled, 'she saw me! Oh, Jesus, Ave, she saw me!' and went running into the kitchen.

The two men were sitting at a small round table near the window, eating the pizza Cal had brought back from the local Pizza Hut.

'What do you mean?' Avery asked.

'I opened the door, she was looking out at me.'

'So what'd you do?'

'Slammed the door shut.'

'So it was just a glimpse, right?'

'But she saw me,' Kellie said, more softly now, like a child trying to explain to her parents that the monster under the bed actually did exist. 'She'll be able to identify me. Later. When we let her go.'

'She won't remember what you looked like. It was just a glimpse, am I right?'

'Yes, but . . .'

'We'll put on the masks. Don't worry, it'll be okay. It was just a glimpse.'

'What'd she do?' Cal asked. 'Get the blindfold off?'

'I opened the closet, she was looking at me with her eyes wide open,' Kellie said, nodding.

'We'll wear the masks from now on,' Avery said. 'You want some pizza?'

'Is it any good?'

'It's delicious,' Cal said. 'Did she look scared?'

'She looked angry.'

'She's supposed to look scared. I'll go scare her when I finish my pizza here. I'll put on my mask and scare the shit out of her.'

'You keep away from her,' Avery said.

'Why'd you open the closet, anyway?' Cal asked.

'See if she wanted anything to eat. We're not supposed to starve her to death, are we?'

'We're supposed to get two hundred and fifty thousand bucks, is what we're supposed to do,' Avery said. 'And then we're supposed to return her safe and sound, end of story.'

'That's what I'm saying, safe and sound,' Kellie said. 'That means feeding her, am I right?'

'We'll feed her, don't worry,' Avery said.

'Oh, we'll take very good care of her, don't worry,' Cal said, and bit into his pizza. Avery gave him a look. 'What?' Cal asked.

'Just stay away from her.'

'Was Kellie went near her, not me.'

'I'll talk to her later,' Avery said. 'When I finish here. Make her understand nobody's going to hurt her.'

'She sure looked mad.'

'Needs a little scare, is what she needs,' Cal said.

Avery looked at him again.

'Just kidding,' Cal said, and held up his hands defensively.

'Have some pizza,' Avery told Kellie.

He seemed very calm, she thought.

Maybe too calm.

The girl had seen her face.

CHANNEL FOUR'S offices were in a skyscraper on Moody Street, just off Jefferson Avenue. Hawes approached the imposing glass and stainless-steel structure through a small pocket park with a waterfall flowing over its rear granite wall. Sitting at round metal tables in bright Sunday afternoon sunshine, half a dozen elderly people drank their cappuccinos or munched on their sandwiches. Hawes wondered what it was like to be old like that, fifty, sixty years or so.

Security was tight here.

A square-shield uniformed guard was standing alongside another man checking names at a lectern-sized desk. Hawes had called ahead, and so Honey Blair was expecting him. But the guy behind the podium asked him to sign in, and then he opened the manila envelope to check the video inside (even though the envelope was imprinted with the words POLICE DEPARTMENT – EVIDENCE) and then he called upstairs before allowing Hawes to proceed to the elevators.

Honey was waiting in the seventh-floor hallway for him.

She was wearing tan tailored slacks and a green cotton knit sweater. Apparently, she favored the short skirts and revealing tops only on camera. She took the evidence envelope from him, and unclasped it to check on the video inside, just the way the guard had. Satisfied, she nodded curtly, said, 'Thanks, I appreciate it,' and was turning to go when Hawes said, 'Hey.'

She stopped.

'We're sorry,' he said. 'We were doing our job.'

'By stopping me from doing mine,' she said. 'You cost me . . .' She looked at her watch. 'It's three o'clock. This tape should've aired at eleven last night. Now it won't go out till the Five O'Clock News. That's seventeen hours you cost me. My scoop went right down the drain.'

'It'll still . . .'

'Be old news by the time anybody sees it.'

'It'll still get a lot of attention. It's a very good tape.'

'Oh, you watched it, huh?'

'Evidence,' he said, and shrugged somewhat boyishly.

'You probably shouldn't have done that.'

'I probably shouldn't have told you I did that.'

Honey nodded. Looked at him.

'Want to watch it again?' she asked.

AVERY HANES knocked on the closet door.

'I'm going to open the door,' he said. 'Don't do anything foolish. No one's going to hurt you. Okay? I know you can't talk, but if you understand me, just kick the door, okay? We're going to let you out of the closet, okay? So kick the door if you understand.'

There was a sharp kick on the door.

Then another one.

Then several in succession.

Sharp angry kicks.

'I'm not sure you're ready for this,' Avery said.

Another series of kicks.

'I'm not sure at all,' he said.

And waited.

There were no further kicks.

He took the key Kellie had given him, inserted it into the hanging lock, twisted it, and then removed the lock from its hasp. He picked up the AK-47 from where he'd momentarily placed it on the floor, and cautiously opened the door.

She was sitting on the floor with her back to the rear

wall of the closet, knees bent, long legs tucked under her, skirt tattered, panties showing. Her brown eyes were wide at first. She blinked them against the sudden light that flooded in.

'Nothing stupid now,' he said.

She opened her eyes again.

He was still wearing a dumb Halloween mask. One of those rubber things you pulled over your entire head. He was Yasir Arafat. She looked straight into the mask. Tried to read the eyes in the holes of the mask.

'Take a good look,' he said. 'They're brown. Like yours.'

She craned her neck, lifted her chin, shook her head violently from side to side, telling him she wanted the gag removed.

'You'll scream,' he said.

She shook her head no.

'If you scream, I'll have to hurt you,' he said.

She kept shaking her head no.

'Are you hungry?'

She nodded. Then shook her head strenuously again and again and again, asking him to please remove the goddamn gag.

'Promise me you won't scream.'

She nodded. Rolled her brown eyes heavenward in solemn promise. He smiled.

Reaching behind her head, he felt for the knot in the twisted rag, found it.

'Turn,' he said.

She turned her head.

He put down the rifle for a moment, started plucking at the knot with the fingers and thumbs of both hands. She spit out the gag the moment she felt it coming loose. Kept coughing. He was afraid she might scream. He was ready to hit her if she screamed. He didn't want to hit her, but he would if she screamed.

'You okay?' he asked.

She nodded.

'Hungry?'

She nodded again.

'I'll untie your feet,' he said.

She nodded.

'You won't try to run, will you?' he asked.

Not until you untie my hands, too, she thought.

'I won't try to run,' she said.

Her throat felt dry, the gag in it all that time.

'If you scream, remember . . .'

'I won't scream.'

'I'll hit you.'

'I remember.'

'Good. So let me untie your feet now.'

Good, she thought. One step at a time.

She stretched her legs out toward him. Suddenly realized she was half-naked in the tattered costume. Almost pulled her legs back. He seemed not to notice. He took a sling blade knife from his pocket, snapped open the blade. It cut through the duct tape like water. She was more afraid of the knife than the rifle.

'Want to stand now?'

'Yes.'

'Want to try standing?'

He closed the knife, put it back in his pocket. She wondered all at once how they'd known where to find her last night. There hadn't been any publicity about the cruise . . . well, she supposed anyone who'd been invited might have talked about it. It occurred to her that someone who'd worked on the video might be in on this. She started running faces through her mind. The grips, the stage hands, the prop guy, the lighting people, the sound technicians. Was one of them an accomplice here?

'You have to believe we're not going to hurt you,' he said.

'I believe you,' she said. 'What is it you want?'

'Just to get you back home safe and sound,' he said.

'I mean . . . how *much* do you want?'

'That's none of your business.'

'Who do you expect to pay it?'

'Barney Loomis.'

He knew Barney's name. He was going to ask Barney for the money, however much it was, unless he'd already asked him. This had to be an inside job. It had to be someone familiar with . . .

'I'll be calling him tomorrow morning. We'll arrange an exchange as soon as possible.'

An exchange, she thought. Me for the money.

How much money? she wondered.

'Everything will be fine,' he said. 'You have to believe me. We don't want to hurt you, and we don't want any trouble. Just don't scream, and don't do anything foolish, okay?'

'I won't do anything foolish,' she promised.

''Cause no one will hear you, anyway,' he said. 'There's no one for miles.'

She said nothing. Was he lying to her?

'Let's get you something to eat, okay?' he said.

'I have to pee,' she said.

THERE WAS A palpable air of excitement in the small dark screening room.

Honey and Hawes sat side by side on cushioned movie-theater seats, six rows of them, eight seats to the row, cup holders on the arms of each seat. They were sitting in the third row. Hawes felt privileged. This was a room reserved for top brass. That was part of the excitement. He was a mere flatfoot being treated like a VIP by a beautiful television celebrity.

Another part of the excitement had to do with the video itself. Watching it on a sixty-inch screen in this exclusive chamber was a very different experience from watching it on a vintage television set in a stuffy little swing room with a patrolman snoring on a cot not twelve feet away. The tape seemed more vibrant here. The tape seemed more immediate.

Moreover, Hawes was watching it through Honey's eyes as well, and Honey was reacting not merely to its immediate unreeling but to the expectation that it would be aired on the Five O'Clock News, not an hour and a half from now. When the two masked perps came down those mahogany steps, she actually grabbed Hawes's hand and squeezed it. When the left-handed perp hit the black dancer, she yelled, 'Oh Jesus *Christ!*' And when he slapped Tamar, she winced and turned her head into Hawes's shoulder. He almost came in his pants.

'Do you know how many people will be watching this?' she asked. Her eyes were glowing. She could hardly sit still.

'How many?' he said.

'Thirty million.'

'That many watch the local news?'

'Who's talking local? We'll air it here in the city at five, and then give it a second shot when we go network. At six-thirty tonight, every man, woman, and child in the United States will be seeing it! Oh *wow,* Cotton!' she said, and impulsively leaned over to kiss him on the cheek.

Oh, wow, he thought.

108

THE TWO PATROLMEN riding Adam Four in Majesta's One-Oh-Four Precinct had been briefed at roll call before relieving on post at a quarter to four. They knew they should be on the lookout for a black Ford Explorer with the license plate number KBG 741, but they had no expectation of ever finding it. Most stolen vehicles ended up in chop shops ten minutes after they were boosted.

So they drove along relatively peaceful Sunday afternoon streets in a neighborhood that used to be Italian but was now largely Muslim, more worried, to tell the truth, about some fanatic blowing up a movie theater or a local bar than they were about finding a suspect Ford Explorer, when all at once, and lo and behold, there it was!

'Check it out,' the driver said.

The cop riding shotgun opened his notebook and glanced at the license plate number he'd scribbled into it at roll call.

'That's it,' he said, sounding surprised.

'I'm gonna play the Lotto tomorrow,' the driver said, and got on the pipe to his sergeant.

AT FOUR-TWENTY that afternoon, Barney Loomis signed himself and Carella into the Rio Building downtown on Monroe Street, led him through the vast and silent Sunday afternoon lobby, and then into an elevator that whisked them to the twenty-third floor.

The reception area was vacant and still.

The Bison Records logo – a big brown buffalo on a black platter – stared down at them from behind an empty desk. Loomis touched four numbers on the code pad alongside the entrance doors, and then led the way down the hall. The walls were decorated with Bison recording artists. Carella recognized only Tamar Valparaiso among them.

Loomis's private office had two vast windows that looked out at the city's skyline. There was a huge black desk, black leather and chrome chairs, expensive audio equipment, a huge flat-screen television set, a bar in wood that matched the desk, and what appeared to be a genuine Picasso on one of the walls.

'What time will this man be here?' Loomis asked.

'I told him four-thirty.'

'Will he know what to do?'

'Oh yes.'

Curt Hennesy arrived at four-thirty-five. The security guard downstairs called up to make sure it was okay to let him in — even though Hennesy was a Detective/Third who'd showed his shield and his ID — and Loomis was in the reception area to meet him when he got off the elevator. He was carrying two rather large aluminum suitcases, which he set down while Loomis punched in the four-number code again.

'Fort Knox here,' he commented.

'Well, the music business,' Loomis said.

Hennesy picked up the suitcases again, and followed Loomis down the hallway to his office.

'You in charge here?' he asked Carella.

'Carella,' Carella said. 'Eighty-seventh Squad.'

'Hennesy,' Hennesy said. 'Tech Unit. What do you want done here?'

'Tap and Tape, Trap and Trace,' Carella said.

'Can I see your court orders?'

Carella fished them from his inside jacket pocket. Hennesy read them silently.

'Piece of cake,' he said. 'Do you have a private line, Mr. Loomis?'

'Yes?'

'Is it likely your caller's going to use that number?'

110

'There's no way he would know that number.'

'Mmm, not so peachy apple pie after all,' Hennesy said. 'What you're saying, to reach you he'd have to call the main number here, is that it? Bison's number?'

'Yes. I suppose so. Yes.'

'And the call would go through the switchboard, is that right?'

'Yes.'

'Well, unless you want me to rewire your entire setup so that every call Bison gets is switched directly to your office . . .'

'No, I wouldn't want that.'

'I didn't think so. So let's see,' he said, thinking out loud. 'The call still has to go through the switchboard. Your operator doesn't have to know anything, it's business as usual. Okay, so she puts the call through to you here, right. Let me get to work here,' he said, and took off his jacket, and looked for someplace to hang it . . .

'I'll take it,' Loomis said.

. . . and opened one of the aluminum suitcases.

'What I do most of the time,' he said, taking from the suitcase an assortment of tools which he was about to put on Loomis's polished desk top before he saw the alarmed look that crossed his face, and spread them on the carpeted floor instead, 'I usually install wires in places the wise guys hang out, you know? We get a court order same as for a search warrant because that's what we're doing, we're seizing conversations, even if it's from bad guys talking. You ever hear of Stephen Sondheim?' he asked.

'Yes?' Loomis said.

'Yes?' Carella said.

'How come he never read the book *Wise Guys?* How come he never heard the expression "wise guys"? How come he writes a musical about two brothers, one's a welterweight boxer, the other's an architect, and he calls it *Wise Guys* when they ain't even gangsters? He's supposed to be very intelligent, how come he don't know these things? Anyway, this'll be the same thing here, we'll be seizing a conversation . . . that's why you needed your court orders, Carella, well I guess you knew that, huh? If you expect this to stand up in court later on, anyway. The way this'll work, I'll set up a Tap and Tape so that your law enforcement people, *us*,' he said, and winked at Carella, 'can wear ear phones and listen to every call coming in, while meanwhile the recording equipment is voice-activated and starts whenever the guy even breathes into his phone. Meanwhile, the Trap and Trace'll give us the number he's calling from. Simple as A, B, C, right?' he said. 'So get to work, Curt,' he told himself, 'instead of passing the time of day here with these nice gentlemen.'

CARLIE EPWORTH, the technician who'd led the team that had scoured the *Hurley Girl* stem to stern, called the 87th Squad at six that night and asked to talk to Detective Kling. Kling had already gone home.

Epworth left a message saying they'd come up negative for latents on the boat, but that they had some fiber and hair samples for possible matching purposes later on if they made an arrest.

At a quarter past six, fifteen minutes before Honey Blair's kidnapping tape went network on the 'Nightly News,' a detective named Henry D'Amato called the 87th Squad and asked to talk to Detective Bert Kling, who had put out an APB on a black Ford Explorer with the license plate number KBG 741. He was informed that Kling had already gone home. D'Amato left a message saying they had recovered the suspect vehicle, and it was behind the station house at the One-Oh-Four in Majesta, awaiting further disposition. He said he'd be there till midnight if Kling wanted to get back to him.

Detective Hal Willis, who'd been briefed on the kidnapping out on the river, thought this was important enough to call Kling at the number he'd left. Kling agreed. He called the One-Oh-Four at once.

'Did you check with DMV?' he asked D'Amato.

'Yeah. It's registered to a woman named Polly Olson, you want the address?'

'Please,' Kling said, and listened, jotting down the address. 'Was it reported stolen?' he asked.

'Didn't have a chance to check that,' D'Amato said.

'I'll get someone on it,' Kling said, and thanked D'Amato, and then immediately called Willis back.

'Hal,' he said, 'we've got a make on that Ford Explorer, it's registered to a woman named Polly Olson at 317 Byrd Street, I think that's over by the Ship Canal. You want to check our boosted vehicles sheet, see if the Ford's on it? Either way, you ought to run on down there, see where she was last night while the Valparaiso girl was being abducted.'

'Why? You think she was part of it?'

'I only know this is the car that was spotted at the marina. And it's hers. So let's see what she has to say.'

'Well, the way I look at it,' Willis said, 'there are only two possibilities here. Either the car was stolen, in which case the lady thanks me for finding it, or else it was used in a kidnapping, in which case I knock on her door and the lady shoots me in the face.'

'Maybe you ought to petition for a No-Knock,' Kling said, half-seriously.

'What judge in his right mind would grant me one?'

'Then you've got nothing to worry about, right?'

'Tell you what,' Willis said. 'Why don't *you* run on

down there to talk to her?'

'I'm off duty,' Kling said, and hung up, and immediately called the Mobile Crime Unit.

'Al Sheehan,' a man's voice said.

'Hey, Al,' Kling said, 'this is Bert Kling at the Eight-Seven. We're working a kidnapping that went down last night . . .'

'Hey, yeah,' Sheehan said. 'I was one of the techs who swept the *River Princess*. Something, huh?'

'I'll say. Al, we picked up a vehicle may have been involved, it's a black Ford Explorer parked behind the One-Oh-Four in Majesta. Detective named Henry D'Amato'll be there till midnight, he's got the keys. You want to do your number on it, see if the bad guys left anything for us?'

'The One-Oh-Four, huh? That's way the hell out in the sticks.'

'Half-hour ride,' Kling said.

'I'm in the middle of something here, I won't be able to head out till maybe seven or so. That be all right?'

'As soon as possible, okay?' Kling said. 'Let me give you a number where you can reach me.'

It was six-thirty when he got off the phone.

Across the room, Sharyn Cooke was just turning on Channel Four's network news.

In his office, Barney Loomis and Steve Carella were about to watch the same broadcast.

THE THING that impressed Loomis most was her performance.

Forget the fact that she was lip-synching, forget the fact that she and the black dancer – Joshua, was it? Jonah? – missed a few steps while they were furiously reenacting the rape they'd executed so masterfully on the video. Even forget the fact that she seemed a bit nervous performing live in front of a scant hundred or so people, what would she do when they booked her into a goddamn *arena?* With thousands and thousands of screaming fans?

Forget all that.

What came over in this three, four minutes of tape — now being broadcast into God knew how many homes all over the country — was the sheer conviction of Tamar's performance. There was a raw power to her voice, yes, but there was a sweetness, too, a poignant plea for innocence in a world gone suddenly brutal, the voice of a lark in a meadow swirling with hawks. Whatever else came over — her luminous beauty, her sexuality, her sensuality, her youthful exuberance, yes, all of those — it was her complete honesty that most impressed. And thrilled. And dazzled.

Long after her song was interrupted by the ugly reality of sudden violence, long after the two intruders carried her up those mahogany steps and out of the viewer's immediate stunned proximity, her glow lingered like a shining truth. Tamar Valparaiso hadn't been trying to sell anything but the purity of the moment. And in this moment, at six-forty-five on a Sunday night all across America, the verity she was selling all over again was 'Bandersnatch.' There was no way that anyone watching this news report could ever doubt . . .

'Well, this is what I've done,' Hennesy said, coming in from the hallway. 'I've got it set up so that . . .'

'Shhh,' Loomis warned.

Hennesy turned to watch the television screen.

On the screen, one of the masked men tossed Tamar over his shoulder.

The other one shouted, 'You move, she dies!' and they backed away up the stairs and out of sight.

The tape ended.

The network news anchor came on again.

He could be seen visibly sighing.

'That was last night at ten-fifteen,' he said. 'So far, there's been no word from the men who abducted Tamar Valparaiso.'

He paused, looked meaningfully into the camera for just an instant, and then said, 'In Moscow today . . .'

Loomis turned off the set.

'When they *do* call,' Hennesy said, 'here's what'll happen. The Tap and Tape I've hooked up is a more sophisticated version of the REMOB every telephone lineman . . .'

'What's a REMOB?' Loomis asked.

Carella didn't know what it was, either.

'Stands for "remote observation,"' Hennesy said. 'Telephone repairmen use it to check the "condition of the line," or so they say. I personally think they get their jollies eavesdropping on phone phucks. Anyway, I found some unused pairs in the cable here, and set up my relay. Whenever the switchboard puts anyone through to your phone, the relay gets activated, connecting your line to the caller's. Carella here will have the option of just listening or automatically recording. At the same time, the Trap and Trace will be locating the caller's number. So you're in business. That'll be twelve dollars and thirty-seven cents,' Hennesy said and grinned like a kid on Halloween night.

5.

DETECTIVE AL SHEEHAN called Kling at a quarter to eight that night. He reported that they'd gone out to the One-Oh-Four and thoroughly examined the recovered Ford Explorer. The car had been wiped clean.

'We're dealing with professionals here,' he said. 'Or else, guys who've seen a lot of movies.'

Kling thanked him and went back to watching a quartet of talking heads on one of the cable channels.

One of them was saying she felt the 'Bandersnatch' tape would only inspire further violent crimes like rape and female abuse.

'Bullshit,' Sharyn Cooke announced.

She was in the small kitchen of the apartment she shared with Bert Kling when she wasn't in his apartment over the bridge. Why they didn't just move in together and save one of the rents was something they talked about every so often. As it was, their separate work schedules often dictated which apartment they used on any given night.

Sharyn Everard Cooke was the police department's Deputy Chief Surgeon, the first black woman ever to be appointed to the job – though 'black' was a misnomer in that her skin was the color of burnt almond. She wore her black hair in a modified Afro, which – together with high cheekbones, a generous mouth, and eyes the color of loam – gave her the look of a proud Masai woman. Five-feet-nine-inches tall, she considered herself a trifle overweight at a hundred and thirty pounds. Bert Kling thought she looked just right. Bert Kling thought she was the most beautiful woman he'd ever met. Bert Kling loved her to death.

The only problem was where to sleep.

Sharyn's apartment was at the very end of the Calm's Point subway line, some forty minutes from Kling's studio apartment across the river in Isola. From his apartment, it took him twenty minutes to get to work in the morning. From her apartment, it took him an hour and fifteen minutes. Sharyn still had her own private practice, but as a uniformed one-star chief, she was obliged to work fifteen to eighteen hours a week at the Chief Surgeon's Office, which was located in Rankin Plaza in Majesta. Majesta was forty-five minutes by subway from Kling's apartment. So it all got down to where they should sleep on any given night.

Because of the kidnapping, and because Kling had to report in at seven-forty-five tomorrow morning, they had planned to spend that Sunday night in his apartment. But at seven A.M. tomorrow, before she went to the office in Rankin Plaza, Sharyn had to be at St. Mary Magdalene's in Calm's Point, where three cops were in the Burn Unit after a blazing building collapsed on them.

So here they were.

'Strawberry or chocolate swirl?' she asked Kling.

'Is that a trick question?' he asked.

She was looking into the freezer compartment of her refrigerator.

'The chocolate swirl is low-fat,' she said.

'I'll have the strawberry,' he said.

'Racist decision,' she said, and at that moment, one of the talking heads on television said, 'The lyrics are racist right from the last word in the second line.'

Sharyn took her head out of the refrigerator.

Kling looked up from the Sunday newspaper in his lap.

'Which word are you referring to?' the hostess of the show asked. She was a white woman, one of innumerable blondes with long straight hair who proliferated on American cable television like amoebae in a petri dish. She called herself Candace Odell. Her guests called her Candy. The guest she was talking to was Jennifer O'Malley, also white, a redheaded columnist for one of the Chicago newspapers.

'The word I'm referring to is "wabe"' Jennifer said.

'How do you find that word racist?' Candace asked.

Her two other guests were black, one male, one female. The man's name was Halliday Coombs. He was a radio commentator in Albany, New York. The woman's name was Lucy Holden. She was a writer for a magazine based in Los Angeles. So many names to remember, so many people to keep track of. But America was a big country. And Candace was good with names. Besides, the screen was divided into four equal segments, so that a viewer could see either all four participants at the same time, or just the one the director decided to zoom in on. The camera was on all four of them just now. Made it easier to remember their names and faces.

Sharyn carried a little bowl of strawberry ice cream into the living room, and then sat down next to Kling with her own bowl of low-fat chocolate swirl.

'Think about it,' Jennifer said slyly. '"Wabe."'

Three of the heads seemed to be thinking furiously. Jennifer's head appeared to be smirking.

'Let's watch "Sex and the City,"' Sharyn said.

'Shhh, this is about "Bandersnatch,"' Kling said.

'Bander-*who*?'

'The kidnapping, shhhh.'

'How do black people pronounce the word "wave"?' Jennifer asked.

'I pronounce it "wave,"' Lucy said.

'So do I,' Halliday said.

'So do I,' Sharyn said.

'But I must admit . . .'

'You never heard the joke with the punch line, "Oberlookin' d'ribber"? For "Overlooking the river"?'

'That's a racist joke,' Candace said.

'Tell me about it, Blondie,' Sharyn said.

'How come you never call *me* Blondie?' Kling asked.

'You want me to call you Blondie?'

'I know that joke,' Halliday said, nodding. 'And it *is* racist, yes. But I must admit I can also see a covert connection between "wabe" and "wave."'

'I can't,' Lucy insisted.

'Neither can I,' Sharyn said. 'How about you, Blondie?'

'Let me taste that chocolate swirl,' Kling said.

'Uh-uh.'

'Why not?'

''Cause once you taste black, ain no goin back,' Sharyn said.

Lucy Holden had her arms folded across her breasts now, clear and unmistakable body language.

'I'll bet Blondie thinks that's a stroke of pure genius,' Sharyn said. 'Inviting a redheaded Irish girl to find all the racist references while the beautiful sistuh with attitude takes the high road.'

'The same sort of black English has its echoes in the word "raths,"' Jennifer said. 'Go to any ghetto in America, you'll hear African-Americans calling rats "raths." The same way they'll use the word "mens" for "men." Or "underwears" for "underwear."'

'I have never in my life called a rat a *rath*,' Lucy said.

'Have you ever in your life even *seen* a rat?' Jennifer shot back.

'Who do you find more attractive?' Sharyn asked. 'The redhead or the sistuh with attitude?'

'Is that another trick question?' Kling asked.

'The one place I really detect clear racism is in the use of the words "Jubjub bird,"' Halliday said. '"Beware the Jubjub bird." That is clearly a racist warning.'

Lucy Holden rolled her eyes.

'How do you find that racist?' Candace asked.

'Well, Candy, I don't know what I'm permitted to say on the air here.'

'This is cable, go right ahead.'

'I'm sure the Jubjub bird refers to the Johnson.'

'The *what!*' Sharyn said, and burst out laughing.

'Uh-huh,' Candace said. 'Do you agree, Jennifer?'

'Absolutely.'

'That the words "Jubjub bird" as used in the song, refer . . .'

'Actually, those words are *code* for the Johnson,' Halliday said.

'Jennifer?'

'Code words for the Johnson, yes,' Jennifer agreed, nodding.

'And what *is* a Johnson?' Candace asked, and smiled encouragement.

Sharyn was leaning forward now, clasping her knees, her eyes wide, her mouth virtually hanging open. There was a long hesitation. The screen was split into two parts now, showing Jennifer's face on one half and Candace's on the other. Jennifer's face was blank. It suddenly occurred to Sharyn that neither of these two erudite white women knew what a Johnson was. She kept watching the screen, waiting. This was the highest suspense she'd seen on television since the O. J. Simpson white Bronco chase out there in the wilds of Los Angeles.

The camera came in on Halliday again. He looked seriously concerned. 'Well,' he said, 'as I said earlier, I don't know what I'm permitted to say here.'

'Oh for God's sake!' Lucy's voice erupted, and suddenly the screen was filled with her face alone. 'The Johnson is a man's *penis!*' she shouted in closeup. 'As in the expression "Slobber the Johnson," which means "Kiss the . . ."'

'We have to break now,' Candace said at once, her smiling face suddenly filling the entire screen. 'We'll be back in just a moment to pursue the question raised by Tamar Valparaiso's new video and CD. Is it "Race or Rape"? You decide! Stay with us.'

'You want to stay with these fools, Blondie?' Sharyn asked. 'Or you want me to take off my unner'wears and slobber yo ole Jubjub bird?'

Kling got up to turn off the television set.

WILLIS FIGURED 317 Byrd Street was six or seven blocks away from the spot on the Ship Canal where two detectives from the Three-One had allegedly drowned a pair of prostitutes who'd accused them of complicity in their illegal evil sex deeds. In a city of contrasts, the newly gentrified Byrd glistened like a rare jewel in a tarnished brass setting. Here there were the coffee houses and the elegant restaurants, the crafts shops and boutiques, the book stores and even a multiplex movie theater. Lining The Canal a dozen blocks away, there were bars that served as whore houses to the hundreds of merchant seamen and sailors who poured into the area every day of the week.

According to the Eight-Seven's hot car sheet, Polly Olson hadn't reported her Ford Explorer missing till eight-thirty this morning, a good ten hours after the kidnapping last night. This may have been mere oversight, or it may have been a clever diversion by a woman setting up an alibi. Who me? Involved in a kidnapping? Hell, my car was *stolen,* I *reported* it stolen! In which case, Polly Olson might very well have been the woman accomplice on the Valparaiso kidnapping. In which case her two AK-47-toting pals might very well be with her tonight. Willis did not want to get shot tonight.

In fact, he did not want to get shot ever again.

The last time he'd got shot was in the thigh, and he thought that might be the last dance for him, verily, though it turned out he was still here, wasn't he? And Parker hadn't been along that night when a punk named Maxie Blaine from Georgia had virtually emptied a nine at the five cops coming through the door, luckily – or unluckily, depending on your viewpoint – hitting the smallest target of them all. Willis had never been in a shootout with Parker by his side, so he didn't really know what kind of a backup he might make, but if there was going to be any gunplay within the next ten minutes or so, he could think of a lot of cops with whom he'd rather be paired.

Neither did he like what he saw when they got to the entrance door of the building. There was a vertical row of bell buttons with lettered names alongside them and an intercom speaker above them. They would have to announce themselves before they were buzzed in.

Parker knew just what he was thinking.

'Hit every fucking button,' he said, and without waiting for Willis to comply, he hit ten or twelve buttons.

Six or seven voices answered at once.

'Police!' Parker yelled. 'There's a burglar on the roof. Buzz us in!'

Only one answering buzz sounded, but it was enough to release the latch on the inner door.

'I learned that from Carella,' Parker said, grinning.

They climbed the steps to the third floor. The same choice greeted them outside apartment 3C. To be or not to be?

Willis knocked.

'Yes?' a woman's voice said.

'Police,' he said, and stepped to the side of the door in case anyone inside decided to pump a volley through it. 'We found your car, ma'am,' he said. 'Want to open the door, please?'

Which gave her the option of going out the window and down the fire escape, which was better than her shooting at them through the wood.

They waited.

'Terrific!' they heard her say.

There was a rush of footsteps to the door. They stayed well back on either side of the jamb until they heard a series of locks and chains falling and tumbling, and finally the door opened and a woman in a red bathrobe over a long white nightgown opened the door wide and smiled out at them. She was a woman in her early fifties, Willis guessed, hair up in curlers, wearing pink bunny slippers, he now noticed, face scrubbed clean, beaming out at them in unexpected pleasure. Wow, they had really located her car!

Or else she was putting on one hell of an act.

'I thought that old buggy was a goner for sure,' she said. 'Where'd you find it?'

'Are you Polly Olson?' Willis asked.

His eyes were looking past her into the apartment where a microwave dinner in a black plastic dish rested on a coffee table in front of which a television set was going.

He was looking for two possible accomplices with two possible AK-47s. Parker was looking for the same thing. Their eyes must have been darting.

'How rude of me,' she said, 'come in, come in,' and stepped aside, either to welcome them or to allow a clean line of fire for her shooter buddies. They stepped into the apartment. Nobody shot at them. Willis felt somewhat foolish.

'Ma'am?' he said. 'Is it your Ford Explorer that was stolen?'

'It sure was! Man, that was fast!' she said. 'You boys are to be commended.'

'When did you report the car missing, ma'am?' Parker asked, getting straight to the point. He was due to be relieved at eleven-forty-five, and it was now close to that — well, actually, it was only eight-thirty, but he didn't want to be delayed by a lot of bullshit here.

'This morning. When I went down right after break-fast,' she said. 'I get up early every morning to move the car. It's alternate side of the street parking here. We can park it all night, but we have to move it in the morning. Even weekends. This is a busy street here, deliveries all the time.'

'So you went down at what time, lady?' Parker asked impatiently.

'Just before eight o'clock. It's illegal to park between eight A.M. and six P.M. I was going to move the car across the street, and then walk over to church. As it was, I missed the nine o'clock mass because I had to report the car miss-ing and all. From where I'd left it.'

'Where was that, ma'am?'

'Right in front of the building. It would've been safe there until eight o'clock. Which is why I went down a few minutes before. Only to discover somebody had already moved it *for* me. I came right upstairs and called the police. Took me forever to report it stolen. I missed nine o'clock mass, I told you.'

'What time did you move it last night, ma'am?'

'Five to six. That's what the signs say. Eight A.M. to six P.M.'

'So it had to've been stolen sometime after six last night, is that right?'

'Well, yes,' she said. 'I was home all last night. Watching television,' she said. 'Same as tonight,' she said, and her voice was suddenly so forlorn that Willis wanted to give her a hug. Her mention of the television set caused all of them to turn toward the screen, where for perhaps the twentieth time that day, the Valparaiso kidnapping tape was being aired.

'Do I have to go for the car right now?' she asked, looking suddenly frightened. 'I mean . . . can it wait till morning?'

'Yes, ma'am, it can wait till morning,' Willis said, and was starting to give her the address of the One-Oh-Four, when all at once he heard himself saying, 'In fact, I can stop by and drive you there, if you'd like.'

'Why that would be very nice, young man,' she said.

'Ten o'clock be all right?' he asked.

'Ten o'clock would be fine,' she said.

In the hallway outside, Parker said, 'Love at first sight, Harold?'

'Fuck you,' Willis explained.

CARELLA was complaining that he felt like the father of the bride. Sitting beside him on the living-room sofa, Teddy watched his lips and his signing hands, and then she herself signed, *Well, in a sense you are.*

'No, darling,' he said, enunciating every word clearly,

126

emphasizing them with his hands so that she wouldn't miss their meaning or their importance to him, 'not in *any* sense am I the father of the bride. I am the *son* of the bride, and I am the *brother* of the bride, but I am not in any way, shape, or form the *father* of the bride.'

Yes, but to your mother and Angela, you are the father *of the bride,* Teddy insisted.

'Their perception has nothing to . . .'

You're the person who'll be giving them away.

'I know that. But that doesn't make me the *father* of the . . .'

At least they're not asking you to pay for the wedding.

'Oh, that'll be the day!' Carella said, and got off the sofa and began pacing. 'My mother's marrying a big ginzo from . . .'

Steve! her eyes snapped, and her fingers crackled.

'Is what he *is,*' Carella said. 'He speaks English the way my *grand*father did when he first came to this country.'

Luigi happens to speak English . . .

'Luigi! Couldn't he have picked a more . . .'

. . . as well as you do. And he's a very nice . . .

'. . . wop-sounding . . .'

You ought to be ashamed of your . . .

'. . . name? Luigi! Jesus *Christ!*'

Well, I'm not going to shout over you, Teddy signed, and folded her hands in her lap.

The room went still.

'I'm sorry,' he said.

You should be, Teddy signed. *It's going to be a lovely wedding.*

'I'm sure it will be,' he said. 'I'm sorry.'

But he was sure it would not be. Because the issue here wasn't that his mother was about to marry a man from Italy, a real *Italian,* mind you, not somebody who was born here and who called himself Italian for God knew what obscure reasons, but someone actually *from* Italy, this was not the issue. The issue was that his mother was getting married at *all.* And so soon after his father was murdered. Before the funeral meats were cold, so to speak.

Which was the *other* thing that rankled about this double wedding impending in June, next month, right around the corner, for which he had been unanimously declared father of the bride when he didn't even choose to be either brother or son of the bride, *brides,* damn it! Of all the men in this vast city, of all the available bachelors pounding on her door and sniffing at her heels, why had his sister chosen the man who'd prosecuted the case of the *People* v. *Cole,* and lost that case, allowed his father's murderer to walk free until another day? Why this particular man? Was there something fucking Electral about this? Something Carella was missing?

The telephone rang.

He looked up at the grandfather clock.

It was nine-thirty.

He went into the hall to answer it.

'Hello?' he said.

'Detective Carella, please.'

'Speaking.'

'This is Special Agent Stanley Endicott,' the voice on the other end said. 'Is this Carella?'

'Yes, it is.'

'I'm not waking you, am I?'

'No, I'm awake.'

'I'm in command of the Joint Task Force here at Federal Square,' Endicott said. 'We've been assigned the Valparaiso kidnapping, and I understand you were the officer who caught the initial complaint, is that correct?'

'Well, the Harbor Patrol was actually the first to

respond,' Carella said, and wondered why whenever the FBI appeared on the scene he automatically started covering his ass.

'But you conducted the initial investigation, isn't that correct?'

'Yes, it is,' Carella said.

'Aboard the *River Princess,* is the information I have here.'

'Yes.'

'And you've been working the case since, more or less.'

Carella liked to think the old Eight-Seven had been giving it their all, but he said nothing.

'Have you come up with anything so far?' Endicott asked.

'We've been tracking a trio the Harbor Patrol stopped on the river, shortly before the kidnapping. We've got a name for the guy who rented a boat that may have been used, but that's all we've got. There's nothing on him in the computer, local, state, or federal. We're thinking he used a phony credit card.'

'What was the name?'

'Andy Hardy,' Carella said.

'Oh really?' Endicott said, and chuckled.

'We also have an eye witness to the boat coming back in before midnight last night . . . well, he didn't actually *see* the boat, but he gave us a good description of the three people who might've been on the boat . . .'

'*Might've* been,' Endicott said.

'We're fairly certain they're the ones who brought the boat in. A man and two women. They drove off in a black Ford Explorer . . .'

'*Fairly* certain,' Endicott said.

Carella was silent for a moment.

Then he said, 'Do you want this or don't you?'

'I'm all ears,' Endicott said.

'So cut the editorials, okay? We've been busting our asses on this ever since we caught it.'

'I'm sure you have.'

'Look, call my lieutenant, okay? He's got all our reports, he'll give you everything you . . .'

'I'd rather hear it from you.'

'The Explorer was reported stolen at eight-thirty this morning. We checked with the owner, last time she saw the car was six last night, when she moved it per parking regulations. The boat the three hired – which may or may *not* have been the one used on the gig, before you repeat it back to me – was dusted by Mobile Crime top to bottom. It was wiped clean as a whistle. Also, we've set up a Tap and Tape *plus* a Trap and Trace in Barney Loomis' office. We expect . . .'

'So he told us.'

'We expect the perps to call with a ransom demand sometime tomorrow. The office was closed today, and they have no way of knowing his home number. Plus, the girl's parents are divorced and living, one in Mexico, the other in Europe someplace. So Loomis is the one the perps'll most likely contact.'

'So he told us,' Endicott said again.

'That's what we've done so far, and that's what we've got.'

'Which is essentially nothing,' Endicott said.

'Well, as I mentioned earlier,' Carella said, 'maybe you ought to talk to my lieutenant. He can give you any further . . .'

'No, no, you've done splendidly,' Endicott said. 'Not your fault these guys are smart. How about the crime scene itself? Has the lab come back to you with anything yet?'

'They said I'd have their report by six tonight. I waited in the office till seven.'

'Think it might be there now?'

'Possibly. I can call the squadroom . . .'

'If it's there, maybe you can bring it along with the rest of the stuff.'

'What stuff do you mean, Agent Endicott?'

'It's *Special* Agent Endicott, by the way, but you can call me Stan. What do people call you, Detective? Stephen? Steve? It says here Stephen Louis Car . . .'

'Steve. People call me Steve.'

'Steve, I'd like to go over whatever evidence you gathered at the scene . . .'

'There wasn't much.'

'What*ever* there was. It'd be in your DD report, wouldn't it?'

'Yes, it would.'

'Your various conversations with eye witnesses . . .'

'Yes.'

'Your own evaluation of the crime scene . . .'

'Yes, that would all be in our report.'

'Photographs . . .'

'Those would be coming from the lab.'

'Plus whatever else you may have got from Mobile this evening.'

'If there *is* anything else, yes, Stan. It was a big crime scene, they were very busy there, inside *and* outside the boat. The perps came up a ladder, you know, on the side of the boat . . .'

'So you're saying there might be footprint casts . . .'

'I'm saying I don't know *what* they got or didn't get. Footprints or whatever. That's why I'm waiting for the report. The perps were wearing gloves, so the likelihood of latents is nil. But they came down these highly polished steps into the ballroom, and they moved across a dance floor with another sensitive surface . . .'

'That's the kind of stuff I mean,' Endicott said. 'Your first hand impressions of the scene. To supplement whatever you've got in writing. When do you think you can get down here?'

'Down where?' Carella asked.

'Why, Federal Square, Steve.'

'How about first thing tomorrow morning?' Carella said.

'How about right now?' Endicott said. 'The Squad's all here . . .'

The Squad? Carella thought.

'. . . and we'd love to get a jump on this before those sons of bitches call tomorrow. Think you can stop by your office first, see if that MCU report is in, and then head right on down here? It's One Federal Square, nineteenth floor. We'll be waiting,' he said, and hung up.

Carella looked at the phone receiver.

The Squad, he thought. Is that what the Joint Task Force calls itself, The Squad?

He put the receiver back on the cradle.

The Squad.

'I have to go in again,' he told Teddy.

It was not the first time she'd ever heard those words, but she pulled a face anyway.

6.

THERE WAS ONLY one building in Federal Square, and it was appropriately addressed One Federal Square. A forty-story limestone structure lit from below with daggers of light, it would have looked imposing, and a bit intimidating, even if it were not the sole edifice on a plot of ground some fifty yards square.

The Joint Task Force, a team of six crack FBI agents and an equal number of elite police detectives, occupied floors nineteen and twenty of the building. You could not enter those floors without a key. Carella did not have a key, which was why someone was meeting him downstairs in the lobby.

The someone was Detective-Lieutenant Charles 'Corky' Corcoran.

In this whole wide world, there is no one with the surname Corcoran who does not also possess the nickname Corky. That is an indisputable truth. Male or female, if you are a Corcoran, you are also a Corky. Charles Farley Corcoran had been 'Corky' when Carella met him some twenty-odd years ago at the Police Academy, and Carella guessed he was still Corky tonight, though there was clipped to his suit jacket pocket an ID card and a gold, blue-enameled detective shield hammered with the word LIEUTENANT. Beaming a toothy smile, blue eyes crinkling in a face stamped with the map of Ireland, he extended his hand and said, 'Steve, long time no see.'

His grip was firm and dry and warm. He looked as fit and as young as he had, lo those many·years ago, when they were both rookies climbing ropes and firing pistols in the Academy.

'Welcome to The Squad,' he said.

The Squad, Carella thought. Supreme egotism in that the designation completely dismissed every detective squad in this city and declared itself *The* Squad, *The* One and Only Squad. Welcome.

'Nice to be here,' Carella said.

He was thinking he had not got to bed till almost eight-thirty this morning after being up all night on the kidnapping. He had been awakened by Byrnes at twelve-thirty and had spent the rest of the day either in court chasing court orders, or up in Loomis' office supervising the installation of the telephone-surveillance equipment. It was now ten-thirty P.M., and he was beginning to feel just a wee bit weary.

The usual modulation from night shift to day shift took place over a period of two days. You worked the midnight-to-eight A.M. shift for a full month, then you took two full days off and came back to work at eight in the morning, the theory being that you'd caught up on your sleep by that time, just like a business traveler adjusting to jet lag.

Sure.

'You're looking good, Steve.'

'Thanks. Do I still call you Corky?'

'Most people call me Charles these days,' Corcoran said. 'Or Lieutenant.' Still smiling, he said, 'Come meet the team,' and led Carella across a vast lobby paved with massive blocks of unpolished marble to a bank of elevators simply marked 19–20. There were only two buttons and a keyway in the elevator that arrived. Corcoran took a key ring from his pocket, slid a small key into the keyway, twisted it, and hit the button for 19.

'I understand you've done some good work on this case,' Corcoran said.

'Thank you,' Carella said.

The elevator whirred silently up the shaft. The door slid open onto the nineteenth floor. The men stepped out into a corridor that ran past a warren of tiny work cubes, occupied with men and women at computers. Carella followed Corcoran to an unmarked door at the end of the hall. He opened the door and allowed Carella to precede him into a room.

There were six smiling men in the room.

Carella recognized only Barney Loomis, who was wearing a brown jacket over beige slacks, a brown turtleneck sweater, and brown loafers. Three of the other five men were both wearing dark blue suits, white shirts, blue ties, and highly polished, black, lace-up shoes. Carella figured them for FBI. They even looked somewhat alike, all three of them square-jawed and dark-haired, sporting the sort of conservative haircut made famous by Senator Trent Lott, although presumably their own barber was not in Washington, D.C.

The Trent Lott Cut was a precision-tooled hairstyle that fit its wearer's head like a carefully stitched toupee. This tailored-rug look was softened somewhat on the trio of agents – Carella guessed one of them was Endicott – because they were each in their thirties and were therefore presumed to be hipper than they actually were, especially since they carried nine-millimeter Glocks and FBI shields. The other two men could only be city detectives. Something in the way they carried themselves, something in their somewhat unpressed look, city detectives for sure. So what Carella had here was three smiling Feebs, two smiling dicks – well, three, when you counted Lieutenant Charles 'Corky' Corcoran, standing behind him and

135

presumably smiling as well – and last but not least . . .

'Detective Carella,' Barney Loomis said, also smiling and stepping away from the other men, his right hand extended. 'Glad you could come down.'

Carella took his hand.

One of the FBI agents stepped away from the other blue suits. 'I'm Stan Endicott,' he said. 'Special Agent in Charge. Welcome aboard.'

Carella had been taught by a sergeant at the Academy never to trust a smiling man with a gun in his hand. He wondered if that same sergeant had ever said anything about a roomful of smiling men in suits, all of whom were packing if the bulges under their jackets were any indication.

'Meet the rest of the team,' Endicott said, and introduced first his lookalike in the blue suit, 'Special Agent Brian Forbes,' and then another FBI agent whose name flew by like the Twentieth Century, and then the pair of city dicks, one of them a Detective/First, the other a Detective/Second. Carella thought he recognized one of the names as belonging to a man who'd made spectacular headlines breaking up either a dope ring or a racketeering scheme or something of the sort – but what had Endicott meant by 'Welcome aboard?' Or Corcoran by 'Welcome to The Squad?'

Everyone was still smiling.

'I brought that stuff you asked for,' Carella said, and walked over to the large conference table in the center of the room and put down his dispatch case. Through the huge windows facing South, he could see across the square to the new red-brick Police Headquarters building, ablaze with light even at this hour. He snapped open the latches on the case, lifted the lid, and removed from it first a sheaf of his own and Hawes' typed DD reports . . .

'Our reports on the crime scene witnesses,' he said.

. . . and then the reports Meyer and Kling had filed on their visits to the marina and their interview with the marina watchman . . .

'These are about the boat and the stolen Explorer.'

. . . and then the report Willis had typed up on his and Parker's visit to Polly Olson.

'Also,' he said, 'the report from Mobile was waiting when I got there. I haven't looked at it yet. I can leave it here with the other stuff, if you like.'

'He still doesn't get it,' Corcoran said, smiling.

Carella wondered if his fly was open.

'What?' he said.

'You'll be working with us,' Endicott said.

Carella figured they must be shorthanded. Some detective out sick or on vacation. Supposed to be twelve men on the Joint Task Force, only six of them in the room here, still smiling like drunken sailors.

'We thought Mr. Loomis should be working with someone he liked and trusted.'

'Actually, I asked if that would be possible,' Loomis said, and nodded.

'Will that be okay, Steve?' Endicott asked.

'Well . . . sure,' Carella said.

'Now you're pissing with the big dogs,' Corcoran said, grinning, and clapped Carella on the back.

Hard.

FAT OLLIE WEEKS was watching a cable television channel whose slogan was 'Equal and Equitable,' which they hoped conveyed the promise of commensurate and unbiased reportage on any subject their reporters tackled. Tonight's burning question was 'Gay or Fey?' and its subject matter was the Tamar Valparaiso video

Bison Records had generously provided.

The moderator was a man named Michael Owens, who was familiarly called 'Curly' Owens by his colleagues because he happened to be bald. This reverse spin was something called 'irony,' a favorite figure of speech practiced in English-speaking countries where it was thought clever to express a meaning directly contrary to that suggested by the words themselves. Curly was, in fact, the very opposite of hirsute, his condition exacerbated by daily shavings and waxings that gave his head the appearance of an overripe melon.

His two guests tonight were at opposite ends of the political and cultural spectrum in that one of them was a minister who represented a Christian Right activist organization that called itself the 'Citizens for Values Coalition,' or the CVC, and the other was a homosexual who was speaking for a group that called itself 'Priapus Perpetual,' or PP for short.

Ollie didn't choose to waste time watching a fag who called his prick a pee pee debating a priest who was probably a fag himself, but he happened to be eating at the kitchen table right then, and the clicker was on the coffee table in front of the TV set, and he didn't feel like walking into the adjoining room to go switch channels. Besides, he had just watched the clip from the Valparaiso video, and he had to agree that the little lady was splendidly endowed, ah yes, so maybe these two jackasses would have something interesting to say about her obviously fey assets. Ollie supposed the word 'fey' had something to do with female pulchritude, otherwise why had it been positioned opposite the word 'gay'?

'Well, you've seen the video,' Curly told his guests. 'So which is it? Gay or Fey?'

The minister's name was Reverend Karl Brenner. He was a man with a long sallow face and snow-white hair, wearing for tonight's show Benjamin Franklin spectacles and a rumpled, dark gray suit with a white collar, the fuckin hypocrite, Ollie thought. Brenner himself thought the words 'gay' and 'fey' were synonymous; he had no idea what they were supposed to be debating here. If a man was fey, he was, ergo, gay. And the African-American man on the video was obviously both fey *and* gay.

The representative of Priapus Perpetual was named Larry Graham. He knew that the widely accepted meaning of 'fey' was 'strange or unusual' but he himself had been considered strange or unusual long before he became gay. Dressed tonight in a purple turtleneck sweater over which he had thrown a beige cashmere jacket, he sat looking smug and self-satisfied, the little fag, Ollie thought. Actually, Graham was as bewildered as the reverend was, even though he realized the question wasn't being asked about the black dancer who'd played the Bandersnatch, but rather about Tamar Valparaiso herself, whose father had warned 'Beware the Jabberwock, my *son,*' mind you, and had later exulted, 'Come to my arms, my beamish *boy,*' don't forget.

As Graham saw it, the question being asked was: Who or what is this person with the exuberant breasts in a torn and tattered costume? A girl or a boy? A daughter or a son? A male or a female? In short, gay or fey? A revealed homosexual or merely a female eccentric, a whimsical adolescent girl, or – dare one even suggest it – a visionary? A Joan of Arc, mayhaps, wielding an invisible vorpal sword?

'What do you say, gentlemen?' Curly asked, and then immediately said, 'Ooops, excuse me, Larry,' and then, compounding the felony, said, 'But that's what the debate tonight is all about, isn't it? *Is* the person on that tape supposed to be homosexual, like Larry Graham here, who admits it freely? And if so . . .'

'Of course he is,' Graham said.

'Reverend?'

'Are we talking about the African-American in the mask? If so, he is very *definitely* homosexual.'

'And how do you know *that?*' Graham asked at once.

'Well, the very way he *moves,*' Brenner said.

'He moves like a dancer,' Graham said.

'Fred Astaire didn't move that way. Neither did Gene Kelly.'

'Besides, we're not talking about the *dancer.* The question does not refer to the *dancer.*'

'It certainly doesn't refer to the *girl,*' Brenner said.

'That's exactly the metaphor,' Graham said.

The Reverend Brenner didn't know what metaphor meant, either. He thought it meant simile. If so, was this little homosexual person here implying that the girl being assaulted was somehow a simile for a homosexual?

'I do not see any connection,' he said. 'The problem with organizations like yours, Mr. Graham, is that you presuppose everyone in the world is either *already* homosexual or else would like to *become* homosexual. That is the implicit threat to family values, and the entire reason for the existence of groups like CVC . . .'

'I do believe, yes,' Larry said, 'that "Bandersnatch" is about a young boy coming out of the closet, yes. If we study the video carefully, we . . .'

'Oh, please,' Brenner said, 'that's utter nonsense.'

'Why don't we take another look at it?' Curly said, and to someone off camera, 'Can we roll it again, boys?'

Ollie thought, Good, let's watch the striptease again.

This was not the tape Honey Blair and her crew had shot

on the night of the kidnapping. This was the studio-shot video with its animated footage and a skimpily but fully clothed Tamar larking under a yellow sky with pastel colored clouds and whimsical budding flowers and fanciful floating insects while the sound of a synthesizer . . .

She looks like a shepherd boy, Ollie thought, and suddenly understood what Larry Graham had meant a moment ago.

She did not look like a boy for very long.

Within seconds after the black guy in his gray mask came whiffling out of the woods, he was clawing and biting at her and tearing her clothes to ribbons, exposing a ripe female form that Ollie was sure would promote perpetual Priapic emissions from teenage boys all over America, not to mention even more mature males in the population.

'That's exactly what I mean,' Graham's voice said over the video. 'The boy has to recognize himself as female before he can realize his full power.'

Bullshit, Ollie thought, and the telephone rang.

He hit the mute button and picked up the receiver.

'Weeks,' he said.

'Oll?'

Patricia.

He grinned.

'Hey,' he said, 'how are you?'

'Fine, Oll,' she said. 'Whatcha doing?'

'Watching television. You familiar with this kidnapping the 8-7 caught?'

'Yeah, this new singer.'

'Some fag is saying she's a boy.'

'Get out,' Patricia said.

'Did you see the video?'

'Sure, it's all over the place.'

'That's some boy, huh?'

'I'd like to look like a boy like that,' Patricia said.

'You look fine just the way you are,' Ollie said.

'Thanks, Oll,' she said, and was silent for a moment. 'I was calling to . . . uh . . . see if we're still on for Tuesday night,' she said.

'Why shouldn't we still be on?'

'I just wondered, that's all. Also, there's this old movie playing at the Atlantis — that's like an art house, y'know — I thought I'd like to see again, if you'd like to see it. It's with Al Pacino, it's called *Looking for Richard*. That's Richard the Third, the Shakespearean character, y'know. Well, it's also a real king, but Shakespeare wrote the play.' Patricia hesitated again. 'Do you think you might like to see it?'

'Sure,' Ollie said. 'Whatever you say, Patricia.'

'You're sure?'

'Positive.'

'Good. You'll like it, I promise. It's not at all what you expect Shakespeare to be.'

'Hey, I *love* Shakespeare,' he said.

'Well, good. Then I made a good pick, huh?'

'You certainly did.'

He had never seen a Shakespeare play in his entire life.

'Also, how should I dress?' she asked. 'I told you, I'll be working Tuesday . . .'

'Me, too.'

'So I won't have time to go home and change . . .'

'Me, neither. Just put on what's in your locker. Whatever you wear to work that morning.'

'It won't be anything fancy,' Patricia said. 'Just slacks and a sweater, probably.'

'That'll be fine.'

'Okay then. You working tomorrow?'

'Oh sure.'

'See you up the precinct then.'

'See you,' Ollie said.

There was a click on the line.

He sighed heavily and put the receiver back on its cradle.

The fag and the priest were still going at it.

He hit the mute button again.

'. . . sending this message to adolescent boys all over America,' the Reverend Brenner was saying. 'If you want to slay wild dragons . . .'

'It isn't a dragon,' Graham said.

'. . . then you have to declare yourself to be homosexual! What kind of a message . . . ?'

'I'm sure that isn't Tamar Valparaiso's mess . . .'

'You just *said* the boy in that video . . .'

'Gentlemen, gentlemen!'

'I'm sure her message is simply "Be what you wish to be. In choice, there is freedom."'

'Oh, are we going to get into the *abortion* issue now?'

'Not on my time,' Ollie said out loud, and turned off the set, and wondered if any of that scrumptious apple pie his sister had baked was still in the refrigerator.

WHAT WAS CALLED CSI in some cities was called MCU here in the big bad city, and never the twain shall meet. The Mobile Crime Unit had struck out twice last night, once on the Rinker and again on the Ford Explorer, but that didn't mean they weren't as sharp or as perceptive as their television counterparts. On the contrary, the package they had messengered over to Carella at seven-thirty this evening, and which he now presented to The Squad downtown, included one piece of very important information.

As expected, there'd been no latent fingerprints on any

of the railings or bulkheads the perps may have touched in boarding the *River Princess* and then descending into the ballroom where Tamar was performing. The intruders were wearing gloves. So much for that.

But they were also wearing running shoes with identifiable soles. And whereas they hadn't left any recoverable footprints on the rubber ladder-treads that ascended to the second level of the yacht, they had left behind some discernible prints on the mahogany steps and the parquet dance floor inside.

Together, Carella and The Squad looked over the report prepared by an MCU Detective/First named Oswald Hooper.

The report stated, unsurprisingly, that the recovered footprints had been left behind on stairway and dance floor by two separate males wearing running shoes later identified from laboratory comparison soles as Reeboks. That the persons wearing the shoes were both male was established by the size and type of the shoe and also by the angle of the foot, definitively different for male and female.

What was revealing about the separate prints, however, was the separate walking pattern for each man. The pattern for the man whose prints were consistently recovered on the *starboard* side of the stairway and dance floor was remarkably different from the pattern for the man who'd been on the *port* side of all the action.

'Starboard is right, port is left,' Corcoran told Endicott.

Endicott gave him a look intended to convey the knowledge that his father had taken him sailing on Chesapeake Bay when he was still a toddler. Corcoran missed the meaning of the look.

'The guy on the right was the one who did all the hitting,' Carella said. 'Have you seen the tape yet?'

'Only on television,' Endicott said.

Forbes, the other FBI agent, said, 'It's all over the place.'

'I've requested a copy from Channel Four,' Corcoran said.

'Are they giving you one?' Carella asked, surprised.

'Why not?'

'Well, when I seized it as evidence, they threatened to sue the city.'

Corcoran raised his eyebrows and gave him a look intended to convey the knowledge that this was the Joint Task Force here, kiddo, this was The *Squad*.

'Well, good luck,' Carella said, and shrugged, but he felt he had been reprimanded. Or perhaps warned. And he realized all at once that Lieutenant Charles Farley Corcoran did not want him on this team. He almost walked out. Something kept him there. Maybe it was the fact that Barney Loomis had requested his presence as someone he liked and trusted.

'What's this about a walking pattern?' Endicott asked, and they all went back to reading Hooper's report.

Apparently, the man on the left possessed a normal walking pattern. That is to say, an imaginary line drawn in the direction of his walk had run through the inner edges of his heel prints. The distance between the footprints of a man walking slowly would be about twenty-seven inches. The distance for a running man would be forty inches. A man walking fast would measure thirty-five inches between footprints. The guy on the left had been moving very fast. Thirty-three inches between footprints. But it was a normal walking pattern, and not a broken one.

The guy on the right, however – the one who'd rifle-stocked the black dancer and slapped Tamar Valparaiso –

had been moving more slowly, twenty-eight inches between footprints. And his walking line indicated that he was partially leaning on his left foot and slightly dragging the right foot.

'Leaning?' Endicott said.

'Dragging?' Corcoran said.

Carella almost said 'Shhhhh.'

Absent any perfectly flat footprints for the right foot, Hooper's report went on, *and given the slower gait and broken walking line, it would be safe to conclude that the suspect sustained a past injury to the right leg that manifests itself now in an existent noticeable limp.*

'*That's* what it was!' Carella told them.

He was referring to what he'd noticed on the tape, but hadn't been able to pinpoint until just this minute. None of the others knew what the hell he was talking about.

'So what do we do?' Endicott asked. 'Put out a medical alert?'

'The report says "*past* injury,"' Corcoran said.

'How far in the past? Could've been last week.'

'A physician's bulletin can't hurt,' Carella said.

'You want to take care of that?' Corcoran suggested.

And all at once, Carella got it.

He was going to be the errand boy.

'What's my role here going to be?' he asked. Flat out. Head to head.

'What would you like it to be?' Corcoran asked right back. Straight on. Toe to toe.

'I don't want to be a gopher, that's for sure.'

'Who says that's what we want?'

'What *do* you want?'

'I think it's what *I* want that counts, isn't it?' Loomis said, stepping in. '*I'm* the one those men will be contacting, *I'm* the one they'll be expecting to pay the ransom,

146

whatever *that's* going to be. If you don't mind, gentlemen, I believe Detective Carella is as qualified as any man in this room to handle whatever may come up in the next few days. So I'd appreciate it if you didn't assign him to running out for coffee and sandwiches.'

'I'd be happy to put out that physician's alert,' Carella said.

'Thank you, Steve,' Loomis said.

'I'll get someone in the cubbies to do it, don't sweat it,' Corcoran said.

'Who*ever* does it, let's get it *done*,' Endicott said, reminding everyone that he was the SAC around here. 'Let's take a look at these DD reports, see if anything pops out at us. Steve, you want to walk us through?'

THE WHOLE IDEA of this thing was to keep the girl alive for forty-eight hours. That was all the time they needed.

Avery had got all the fake stuff for the gig from a man he'd done business with before, a purveyor of false identity documents like social security cards, birth certificates, divorce decrees, gun permits, college diplomas, drivers' licenses, press credentials, and of course credit cards that actually worked when you used them. The man's name was Benny Lu, or at least that was the name he used here in the United States, preferring the nickname to the full Benjamin Lu that was on his Hong Kong birth certificate, if even that was real. Benny had migrated to the United States four years ago, after he'd almost been busted by Hong Kong's ICAC.

Avery had met him two and a half years ago, when he'd needed several false documents in order to casually prove to a certain rich fat lady in Palm Beach that he was, in fact, one Judson Fears of Gloucester County, Virginia, before she would let him into her luxurious waterfront mansion and incidentally her bed, the suspicious old bitch. He had later run off with $200,000 worth of her nice jewelry, thank you, but it served her right for not accepting him at face value, and besides, the jewelry was insured.

'I used to work in a Hong Kong restaurant,' Benny told him the first time they met. Benny was tall and slender, with a droll smile and eyes that always seemed amused. He had the long narrow fingers of a Flower Dancer, precious assets in the delicate operations he performed. 'I was making coolie wages,' he told Avery, 'until I realized I was in a position to be of valuable assistance to certain people who had need of certain information.'

Avery thought it odd that a Chinese man would use an expression like 'coolie wages,' but he made no comment because he believed it was important for a person to listen carefully while he was being educated.

'This was six years ago,' Benny said, 'when the economy in Japan was still very big. You had all these Japanese tourists coming to Hong Kong, spending lots and lots of money, and paying for everything with credit cards. These certain people came to me with what is called a "skimmer." What it is . . .'

A skimmer, Avery learned, was a battery-operated, wireless device that cost some three to five hundred dollars, and that fit easily into the inside pocket of Benny's jacket. Whenever Benny swiped a customer's credit card through this little machine, it read onto its very own computer chip all the data embedded in the card's magnetic security stripe.

'I'm not just talking name, number, and expiration date,' Benny said, grinning at the simplicity of it all. 'What the skimmer *also* copies is the card's verification code. This is what's electronically forwarded from the merchant to the card company's central computer any-time a purchase is made. The code tells the company the card is valid. Once you've copied that code, you have everything you need to make an exact clone of the card.'

He was still grinning three weeks ago, when Avery went to see him again. Benny Lu lived in a small develop-ment house out on Sands Spit, a half-hour drive from the city. Avery told him what he needed. A fake credit card that would enable him to rent a car . . .

He told Benny he'd be renting a car instead of a boat because over the years he had learned that you shouldn't trust anyone but your mother, and maybe not even her . . .

. . . and a fake driver's license to back up the name on the phony credit card.

'Piece of cake,' Benny Lu said, grinning.

His basement looked like a computer nerd's hangout. Benny himself looked a little like Fu Manchu in the silk robe he was wearing, which he told Avery his sister who still lived in Hong Kong had sent him for Christmas.

'She says it's no different under the Chinese,' he assured Avery, who didn't give a rat's ass about Hong Kong *or* the British *or* the Chinese. All he cared about was getting the stuff he needed. It was raining outside the basement win-dows. This was now the end of April. The kidnapping scheme had already been underway for almost two months by then.

When Benny was skimming credit cards for the Hong Kong gang, he was paid a thousand Hong Kong dollars for every name he delivered, which at the time was the equivalent of about a hundred and fifty U.S. bucks. He would skim three or four cards every day except on his day off, which was Wednesday. This averaged out to some-thing like a thousand bucks a week, not enough to buy his own restaurant but plenty of extra spending money if only the Hong Kong credit card dicks hadn't busted the gang, and almost busted him in the bargain.

Here in the U.S., Benny paid a hundred bucks for each name skimmed by his people in restaurants and gasoline stations. He got his supply of blank plastic cards from a manufacturer in Germany who mass-produced them and sold them to him (and many other counterfeiters like him) for two hundred bucks a card. Using a thermal dye printer, Benny stamped American Express, Visa, or Master-Card graphics onto the face of a blank card, embossed it with the name and account number of a skimmed card's true owner, and then embedded the stolen code onto the counterfeit's pristine magnetic stripe. He sold the clones for two thousand bucks a pop, cheap at twice the price when you considered that whatever you charged on the electronically identical card wouldn't be discovered until the genuine card's owner got his bill a month later.

'Sign the name on this sheet of paper a dozen or so times before you sign the back of the card,' Benny told him. 'So it'll have a natural flow to it.'

'Andy Hardy?' Avery said. 'That's the guy's name?'

'That's his name, that's right. That's the name on the original card.'

'Like in Mickey Rooney?'

'Who's Mickey Rooney?' Benny asked.

'Don't they show old movies on television in Hong Kong?'

'Sure, but who's Mickey Rooney?'

'He was Andy Hardy.'

'I don't get it.'

'You never heard of Judge Hardy?'

'I try to stay far away from judges,' Benny said.

Avery shrugged, and then signed the name 'Andy Hardy' ten times before he signed the back of the card. He was now in possession of a credit card with the name ANDY HARDY embossed on its front in raised letters, and his own 'Andy Hardy' signature on the back of it.

'How long will this fly?' he asked Benny.

'Should take you through the end of May at least.'

Which was world enough and time.

Replicating a driver's license was a simpler and much less expensive matter.

Benny explained that in his line of work a 'template' was a layered graphics file that could be computer-manipulated to hide or reveal images and text. In the good old days two or three years ago, when thirty percent of all counterfeit and false identification seized by law enforcement agencies came from the internet, Benny had purchased driver's-license templates for all fifty states, God bless American enterprise!

Now, while April showers lashed his basement windows, Benny took a digital head-and-shoulders photograph of Avery standing against a blue background. He stored this on one of his computers, together with the scanned 'Andy Hardy' signature Avery had used on the credit card. Loading the template for a Connecticut state driver's license, Benny first called up the photograph, hid it, and then revealed a stored Department-of-Motor-Vehicles signature. When he revealed the photo again, the signature seemed superimposed along its right-hand side. Then, in repeated mouse clicks that first hid and then revealed successive layers, Benny replicated the Connecticut state seal, and a shadow image of Avery's head shot, and the Andy Hardy signature.

Filling in the blank spaces on the template, he typed in the name HARDY, ANDY and an address he pulled from a Connecticut phone book, and below that Avery's actual date of birth, September 12, 1969. Just beneath that, he typed in a date of issue, which he fabricated as July 26 the previous year, and to the right of that the letter M for Avery's sex, and the abbreviation BR for the color of his eyes, and 6'1" for his height. He typed in a false identifying license number across the top of the template, and then an expiration date that was on Avery's birthday, two years after the date of issuance. Lastly, he hid everything he'd already done, and revealed only the bar code Connecticut had conceived as a security feature. When he revealed the license again, the bar code was running along the bottom of it.

Voilà!

He now had on his computer a document virtually indistinguishable from the real thing. All he had to do was print it and laminate it, and Avery would be in possession of a Connecticut state driver's license bearing his own photograph alongside Andy Hardy's name and signature.

The fake license cost Avery three hundred bucks.

For $2,300, he had become Judge Hardy's son.

Everything else was free.

That was because everything else had been stolen.

Including the girl, too, when he thought about it.

Cal was the experienced thief here, experienced in that he'd never been sent away for Auto Theft, of which there had been plenty, believe me, him having started taking cars on joy rides when he was but a mere sixteen. It was a shame his record had to've been marred by that one botched bank holdup, but nobody's perfect.

The first car they'd used was the black Explorer, which they'd driven to and from the marina, and which they'd already ditched this morning after they'd dropped the girl and Kellie off at the house. Scoped the early-morning streets searching for a vehicle parked in a deserted area, found one that looked reliable enough, parked the Explorer behind it while Cal jimmied the door of the prospect car, opened the hood, jump-wired the ignition, and off they went into the wild blue yonder. Nice roomy Pontiac Montana, too.

Avery found it amusing that all these city dwellers owned or leased these big gas-guzzling SUVs with names that sounded all macho woodsy and outdoorsy. These people lived in apartment buildings, and they took the subway to work, and they probably never drove the car further than the nearest movie complex on weekends, but they were all dying to have these big monsters they could drive 'off-road.' Off-road *where?* Avery wondered.

This was the big bad city, man. You didn't need an Explorer or a Montana or a Durango unless you wore leather chaps and a cowboy hat. Or unless you were transporting merchandise worth a quarter of a million bucks. They would use the Montana when they picked up the ransom money tomorrow, two hundred and fifty Gs in crisp new hundred-dollar bills. By then, Cal would have stolen the third and final car – probably another one with a name like Caravan or Forester or Range Rover – which they would use to drive the girl from the house to wherever they decided to drop her off.

At first Avery thought he might have some difficulty finding a suitable house. They needed something isolated, but they all wanted to get out of here as soon after the exchange as possible. Cal would be heading for Jamaica because he dug black girls. Kellie was heading for Paris, France; she had already begun taking French lessons. Because traveling together might be dangerous, Avery would be going to London first, and would join her a week later.

The house he'd found was in the direct flight path of

the city's international airport, perched on the edge of South Beach, not one of the county's better resort areas. Even so, during the summer, and because of its location on the sea, the house would have carried a price tag of five, six thousand a month. A big old gray ramshackle structure furnished with rattan furniture and lumpy cushions that smelled of mildew, it was flanked by two similarly dilapidated buildings, empty now during the transitional days of April and May.

When the real estate agent told him the owner was asking three thou a month, Avery asked, 'For what? A house nobody wants because of all the air traffic zooming and roaring overhead?' The agent argued that in these days of extended airport hassles and long delays the house's proximity to the airport was a plus. It must have also occurred to her that closeness to the airport might be desirable to terrorists as well – I mean, what the hell, did Avery look like some kind of fucking terrorist? The questions she'd asked, the identification she'd pored over – the fake Andy Hardy stuff, ha ha, lady – you'd think Avery was about to build a bomb instead of just kidnap a girl!

The girl was now safely ensconced in the house, and tomorrow morning Avery would make the first of his phone calls. The phones themselves – but that was another story.

By tomorrow night at this time, he'd be in possession of two hundred and fifty thousand bucks!

Thank you, Barney Loomis, and God bless us every one!

7.

THERE WERE MARCHERS outside the Rio Building when Carella got there on Monday morning at eight o'clock. The marchers were carrying hand-lettered signs on wooden sticks.

Some of the signs read: ROCK RACIAL PROFILING!

Others read: TAMAR IS A RACIST!

Yet others read: WHY A BLACK RAPIST?

The marchers were chanting, 'Ban Bandersnatch! Ban Bandersnatch! Ban Bandersnatch!'

Television cameras were rolling.

Carella was not surprised to see the Reverend Gabriel Foster at the head of the procession.

Six-feet-two-inches tall, with the wide shoulders and broad chest of the heavyweight fighter he once had been, his eyebrows still ridged with scar tissue, Foster at the age of forty-nine still looked as if he could knock your average contender on his ass in thirty seconds flat. According to police records, the reverend's birth name was Gabriel Foster Jones. He'd changed it to Rhino Jones when he'd enjoyed his brief career as a boxer, and then settled on Gabriel Foster when he began preaching. Foster considered himself a civil rights activist. The police considered him a rabble rouser, an opportunistic self-promoter, and a race racketeer. His church, in fact, was listed in the files as a 'sensitive location,' departmental code for anyplace where the uninvited presence of the police might cause a race riot.

Foster looked as if he might be promoting just such a

commotion on this bright May morning.

'Good morning, Gabe,' Carella said.

'Ban Bander . . .' Foster said, and then cut himself off mid-sentence and opened his eyes wide when he saw Carella. He thrust out his hand, stepped away from the line of protestors, and grinned broadly. Carella actually believed the reverend was glad to see him. Shaking hands, Foster said, 'Don't tell me you're on this kidnapping?'

'More or less,' Carella said, which was the truth.

'Did you see the video?' Foster asked him.

'I saw the taping they did last night,' Carella said. 'Not the video itself, no.'

'It depicts the girl's rapist as a black man.'

'Well, it depicts a black dancer portraying some kind of mythical beast . . .'

'Some kind of mythical *black* beast,' Foster said.

'The beast in the original poem isn't black,' Carella said.

'That's exactly my . . .'

'And the poem was written in England, back in the 1800s.'

'So why . . . ?'

'There isn't even a *rapist* in the poem. That's what's so fresh about the song. This girl takes a . . .'

'That's exactly my point, Steve! There *is* a rapist now. And the rapist is black.'

'Come on, Gabe. The song takes a powerful stand *against* rape! You can't object to that.'

'I can most certainly object to the rapist being black.'

'It's the *dancer* who's black. Tamar Valparaiso hired a black dancer. Equal opportunity. Do you object . . . ?'

'To portray a black rapist.'

'Gabe, I think you're barking up the wrong tree. I

don't know the girl, but I'm willing to bet my last dollar she isn't a racist.'

'I can smell one a hundred yards away,' Foster said.

'Maybe your nose is too sensitive,' Carella said. 'I have to go upstairs, Gabe. You want my advice?'

'No.'

'Okay, see you later then.'

'Let me hear it.'

'Pack up and go home. You don't want to be on the wrong side of this one. It'll come back to haunt you.'

'Ah, but I'm on the right side of it, Steve. The rapist on that video is vicious and monstrous and black. That's racist. And that's good enough for me.'

'I have to go,' Carella said.

'Good seeing you again,' Foster said, and nodded briefly, and stepped back into the line of marchers. 'Ban Bandersnatch!' he shouted. 'Ban Bandersnatch! Ban Bandersnatch! Ban Bandersnatch!'

The black security guard who took Carella's name and phoned it upstairs glanced through the tall glass windows fronting the street, and asked, 'What's *that* all about?'

'Beats me,' Carella said, and signed his name, and waited for clearance. When it came, he took the elevator up to the twenty-third floor, and went through the still-empty reception area directly to Barney Loomis' office at the end of the hall. The Squad was already there. Loomis was not.

'Steve, ah,' Corcoran said, and immediately looked at his watch as if to imply that Carella was late, which he wasn't. 'Few people you should meet who weren't here yesterday,' he said, and introduced a handful of FBI agents and detectives whose names Carella forgot the moment he shook hands with them.

The office itself had undergone something of a

transformation since late last night. There was now new equipment everywhere Carella looked. In fact, someone he guessed was an FBI technician was busily testing an electronic device set up on a long folding table across the room.

'Let me tell you what we've done here,' Endicott said.

He looked wide awake and alert, wearing this morning a dark gray suit that seemed better tailored than the blue one he'd worn yesterday. Corcoran, in contrast, was wearing brown slacks and a brown V-necked sweater over a plaid sports shirt. Carella himself had worn a suit today. He suddenly felt overdressed for a city detective.

'First off, we've installed a direct line to your office. You pick up that green phone there,' Endicott said, pointing, 'and you've got the squadroom at the Eight-Seven. How's that for service?'

Carella was wondering How come?

'We figured we'd let you guys do what you do best, am I right, Charles?' Endicott said. 'The legwork, the nuts and bolts, the nitty gritty. We get anything to chase, you pick up that green phone, your boys are on it in a minute. Will that work for you?'

'Sure,' Carella said. 'Thanks.'

'Regarding all this other stuff,' he said, 'we noticed that your telephone guy set up a simple Tap and Tape, with a jack for a single listener, but we'll be more people working on this, so we've installed equipment that'll accommodate three more sets of ear phones, you can understand why that would be necessary,' Endicott said, and smiled hopefully, as if seeking Carella's approval.

'More the merrier,' Carella said.

'The other thing . . . the court orders you got yesterday were for the primary landline carriers . . . AT&T, Verizon, Sprint, MCI . . . but there are at least half a dozen other

158

service providers so we've taken the liberty of obtaining court orders for those as well, assuming our boy will be calling from landline equipment – which may not be the case.'

'This is all so much easier since 9/11,' Corcoran said.

'Oh *so* much,' Endicott agreed. 'Though I have to tell you the truth, I've never known a judge to turn down a federal request for a wiretap.'

'Used to be probable cause, probable cause,' Corcoran said, and rolled his eyes.

He was referring to the way it customarily worked. Before a judge could approve an application for electronic surveillance and issue a court order, he had to determine that:

a) there was probable cause for belief that an individual was committing, had committed, or was about to commit an offense covered by law . . .

b) there was probable cause for belief that particular communications concerning that offense would be obtained through such interception . . .

c) normal investigative procedures had been tried and had failed or reasonably appeared unlikely to succeed or to be too dangerous . . .

d) there was probable cause for belief that the facilities from which, or the place where the communications were to be intercepted were being used, or were about to be used, in connection with the commission of such offense.

In each of Carella's applications yesterday, he had cited probable cause. His petitions had been granted in every instance. But Corcoran was saying . . .

'Judges are a lot more malleable since 9/11. Before then, to get a court order for a pen register . . .'

'That's a sort of reverse caller-ID,' Endicott explained.

'Yes, I know,' Carella said.

'We record the numbers dialed *out*.'

'Yes, I . . .'

'. . . you had to show probable cause. Now, you just go in and say the information will be relevant to an ongoing investigation, and by federal law, a judge is required to approve the order. Relevant, can you believe it?'

'Makes it nice,' Endicott said.

'Makes it simple.'

'Anyway,' Endicott said, 'since you'd covered only the landline carriers, we went ahead and obtained additional court orders for the wireless companies, too. These computers you see around the room . . .'

Carella counted four of them.

'. . . tap into our central computers down at Number One Fed. If our boy uses any of the seven mobile-phone providers servicing this city, we've got sophisticated links to all of them, and we'll triangulate in a second.'

Carella nodded.

He didn't know what 'triangulate' meant. He said nothing.

'Want to try your new toy?' Corcoran said, and handed him the receiver on the green phone.

Carella put it to his ear.

He heard the phone ringing on the other end.

'Eighty-seventh Squad, Detective Hawes.'

'Cotton, it's me. Just testing.'

'Testing what?' Hawes asked.

ON ONE WALL of Bison's conference room down the hall, the company had set out a generous buffet consisting of orange juice (or grapefruit juice), croissants (plain or chocolate), Danish pastries (cheese or jelly), bagels (plain, onion, or poppy seed), smoked Norwegian salmon, cream cheese, butter, jellies and jams in a wide variety of flavors, and coffee (either full-strength or de-caf).

The four men seated around the huge rosewood conference table had helped themselves to the sideboard goodies and were now leisurely enjoying their morning repast before getting down to business. They were in a jocular mood. They had a lot to be happy about.

Barney Loomis' plate was brimming, as usual. He demolished his breakfast with obvious gusto now, listening to the chatter all around him, but not distracted by it in the slightest. Gulping down the last of his onion bagel heaped with salmon and cream cheese, he washed it down with the last of his 'hi-test coffee,' as he called it, and began the meeting abruptly by asking, 'Did you see those marchers outside? They're labeling Tamar a racist! What's wrong with these people, anyway?,' never once realizing that referring to the black protestors as 'these people' might in itself be considered a trifle racist.

'Controversy never hurt anybody,' Binkie Horowitz said.

As Bison's Vice President in charge of Promotion, he had checked all his people before this morning's meeting, and was confident that the only thing that could possibly hurt them now was if the kidnappers actually killed Tamar Valparaiso, bite your tongue.

'I'm not so sure,' Loomis said. 'We lose the black market because of those jackasses marching out there . . .'

'We won't lose the black market,' Binkie said, 'don't worry.'

Short and slight, narrow-waisted and narrow-shouldered as well, he resembled a harried jockey whipping a tired nag across the finish line. Leaning over the table, his brown eyes intense, he said, 'We are not at this very *moment,* in fact, losing the black market. We *are,* in fact, averaging *more* spins per hour on all-black radio than we are on the white stations. Take WJAX, for example – which by the way played Alicia Keys' "Fallin'" a hundred and seven times in its first week of release – I checked with our man in Florida first thing this morning, and since news of the kidnapping broke, and especially since the kidnap tape ran last night on network news, they've been playing 'Bandersnatch' every hour and a half, with requests for it pouring in all the time. If the momentum holds at that rate, we're looking at sixteen spins a day, times seven days a week, will come to a hundred and twelve spins in the next week alone, which will top Alicia's hundred and seven for a week on that same station. And I don't have to tell you "Fallin'" was number one all over the country. And JAX is a *top* black station, this isn't some thirty-kilowatt shack in rural Mississippi. We don't have to worry about losing the black market, Barney, I can assure you of that.'

'Tell that to the good Reverend Foster,' Loomis said, going to the sideboard and pouring himself another cup of coffee. 'He's a national player, he'll be all over cable television in a minute and a half.'

J. P. Higgins, Bison's VP in charge of Video Production, had been silent until now. Truth of the matter was that he was nursing a hangover this morning, having partied too strenuously aboard the *River Princess* on Saturday night, and having partied privately with the black reporter from *Rolling Stone* last night, celebrating what he considered the fortuitous circumstance of a kidnapping that had thrust Tamar's video into national prominence.

Dressed this morning in sweater and slacks and wearing a blue beret he thought made him look debonair if only he had a mustache, he turned to Binkie Horowitz and, seemingly suddenly inspired, asked, 'Any chance we can get more cable stations to show our video?'

'Why not?' Loomis said from the sideboard, and while he was just standing there, fixed himself another bagel with salmon and cream cheese. 'If Foster's going to join the talking heads, then maybe they'd like to lead in with our actual goddamn video! Let it speak for itself. Hell, that video isn't about *race,* it's about *rape!*'

'That's a good point to make to the radio stations, too,' Harry Di Fidelio said. 'A good talking point. "Bandersnatch" isn't about race, it's about rape. Race, rape, they almost rhyme, in fact. What they call a slant rhyme.'

Dressed this morning in a dark blue suit with a white shirt and a blue tie, Di Fidelio lacked only laced black shoes to blend right in with most of the FBI agents down the hall in Loomis' office. Instead, unaware that he might be emulating the fashion preferences of a former U.S. President, he was wearing brown loafers with the blue suit. His socks were brown, too, but that's because he was color blind.

As Bison's VP in charge of Radio Marketing, Di Fidelio was constantly on the lookout for ways to convince the deejays that they actually had something to *talk* about. It was one thing to Pay-for-Play a radio station, and another to sic the indie promoters on them, but if you could give a deejay a truly *personal* reason to plug a record, you were home free. So far, the single had been played on more than 115 Top 40 stations including Z100, WKTU, KIIS, WHYI, KZQZ, WNCI, KDWB, KSLZ, WEZB, and enough damn alphabet soup to feed an army of fans. But if this thing became *really* controversial . . .

'Rape or Race, we could say,' he suggested, and spread his hands on the air to spell out the words. 'Rape or Race. *You* decide.'

'That's not bad,' Binkie said. 'Rape or Race. We fight fire with fire. Go head to toe with Foster or anyone else who wants to bring up the race issue. Hell, our hands are clean, our credentials are spotless,' he said, seemingly unaware of the fact that no one around that table was black.

'Let's shotgun the video all over the place,' Loomis said. 'Use the "Rape or Race" pitch, I like it, spell it all out for them. Maybe get viewers to call in or e-mail, get a poll going, is it rape or race? *You* decide.'

'Rape or Race,' Di Fidelio repeated, spreading his hands on the air again, reminding everyone that this was *his* idea, after all. '*You* decide.'

'Be great if we could get some women's rights groups to champion the video,' Higgins said. 'Get them to say what a brave stand Tamar took, get them to suggest she *herself* may be out there getting raped this very . . .'

'I wouldn't go there,' Loomis said at once.

'Well, we don't really *know* what's happening to her, do we?' Higgins said. His head was pounding. He didn't feel like arguing.

'When they call today,' Loomis said, and looked at his watch, 'I'll ask to speak to her. Before we turn over any money, I want some assurance that . . .'

'Incidentally . . .'

They all turned toward the far end of the table.

A short, slender man wearing a blue blazer, gray flannel slacks, a paler blue shirt, and a gold-and-blue silk-rep tie, sat there with only a cup of coffee in front of him. Jedediah Bailey, the firm's accountant.

'Do you have any idea how much they'll be asking for?'

'Of course not,' Loomis said. 'How would I know how much . . . ?'

'Just asking,' Jedediah said, and spread his hands

defensively, palms outward. He'd merely wanted to ascertain that Loomis could get hold of what would most certainly be a sizable amount of cash in a short period of time. Loomis was the company's sole shareholder and CEO. Were his personal assets liquid enough? That's all Jedediah wished to determine, so sue him.

'I'm hoping we'll have her back by tonight sometime,' Loomis said.

The room went silent.

'You know . . .' Higgins ventured, and then shook his head.

'What?' Loomis asked.

'It wouldn't hurt if this thing dragged on even longer. Few days longer,' Higgins said, and shrugged. 'It wouldn't hurt, really.'

He was the only one in the room who'd dared say it.

THE ENTIRE SQUAD was in the office when Endicott gave Loomis' private secretary her marching orders.

Gloria Klein was in her early thirties, a somewhat plain-looking woman, even in the mini and tight sweater she felt appropriate to her job at a record company. She kept shifting her attention and her pale blue eyes from Endicott to Loomis, as if checking to see that her boss agreed with all this.

'Mr. Loomis won't be taking any calls from people you can identify. If you recognize a name, you tell the caller Mr. Loomis will get back to him or her. Have you got that?'

'Yes, sir,' she said.

'Now, Gloria,' Endicott said, 'if a caller refuses to give his name, or if he says something like 'This is personal,' you ask him to hold, please, and then check with Mr. Loomis before putting him through. Have you got that?'

'Yes, sir. Does this have to do with Tamar, sir?'

No, it has to do with the price of fish in Norway, Endicott thought, but did not say.

'Yes, it has to do with Tamar,' he said.

'Are we expecting a call from her kidnappers, is that it?'

'You don't need to know that.'

'Yes, sir.'

'Anyone whose name you recognize . . .'

'Mr. Loomis will call back.'

'Any strange name, or anyone who won't give a name . . .'

'I buzz Mr. Loomis, check if it's okay to put the call through.'

'Very good, Gloria. And if anyone should ask, there's no one here with Mr. Loomis.'

'Yes, sir.'

'He's alone.'

'Yes, sir.'

'That's it.'

'Thank you, sir,' Gloria said, and made eye contact with her boss again, checking.

Loomis gave a slight nod.

THE PHONE on his desk rang at twelve o'clock sharp.

He picked up.

'Yes?' he said.

'Mr. Loomis, there's someone who says you're expecting his call. He wouldn't give a name.'

'Give me three minutes, and then put him through.'

He replaced the receiver on its cradle, and turned to the others. 'Won't give a name, says I'm expecting his call.'

'Bingo,' Corcoran said, and nodded toward a makeshift

structure not unlike a phone booth, its walls baffled to deaden any sound in the office around him. Loomis entered the booth at once, sat in a chair set up in front of an extension phone. Endicott, Corcoran, and two of his detectives put on ear phones at the monitoring equipment. Carella stood by the green phone that would connect him directly to the Eight-Seven. The three other detectives and the remaining agent were already sitting at phones that linked them to One Fed Square.

The room was utterly silent.

When the phone rang again, its sound burst on the air like a hand grenade.

'Here he is,' Endicott said. 'Just sound natural, hear what he has to say. We'll be on him, believe me.'

The phone kept ringing.

'That's three, four . . .'

'Pick up,' Endicott said.

In the booth, Loomis picked up the receiver.

'Barney Loomis,' he said.

'We have the girl,' the voice on the phone said. 'We want two hundred and fifty thousand dollars in unmarked, hundred-dollar bills. We'll call at three P.M. sharp to tell you where to deliver it. Do anything foolish and she dies.'

'How do I know she's still alive?' Loomis asked at once.

'Would you like to talk to her?'

'Yes. Yes, please. Let me talk to her.'

There was a silence.

'Verizon landline is tracking,' one of the agents said.

'Sweetheart, come here a minute.'

This on Loomis' phone. Somewhat apart, as if the caller were holding the receiver out to someone.

'Verizon says it's a cell phone,' one of the detectives said.

There was another silence, longer this time.

'Tell Mr. Loomis you're okay,' the voice on the phone said. 'No, don't touch the phone!' Sharply. 'Just tell him you're fine.'

'It's AT&T wireless,' the same detective said.

'Get on it,' Endicott said.

A shorter silence.

'Hello?'

'Tamar?'

'Yes, Barney.'

Across the room, an agent was asking an AT&T operator to determine the number of the cell phone and track its location.

'Are you all right?'

'I'm fine, Barney.'

'Nobody's hurt you, have they?'

'No, I'm fine.'

'I'll get the money they want, Tamar. You'll be home soon.'

'Thank you, Barney.'

'How's the CD doing?' Tamar asked.

'Very well, actually.'

'First tower's tracking,' one of the agents reported.

'Am I gonna be a star?'

'Oh, you betcha, kid. A real diva.'

'Good. I have to go now, Barney. He wants me to get off the phone.'

'I'll see you soon,' Loomis said.

The man's voice came on again.

'Okay?' he asked. 'Satisfied, Mr. Loomis?'

'Second tower's got it.'

'Yes. Thank you,' Loomis said.

'Get the money by three P.M.'

'Keep him on,' Endicott said.

There was a click on the line.

'Shit!'

'The way this works,' Corcoran said, yanking off his ear phones, 'is the landline company hands us off to the wireless provider, who tracks the call through the base station towers handling it. It's called triangulation. These are three *radio* towers, you understand, a cell phone is a *radio* phone. The first tower judges a rough distance to the caller. Second tower narrows the choice to two points. Third tower pinpoints the location. Unfortunately, our guy got off before the third tower could zero in.'

'He's out on the Island someplace, that's for sure,' one of the agents said.

'Here comes the info now,' a second agent said, and joined him at the computer. They both turned to look at the printer as it began spewing paper. Two detectives rose from their phones and immediately put on their jackets.

'How does it jibe with Sands Spit?' Endicott asked.

'Rosalita Guadajillo,' the first agent said, yanking the printout free. '3215 Noble. Nowhere near. She's right here in the city.'

'Maybe an accomplice,' Corcoran said.

'Move on her,' Endicott ordered, and the two agents went out the door, followed immediately by the two detectives. Carella, sitting by his new green toy with his thumb up his ass, looked at Special Agent in Charge Stanley M. Endicott.

'We have experience in such matters,' Endicott explained, and shrugged.

'What's happening?' Loomis asked, coming out of the booth.

'We lost him,' Endicott said.

'This is going to be elaborate,' Corcoran said.

'How do you know?'

'We've had experience with these things.'

'She's alive,' Barney said. 'Thank God for that.'

'Everything'll be fine,' Endicott told him. 'You'll see.'

Carella said nothing.

'You pissed off about something?' Endicott asked.

SPECIAL AGENT HARVEY JONES definitely thought he saw cockroaches in the hallway. Which was better than rats, he supposed. His cousin was an agent in Los Angeles, and she told him there were rats in Beverly Hills. Driven down into populated areas because of the drought. Drinking from rich people's swimming pools. Imagine you're a movie star and you go out for your early morning swim in your big private walled pool and a hundred rats are in the water with you! In this part of the city you expected rats — although all Jones had seen so far were cockroaches. In Beverly Hills, you didn't expect rats. Jones had grown up with both cockroaches and rats; he was sensitive to both.

This part of the city was familiarly called *La Perlita,* after an erstwhile notorious slum in San Juan cynically named *La Perla,* which was Spanish for 'The Pearl,' and some pearl it had been, honey. The reincarnation here wasn't much better. Nicknamed by the so-called Marine Tigers who'd first migrated from the island in the early forties (aboard a vessel called the *Marine Tiger,* hence the derogatory appellation), *La Perlita* was still predominantly Puerto Rican and somewhat dangerous, even for four men carrying guns and badges.

A lot in this city had changed since the forties but not *La Perlita.* Maybe nowadays, third- and fourth-generation Puerto Ricans no longer sounded like *banditos.* Maybe nowadays, men going to work in business suits weren't necessarily hit men for drug posses. And maybe nowadays teenage girls wearing short tight satin skirts and stiletto-heeled sandals were only heading to the prom and not the nearest street corner to peddle their wares. But however you looked at it, *La Perlita* was still a sprawling slum rife with drugs, prostitution, and . . . yes, rats. Come to think of it, it was a lot like Beverly Hills, don't write me letters, Jones thought.

As they climbed to the fourth floor of the tenement at 3215 Noble Street, the four men were discussing a TV show Special Agent Forbes had seen on television. Special Agent Forbes was saying he'd been watching this writer on C-Span the other night, giving a book talk in a book store in Seattle someplace, and the writer was telling the audience that he once got a letter from some lady who said she wasn't going to read his books anymore because there were too many *people* in them.

'Can you imagine that?' Forbes asked. 'Too many *people* in them?'

'No, I can't,' Jones said, shaking his head in agreement and amazement. 'In fact, one of the things I like most about this job is *meeting* different people. So how can there be too many people in a *book?*'

'Besides, they aren't *people*,' Detective/First Grade Lonigan said, 'they're *characters*.'

'Who was this writer, anyway?' Detective/Second Grade Feingold asked.

'Some mystery writer,' Forbes said.

'Well, that's different,' Lonigan said, changing his mind. 'In a mystery, you can't have too many people, that's right. That's because all the people are suspects . . .'

'The characters, you mean.'

'Are suspects, correct. So if you can't keep track of them, then you can't possibly figure out who committed the murder, which is the whole point of a mystery, anyway, isn't it?'

Listening, Jones wondered if that was the whole point of a mystery, anyway.

'I still think he was right,' Forbes said. 'A woman telling him there's too many *people* in his book. If she wants fewer people, she should go read "Snow White and the Seven Dwarfs."'

Or 'The Three Little Pigs,' Jones thought, and all four men stopped outside the door to apartment 4C. Because they'd had experience in such matters, they listened at the wood before they knocked. Because they'd had experience in such matters, they also drew their weapons. This was maybe an accomplice to a kidnapping behind this door here.

'Yes?'

A woman's voice. Sounded young. No Spanish accent despite the Spanish handle. Forbes looked at the computer printout again. Rosalita Guadajillo.

'Miss Goo-ah-duh-Jello?' he asked.

'*Gwa-da-hee-yo, sí,*' she said, correcting his pronunciation. 'Who is it?'

'FBI,' Forbes said. 'Want to open the door, please?'

There was a moment's hesitation. FBI? *What!* The reaction was always the same. You could almost visualize the silence behind the closed wooden door, as if the words were popping up in a comic strip balloon. What the . . .!!!!

The door opened just a crack, held by a night chain. In the wedge, they could see part of a narrow foxlike face.

'Let me see some ID,' the woman said. Perfect English. Not a trace of an accent.

Jones held up his badge. So did Forbes. Gold, with a spread-winged eagle crowning what looked like a true warrior's shield, dominated by the large letters *U.S.*

engraved midway between the smaller words *Federal Bureau of Investigation* above and *Department of Justice* below. Not at all like the hanging plastic ID badges they carried on 'X-Files,' those so-called Burbank Studio FBI Cards. Behind the two agents, the city dicks flashed their gold, blue-enameled shields.

The overwhelming ID had no effect.

The door remained fastened by the chain.

'What do you want here?' the woman asked.

'Are you Rosalita Guadajillo?' Jones asked, having no better luck with the name than Forbes had.

'Yes? What is it you want?'

'Few questions we need to ask you, Miss,' Forbes said. 'Could you please open the door?'

There was another hesitation, and then a short sharp click as she closed the door. Forbes figured it wouldn't open again. He was thinking they'd have to come back later, with a warrant, when all at once he heard the chain rattling loose, and the door opened wide, surprising him.

Rosalita Guadajillo was a slender woman in her early twenties, they guessed, some five-feet-six-inches tall, obviously dressed to go out on this Monday at almost twelve noon. Her hair was black, her eyes brown and lined with a greenish tint. She was wearing bright red lipstick and round plastic earrings of the same color, high-heeled strappy black sandals, a short, tight black skirt, and a crisp white blouse unbuttoned some three buttons down to reveal somewhat exuberant cleavage cushioning a red plastic necklace that matched the earrings. Both Jones and Forbes figured her for a hooker, so much for profiling.

'May we come in?' Forbes asked.

He wasn't being polite. He was protecting their asses

against future claims of forced entry, these days.

'What's this about?' Rosalita asked, stepping aside to allow them entry. She was not unmindful of the display of big hardware, but this was *La Perlita* and guns were as common here as *cuchi frito* joints. They walked into a small kitchen still set with that morning's breakfast dishes. Living room with a thrift-shop three-piece set of stuffed furniture. Doors opening on two small bedrooms. Closed door probably led to the bathroom. One of the detectives opened the door. Nobody in there, thank God.

'This your phone number, Miss Guadajillo?' Forbes asked. He was getting close to the correct pronunciation, but still no cigar.

She looked at the printout.

'Yes?' she said.

'You make a call from this phone at noon today?'

'No.'

'To a man named Barney Loomis . . .'

'No.'

'At Bison Records?'

'No. I haven't even tried to use that phone since late last night.'

'You know exactly when you used it last, is that it?' Jones asked.

'Yes, it so happens I do,' she said, getting all huffy. 'Because that was when I tried to call my sitter, and I discovered it was missing.'

'Missing, huh?'

'The phone, huh?'

'Your sitter, huh?'

'I have two kids,' Rosalita said. 'A sitter was with them last night. When I tried to call her, my phone was gone.'

'You have two kids, huh?' Lonigan said.

'Eight and six. A boy and a girl.'

Meant she'd been knocked up the first time when she was sixteen or thereabouts, Lonigan figured.

'Where are these kids now?'

'My mother has them. She keeps them all day. While I work.'

'Doing what, Miss Guadajillo?'

Lonigan figured he already knew.

'I have a boutique on Mason and Sixth.'

'A boutique, huh?' Feingold said.

'Yes. I sell costume jewelry. These earrings are from my shop.'

'Is that a fact?' Forbes said skeptically.

'Yes, it's a fact,' Rosalita said. 'Why do you want to know about my phone?'

'Did you happen to *report* it missing?'

'I just learned about it late last night.'

'What time last night?'

'Around ten-thirty. When we got out of the movies. That's when I tried to call home to see how the kids were.'

'Who's we?' Forbes asked.

'What movie?' Jones asked.

'My boyfriend,' Rosalita said. 'The new Tom Cruise movie.'

'But your phone was missing, huh?'

'My phone was missing, yes. I think I may have left it at the shop. Or else somebody stole it from my bag.'

'You going to the shop now?'

'Yes.'

'Why don't we just come with you?' Forbes suggested. 'See if maybe you left the phone there.'

'*Por que es ese putó selular tan importante después de todo?*' Rosalita asked – which was incidentally Spanish, which neither the agents nor the detectives understood, incidentally.

Besides, it didn't really matter, did it?

The fucking phone wasn't in her shop, anyway.

8.

BECAUSE BOTH MEN were downtown to testify in two separate court cases that Monday morning, Detectives Andy Parker and Ollie Weeks happened to run into each other at the Criminal Courts Building when their respective judges called lunch breaks. Both detectives normally enjoyed testifying since it gave them a chance to bask in the glory spotlight for a few hours, even though they felt the system was designed to put dangerous criminals back on the street again as soon as possible. A trip downtown took them away from the humdrum daily grinds of the 8-7 and the 8-8. Down here in the halls of so-called justice, they almost felt it was all worthwhile.

'Ollie, hey!' Parker called.

'Andy, *vee gates?*' Ollie said, meaning to say *'wie gehts,'* an expression he'd picked up from his lieutenant, but only to prove to all these Jewish lawyers down here in these hallowed marble corridors just how tolerant he was of the Hebrew faith. Ollie guessed the expression meant 'How goes it?' Parker didn't know what it meant, so Ollie could just as well have been saying *'Veh farblondjet,'* which meant 'Get lost,' but which he hadn't yet learned.

Both men were wearing suits and ties. When these shrewd defense-lawyer shysters started working you over, it was always best for the jury to think you were gentlemen instead of roughnecks or rogues like some of the cops you saw on television these days. Actually, Parker and Weeks did occasionally behave like roughnecks and/or rogues, but it didn't pay to let the jury know this when you were testifying that you went in with all the proper No-Knock documentation.

'You feel like Chink's?' Parker asked.

Both men were consummate bigots.

'I know a great place,' Ollie said.

The two detectives strolled in bright May sunshine toward a Chinese restaurant in nearby Hull Street. They could have been bankers or lawyers or stockbrokers, they looked that dandy. Parker had even shaved for the occasion of his court appearance. He told Ollie the 8-7 had caught a spectacular case this past Saturday night, had Ollie seen the tape on TV? Ollie said he had. In fact, he was sick and tired of seeing Tamar Valparaiso on television day and night.

'Did you know somebody stole my book?' he asked.

'No!' Parker said, looking appalled. 'What book?'

'This book I wrote.'

'*You* wrote a book?' Parker said. He considered this something of an oddity, like an elephant in the jungle writing a book. With his right tusk. Or perhaps his trunk.

'Yeah, a novel,' Ollie said. '*Report to the Commissioner.* Some illiterate scumbag stole it from my car.'

'Did you get the guy?'

'Not yet. But I will. Oh, I will, I promise you.'

'I always thought I myself could write a book, some of this crap you read nowadays,' Parker said. 'If only I could find the time.'

Because he didn't wish to rain on Parker's parade, Ollie didn't mention that it also took talent. Instead, he said, 'It does take time, m'friend, ah yes.' What was taking most of his own time these days was trying to remember the exact language in the stolen manuscript, which happened to be the only copy Ollie had, every word of which he felt was perfect. Since Ollie didn't know any professional writers but himself, he didn't realize that what he was doing was called 'rewriting.' And since he had nothing against which to compare his new pages, he had no idea that they were really much better than what he'd originally written. In all truth, it wasn't too difficult to write pages that were better than the original ones, but Ollie didn't know that, either.

'Yeah, this half-spic, half-Russian singer, her parents anyway,' Parker said, getting back to the kidnapping because Ollie's novel was of no interest to him whatsoever. 'You should try to catch the tape on TV,' he said. 'She's half-naked, these great tits spilling all over the place.'

'I *did* catch it,' Ollie said. 'You ever eat here before?' he asked, salivating and shoving through a door that was made of wood but that looked like a beaded curtain.

At noontime, the place was crowded with many of the employees who kept the city's judicial and financial systems running. A hostess wearing a green silk Suzie Wong gown slit to the thigh on her left leg seated the men in a booth some ten feet from the entrance doors, and handed them menus. Parker watched her slitted thigh as she went back to her station. Ollie was already looking at his menu.

'She gets raped by this spade twice her size,' Parker said. 'Tamar whatever the fuck her name is.'

'You wanna try some dim sum?' Ollie asked.

'What's that, them dim sum?' Parker said.

'Or how about some of the specials?'

'Why don't you order?' Parker said. 'I trust you.'

'I do happen to be an expert on Chinese coo-zeen,' Ollie said.

'So order, go on. He's got muscles on his muscles, this jig, prolly got them in the prison gym.'

A waiter padded over to their table. To start, Ollie

ordered eight golden puffed shrimp, six chicken fingers, six pan-fried pork dumplings, and two five-piece orders of barbecued spare ribs. Then he ordered the Hot Lovers Chicken, which was deep-fried chicken sautéed with snow peas, baby corn, and straw mushrooms in a spicy tangy sauce, and the Dry Sautéed Beef, Szechuan Style . . .

'This is real Chinese home cooking,' he told Parker.

. . . and the Mee Goreng, which were spaghetti-style noodles sautéed with various exotic spices, shrimp, tomatoes, eggs, and vegetables . . .

'A specialty in Singapore,' Ollie explained.

. . . and then the Young Ginger Beef, and the Scallops with Lemon Sauce, and the Broccoli with Garlic Sauce, and the Sautéed Fresh Spinach.

'I hope that'll be enough,' he told Parker. 'We can always order more later, if we need it.'

The waiter wagged his head in wonder and went off.

'Why do they always look like they're pissed off?' Parker asked.

'Who?' Ollie said.

'Chinese waiters. They always look like they got a hair across their ass.'

'It ain't that,' Ollie explained. 'It's they got these squinty eyes makes them look like they're frowning.'

'He prac'ly tears off all her clothes,' Parker said.

'Who does?'

'This rapist.'

'You know,' Ollie said, 'sometimes I don't know what the fuck you're talking about.'

Parker explained that on Saturday night, just as the new shift was coming on at eleven-forty, he answered a phone call from this captain in Harbor Patrol who asked to talk to the detective on duty . . .

'So like a jackass, I handed the phone to Carella who

was just walking in, and gave away the biggest case we've had all year.'

'A rape case? That's big in the Eight-Seven? In the Eight-Eight, we get ten, twelve rape cases every ten, twelve minutes.'

'A *kidnapping!*' Parker said. 'Of a goddamn rock star! It's been all over television. Don't you watch television? They been playing the tape every ten minutes. It's getting more plays than the attack on the World Trade Center.'

'I saw it, I saw it,' Ollie said. 'Ah,' he said and spread his hands wide in greeting. The waiter had just arrived with their appetizers.

'What happened,' Parker said, helping himself to the puffed shrimp, 'was this roving reporter from Channel Four was there to tape this girl doing a song from her album . . . you want some of these?'

'Thanks,' Ollie said. He was shoveling chicken fingers and dumplings onto his plate.

'And what should happen but these two black dudes . . .'

'Big surprise,' Ollie said.

'. . . come marching in and grab the girl. It's the biggest thing hit this city since that fuckin councilman got shot. And like a jerk I handed it to Carella on a silver platter.'

'Well, you couldn'ta known,' Ollie said. 'The Harbor Patrol, it coulda been a jumper.'

'Exactly what I thought.'

'Sure, the Harbor Patrol. What else could it be?'

'Or some kinda boating accident.'

'Right, a boating accident.'

Now that food was on the table, he was even less interested in Parker's rape or kidnapping or whatever it was. When food was on the table, Ollie was hardly ever interested in anything else. Which was why it still surprised him that he'd been so interested in Patricia Gomez this past Saturday night when, after all, food had been on the table then, too. By coincidence, he supposed, Parker chose that moment to ask, 'What'd you do this weekend?'

'How do you like this food, huh?' Ollie said, gnawing on a spare rib. 'Is it something, or what?'

'Terrific,' Parker said. 'So what'd you do this weekend?'

'I went out Saturday night.'

'Where'd you go?'

'Billy Barnacles.'

'No kidding?' Parker said. 'They got a band there, don't they?'

'Yeah, the River Rats.'

'So what'd you do, you went there with a girl?'

'No, I went out dancin all by myself,' Ollie said.

'Hey, *that's* right!' Parker said, pointing a spare rib at him. 'That little spic uniform up your precinct!'

He was referring to Patricia Gomez, Ollie figured.

'That was Saturday night, huh?'

'Yeah.'

'Sure, I remember you telling me,' Parker said, and looked sternly across the table at him. 'You went out with her after all, huh? Even though I warned you.'

'Yeah, I went out with her.'

'I lived with a Spanish girl for six months,' Parker said. 'In the end, she cut off my dick for a nickel and sold it to a *cuchi frito* joint.'

'I guess you mean that figuratively,' Ollie said, using a literary term he didn't expect Parker to understand.

'I mean it however you wish to take it,' Parker said, sounding offended. 'You want to go out with Spanish girls, then you better go hide your *cojones* in the olive jar.'

'Anyway, Patricia ain't Spanish, she's Puerto Rican.'

'What do you think I'm talking about? What are Puerto Ricans if not Spanish? Where do you think the term "Hispanic" comes from, if not Spanish? This girl I lived with, her name was Catalina Herrera, they called her Cathy, all her spic friends. They all sound so fuckin *American* nowadays, you sometimes forget they came from some shack on the side of a hill in Mayagüez. I met her when we were chasing the Graffiti Killer, you remember that case? Man, he was up to all kinds of mischief, killed four fuckin people before we got him. Her son was the first victim, a bona fide wall-writer. Cathy was divorced from some guy went back to live in Santo Domingo. Anyway, to make a long story short, one thing led to another, and this and that, and eventually we started living together.'

'So what happened?' Ollie asked. 'Do you wear a prosthesis now?'

Parker didn't know what a prosthesis was. He didn't laugh. Ollie was laughing at his own joke, though.

'What's so fuckin funny?' Parker asked. 'What happened was we had this big drug bust set up for a Tuesday night, and I happened to mention this to Cathy while we were in bed the night before, little pillow talk, you know? She listened very carefully, they have this way of listening, Spanish girls, but who suspects anything, am I right? I mean, we're *living* together, we're like man and wife. Okay, Tuesday night rolls around, we put on the vests, we break out the assault rifles, we're six guys strong who go out to raid this posse run by a guy we know only as *El Zorro Canoso,* which means "The Gray Fox" in case your girlfriend ain't teaching you too much Spanish these days . . .'

'She ain't my girlfriend,' Ollie said. 'We only went out once togeth . . .'

'*El Zorro Canoso.* Twenty-four years old, he's got a full head of gray hair already, probably because he's worried about being sent upstate for a long time. But guess what? Nobody's home. We go in with a warrant, but nobody's there. The place is empty. *El Zorro Canoso* has flown El Coopo. Next thing I know, Cathy comes around wearing a silk Fuck-Me dress she bought at Juno's on Jeff Av, and these high-heeled whore shoes that are all straps, I ask her did somebody die and leave her a fortune? She tells me she hit the numbers, which was bullshit because I knew she never played the numbers. What it turns out . . .'

'She ratted out your bust,' Ollie said.

'How'd you guess? The morning after I told her about it, Tuesday morning this is, the day of the bust this is, she runs to her former husband's cousin, whose name happens to be Bernardo Herrera, who is guess who?'

'Zorro.'

'Bingo, you shoulda been a detective. Her ex-hubby's fuckin cousin is *El Zorro Canoso,* who runs the posse we're about to bust! He thanks her for being such a good relative, and then he lays five bills on her, which is what I meant when I said she'll cut off your dick for a nickel and sell it to a *cuchi frito* joint.'

'Well, Patricia didn't cut off my dick,' Ollie said. 'For a nickel or however much. In fact, she doesn't even *like cuchi frito.*'

'You're missing my point, friend. And what's this on the platter here? It looks like somebody cut off the *chef's* dick.'

'That's the Szechuan beef.'

'It looks like it.'

The men were silent for several moments, eating.

'So did you get in?' Parker asked.

'Come on, what kind of talk is that?'

184

'I'm curious,' Parker said, and lowered his voice, and leaned across the table, and said, 'Well, didja?'

'Come on, Andy,' Ollie said, and sort of jerked his head over his shoulder and slitted his eyes at the booth behind him.

'Nobody can hear us,' Parker said.

'We better hurry here,' Ollie said. 'The judge said one-thirty, didn't he?'

Parker looked at him.

'What?' Ollie said.

Parker kept looking at him.

'Nothing,' he said at last, and went back to his lunch.

FOR THE FIRST TIME in fifteen years, Carella wanted to smoke a cigarette.

Anything but sitting here on his hands.

The four men who'd been sent to find Rosalita Guada-jillo were back.

'Lady's clean as a whistle,' Forbes reported. 'She runs a little jewelry boutique on Mason Avenue, up there in *La Perlita,* sells mostly cheap crap from Third World countries. She went to call her kids last night around ten-thirty, fished in her handbag, no cell phone. Somebody stole it.'

'Our man,' Corcoran said, nodding.

'Smart,' Endicott said.

'He knew we'd be tracing the call . . .'

'Even if he made it from a mobile . . .'

'So he made it from somebody *else's* phone . . .'

'Which is now undoubtedly at the bottom of the river,' Endicott concluded.

'Which means all your equipment here is worthless,' Loomis said, waving his hand at the gear they'd set up all over the room.

'Not entirely,' Endicott said. 'When he calls again . . .'

'*If* he calls again,' Loomis said.

'Oh, he'll call,' Corcoran said. 'The name of the game is money. Until he gets his money, he'll keep calling.'

'And when he calls, we'll be taping it,' Endicott said. 'Voice prints are admissible evidence. We take this guy to trial . . .'

'I don't care about taking him to trial,' Loomis said. 'I already told you that. All I want is Tamar back.'

'Oh, we'll get her back, all right,' Corcoran assured him.

'I don't want her endangered in any way. I want to give them the money, get her back, and that's that.'

'Or vice versa,' Endicott said.

Loomis looked at him.

'Sometimes it's better to get the victim back *first*,' Endicott explained.

'Or simultaneously,' Corcoran said.

'Or at least get proof of life,' Endicott said.

'Proof that she's still alive,' Corcoran explained. 'An ear, or a finger, or . . .'

Barney Loomis went suddenly pale.

Carella wondered what the hell he was doing here.

YEARS AGO in the police department, long before he'd joined the force, a commonly accepted axiom was that if you weren't Irish, you'd never 'cop the gold.' In this case, 'cop' wasn't an abbreviation of 'copper,' which might have made for some nice metallurgical imagery. Instead, 'cop' meant to achieve or to obtain, or more specifically to be *promoted* from a uniformed officer to a detective carrying a gold shield. In this city, so rare was the occurrence of anyone *not* Irish copping the gold, that whenever it did happen to an outsider, the surprised recipient (regardless of his religious beliefs) was automatically asked 'Who's your rabbi?'

Eventually, as more and more police officers of non-Irish descent began making detective, 'Who's your rabbi?' became a standard joke. Indeed, over the syears, the dogma gradually changed to read, 'If you ain't Irish, you'll never make *captain,*' but even that bromide fell into disuse when two black police commissioners were appointed in succession.

Now, in this room full of WASPs – or such was Carella's perception even though Corcoran was Irish-Catholic and Feingold was Jewish and Jones was black – he suddenly felt like a little Wop mutt who had no right pissing with the big pedigreed dogs.

Detective Lieutenant Charles Farley Corcoran and Detective/Second Grade Stephen Louis Carella had been graduated from the Academy on the very same day. Corcoran had been assigned to the Thirtieth, a silk-stocking precinct. Carella had begun walking a beat in the Eight-Seven, a precinct uptown in the asshole of creation.

His first day on the job, uniform all spanking new, shoes polished to a high luster, silver shield shining on his chest, thirty-eight S&W – the mandated weapon back then – hanging in a holster on his right hip, a woman came running out of a building wearing only panties and a bra and screaming at the top of her lungs, he figured somebody was about to rape her. Two minutes later, a guy in his undershorts and a tank top undershirt came running out after her, also yelling bloody murder, which now seemed to be what this was about to turn into. Because right behind him was a *second* woman, fully dressed this time, and carrying in her hands what later turned out to be an ax she'd taken from the fire-alarm box on the third floor of the building. The second woman was yelling 'Bums!' as she came running down the steps of the front stoop, 'Bums! Bums!' It took Carella, bright rookie that he was, maybe thirty seconds to realize she was referring to the half-naked man and woman who'd preceded her out of the building, and another thirty seconds to calculate that the lady with the ax had caught them in bed together.

Stepping into her path, holding up his hand like a traffic cop, which frankly he wished he was in that moment, he said, 'All right, lady, let's hold it right there.'

The only thing the lady was holding right there was the ax.

Wild-eyed, she shoved past Carella . . .

Actually *shoved* past him, pushing him out of her way as if he were some sort of inanimate obstacle keeping her from exacting justice upon the two barefoot bums in their skivvies, who were now running around the corner, out of sight.

While Carella recovered his balance, he tried to remember the rules and regulations that governed when it was permissible for him to draw his gun and fire it. He was certain that assaulting a police officer qualified. He was also certain that carrying a dangerous weapon was another good reason to bring the piece into play. In fact, back then there weren't too many restrictions on when a cop could unholster and/or discharge his weapon. But however justified he may have felt, he was pretty positive he wouldn't get any medals for shooting a fat lady in the back – her back was to him now as she ran for the corner. So he yelled into the suddenly sweaty summertime air, 'Police! Stop or I'll shoot!,' drawing his gun, and hoping against hope that he wouldn't have to shoot anybody his first day on the job.

The woman didn't stop, but neither did he have to shoot her because in that moment she ran around the corner, and by the time he himself reached the corner, and turned it out of breath, all three of them were gone, the two adulterers — if that's what they were — in their scanties, and the fat lady with the ax. A disappearing act! Carella still had his gun in his hand. He felt like a jackass.

'Where'd they go?' he asked a kid on a bicycle.

'Where'd who go?' the kid asked.

Totally vanished.

He went back to the building, where a sizable crowd had gathered, and began asking questions the way he guessed he was supposed to, but all he could learn from anybody was that the woman probably thought there was a fire, which is why she was using an ax to help those people in their underwear get out of the building.

He learned something that first day on the job.

In this precinct, nobody knew anything.

In this precinct, the cop on the beat was the enemy.

When he got home that night and told his mother what had happened his first day on the job, they both had a good laugh over it. The next day, things weren't quite as funny.

The next day a patrolman hoping to cash his paycheck at a bank not too far from . . .

The telephone rang.

It was precisely three o'clock.

ENDICOTT signaled for Loomis to pick up.

'Hello?'

'Mr. Loomis?'

'Yes?'

'Have you got the money?'

'Yes,' Loomis said.

'Hundred-dollar bills? Unmarked?'

189

'Yes.'

'They'd better be. What kind of car do you drive?'

'What?'

'What kind of . . . ?'

'The company provides a car and driver. It's a Lincoln Town . . .'

'Can you drive it yourself?'

'Yes?'

'Is there a phone in it?'

'Yes?'

'Do you know the number?'

'Not offhand. I can get it for you.'

'Get it. I'll call back in five minutes.'

'Wait!' Loomis shouted.

But he was already gone.

'Cell phone again,' one of the agents manning the computers said. 'Sprint. They're checking the number now.'

'One tower got him, and out,' another agent said.

'Someplace in Calm's Point.'

'He knows what he's doing.'

'Here's the number now,' the first agent said, and went to the printer. Reading from the sheet of paper as it reeled out, he said, 'Randall Carter, Jr. 421 Pastoral Way . . . over the river in the next *state!*' he said, sounding surprised.

'Another stolen phone,' Endicott said.

'Probably has a dozen of them.'

'He'll use a different one each time he calls, wait and see,' Corcoran said, nodding sagely.

Everyone else nodded, too.

THE PHONE rang some six minutes later.

Endicott nodded.

Loomis picked up.

'Hello?'

'Have you got that number?'

'Yes.'

'Give it to me. Read it slowly.'

Loomis read the number to him.

'Is this it?' the caller asked, and read the number back to him.

'Yes, that's it exactly.'

'First tower's on him.'

'Okay, this is what I want you to do. You say you've got the money?'

'Yes.'

'Are there any policemen there with you?'

Loomis didn't know what to answer. He looked first at Endicott and then at Forbes. Both men shook their heads.

'No,' Loomis said.

'You're lying, but that's okay. I want you to put the money in a dispatch case, have you got that?'

'Yes,' Loomis said.

'Then pick one of the detectives sitting there with you . . .'

'There are no detectives here with me,' Loomis said.

'Of course not. Find one, anyway, do you think you can manage that, Mr. Loomis?'

Little bit of bitchy sarcasm there.

Loomis ignored it.

'Yes, I think I can find a detective,' he said.

'Well, good. When you find one, I want you to give him the case with the money in it. For safekeeping. To make sure no bad guys try to grab it before it's in our hands. Have you got that?'

'Yes?'

Loomis was looking puzzled now. So were all the people on The Squad. Usually, they told you not to inform the police or the vic would die. Either these guys were complete amateurs or they'd done this a hundred times before and had come up with a new wrinkle. Not having access to the ear phones, Carella was puzzled, too, but only because he didn't know what the hell was going on.

'Second tower's on him. He's in a moving vehicle.'

'At three-thirty sharp . . . that should give you enough time to find a dispatch case and a cop, shouldn't it, Mr. Loomis?'

More sarcasm.

Again, Loomis ignored it.

'Yes, I'm sure that's enough time,' he said.

'At three-thirty sharp, then, I want you and the cop and the case to go down to the limo,' the caller said. 'And I want you to drive the limo out of the garage and onto the River Highway heading toward the Hamilton Bridge. Have you got that, too?'

'Yes.'

'Repeat it.'

'River Highway to the Hamilton Bridge.'

'Who's with you in the car?'

'A detective.'

'*And* the case. Don't forget the case with the money.'

'Second tower's on him.'

'Cingular wireless this time. Getting the number now.'

'Come on, come on,' Endicott said.

'*You* drive, Mr. Loomis. The cop rides shotgun. Tell him to wear a holstered weapon. Have you got all that?'

'Yes.'

'Good. Three-thirty sharp. I'll call you again in the car at a quarter to four. Any questions so far?'

'Yes. When will we get Tam . . . ?'

'All in good time. But listen to this, Mr. Loomis, and whoever else is listening.'

Endicott nodded sourly.

'There are three of us. Two of us will be picking up the cash, while our friend stays with the girl. If there is any sign of police activity at the site, the girl gets killed. If anyone tries to follow us from the site, the girl gets killed. If you try to arrest us after we pick up the cash, the girl gets killed. The girl is our hole card, do you understand? We're showing you the hole card now, so you won't try to bet her life on a losing hand. Tell me you understand everything. Especially about the girl getting killed if there are any tricks.'

'Yes, I understand everything,' Loomis said.

'Keep him on.'

'Especially about the girl getting killed.'

'Especially about Tamar getting killed.'

'Keep him on!'

'Good,' the caller said, and hung up abruptly.

'Damn it, we were almost there.'

'Why do you suppose he wants a cop tagging along?' Forbes asked.

'Peculiar, isn't it?' Endicott said.

'Last thing he should want is a cop.'

'An *armed* cop, no less.'

'You want this number?' one of the agents asked. 'It's a lady in Riverhead.'

'Move on it,' Corcoran told Feingold. 'But it'll be another stolen phone, wait and see.'

'He's so damn sure of himself,' Endicott said.

'Well, he's got the girl,' Corcoran said, 'you heard him. She's his hole card.' He hesitated only a moment, and then said, 'I'll go with you, Mr. Loomis,' and was actually putting on his jacket when Loomis said, 'No.'

They all turned to look at him.

'I want Detective Carella,' he said.

9.

THE CELL PHONE in the car rang at precisely three-forty-five, just as Barney Loomis was driving past the Buford Park exit on the River Harb Highway.

Carella picked up the phone, hit the SEND button.

'Hello?' he said.

'Who's this?' Avery asked.

'Detective Carella,' he said.

'What's your first name, Detective?'

'Steve.'

'Would you mind if I called you "Steve"?'

'Not at all.'

'I have trouble with Italian names, you see.'

And fuck you, too, Carella thought.

'Steve, is Mr. Loomis driving?'

'Yes, sir.'

'Is there anyone else in the car with you?'

'No, sir.'

'Is this the only phone in the car?'

'Yes, sir.'

This was a lie. Carella had another cell phone in the side pocket on the right side of his windbreaker.

'Is it portable?'

'Sir?'

'Can it be taken out of the car?'

'Oh. Yes, sir, it can.'

'Let me talk to Mr. Loomis.'

Carella handed the phone to him.

'Hello?' Loomis said.

'Mr. Loomis, I want you to drive to Exit 17. That should take you ten, maybe fifteen minutes. Make a right turn at the top of the ramp. You'll see a parking area for people who are sharing rides. Park there and wait. I'll call again at four o'clock.'

There was a click on the line.

Loomis put down the phone.

'What'd he say?' Carella asked.

'Exit 17, park there and wait for his next call.'

The cell phone in Carella's pocket rang. He yanked it out, hit the TALK button.

'Hello?' he said.

'Carella? This is Lieutenant Corcoran.'

'Yes, sir,' Carella said.

Back at the Academy, it used to be 'Steve' and 'Corky.' Now it was 'Carella' and 'Lieutenant Corcoran.'

'Have you heard anything yet?' Corcoran asked.

'Yes, sir, he just called.'

'What'd he say?'

'He wants us to . . .'

'What are you doing?' Loomis asked at once.

Carella turned to look at him, puzzled.

'What the *hell* are you doing?' Loomis shouted.

'Hold it a second,' Carella said into the phone, and turned to Loomis again. 'Corcoran wants to know . . .'

'Give me that phone!' Loomis snapped and held out his right hand.

'Wants to talk to you, Lieutenant,' Carella said, and passed the phone to him.

'Lieutenant Corcoran?' Loomis said. 'You listen to me, *Lieutenant* Corcoran. Are you fucking *crazy?* These people told us they're going to kill Tamar if we try any tricks. I consider telling you where we're going – and Christ knows what else you've got planned for the next few minutes — is *exactly* what they warned us about, it's playing tricks. I don't want you trying to find our location, I don't want you sending in the fucking Marines, I just want to drop off the money and await further instructions, have you got that, Lieutenant Corcoran?' Loomis listened. 'Yes, Lieutenant,' he said, 'I am perfectly willing to take responsibility for whatever may happen to Tamar. So don't call this number again, and don't call the number in the car, and I hope to God you haven't got anyone following us right this minute,' he said, glancing in the rear-view mirror. 'Because if anything happens to that girl, I will personally cut off your balls. Is that clear, Lieutenant Corcoran?' Loomis listened again. 'Good. No more god-damn *tricks!*' he said, and nodded curtly, and handed the phone back to Carella.

'Hello?' Carella said. 'Yes, I heard.' He listened. 'Okay,' he said, 'we play it his way. See you later,' he said, and hit the END button, and tossed the phone over his shoulder onto the back seat.

'I don't like that man,' Loomis said. 'I don't like *any* of them up there, you want the truth, Corcoran least of all. He's too full of his own perfume.'

Carella said nothing.

'None of them on that task force has any concept that we're dealing with a human life here,' Loomis said.

'Well, I think they know that, Mr. Loomis.'

'This is all one big game to them. The good guys and the bad guys. Never mind that the kidnappers spelled it all out, exposed their hole card, told us exactly what was at stake. It's still all cops and robbers to them, isn't it?'

'I don't think so, Mr. Loomis. But we'll play it your way,' Carella said. 'And hope for the best.'

They were approaching Exit 15 now. Loomis kept

looking on and off into the rear-view mirror, checking to see if anyone was following. Carella was wondering if maybe it wasn't really all cops and robbers, after all.

That day long ago, it had been cops and robbers, all right, three real cops and three real robbers. The robbers were coming out of a bank on Twelfth and Culver, which was on Carella's beat, and not too far from the station house. At the same time, a patrolman named Oscar Jackson was taking a five-minute break to run into the bank to cash his paycheck from last Friday while his partner, Patrolman Jimmy Ryan, sat at the wheel of their idling cruiser, which he'd just pulled into the curb outside the bank.

Police officers were still called patrolmen back then because there weren't too many female uniforms on the force and there weren't any real problems with gender identity. There weren't many black patrolmen back then, either, but Oscar Jackson was indeed black, and he was just taking his wallet out of his pocket to remove the paycheck from it when these three guys wearing ski masks and carrying sawed-off shotguns came running down the bank steps. Nowadays, they'd be carrying Uzis or AK-47s, but this was back then, when you and I were young, Maggie.

Carella had just turned the corner when he saw Jackson – whom he'd noticed around the station house but whose name he didn't yet know – look up and into the masked faces of the three armed men barreling down the wide front steps of the bank. Jackson didn't need a program to tell him this was a robbery in progress. Neither did Carella. And neither did Patrolman Jimmy Ryan at the wheel of Charlie Two.

All three men unholstered their weapons, Jackson stepping to one side and immediately assuming a shooter's crouch, Ryan coming out of the car and hunkering down behind the hood with his elbows on it and his gun in firing position, Carella fearlessly (but he was young) rushing toward the bank with his .38 in his right hand. All three fired in almost the same instant.

Only one of the robbers returned fire, and he directed his shotgun blast at the cop closest to him, who happened to be Oscar Jackson. Jackson fell to the pavement, bleeding from a devastating wound in his chest. The man who'd shot him dropped at the same moment, felled by three rounds from Ryan's pistol. Carella had to empty his revolver before he dropped both of the other robbers. But the holdup attempt had been foiled and the only casualty was Oscar Jackson, who was dead even before Ryan and Carella knelt over him. His uncashed paycheck lay on the sidewalk beside him, in the widening pool of his own blood.

That day had been cops and robbers, all right, and maybe every day after that had been cops and robbers, too. But that day hadn't been 'one big game,' as Barney Loomis would have it, and neither was today a game, not when a twenty-year-old girl's life was at stake. They'd been ready to proceed according to procedure, but Barney Loomis had called off the dogs. Carella just hoped nobody got hurt today.

'Exit 17 coming up,' Loomis said.

THEY HAD MOVED the girl into the smaller of the two bedrooms, where they'd fastened to the door a hasp and lock similar to the one on the closet door. There was a single window in that bedroom, but it opened onto the beach, and there was nobody on that beach but us seagulls, boss. Besides, the girl was handcuffed to the radiator and couldn't get to the window even if she'd tried.

Avery had warned her that there was no sense yelling for help because then they would have to kill her on the spot instead of delivering her to her benefactors at Bison this very night.

Avery had patiently explained to the girl everything they hoped to accomplish today, had laid it all out in detail, the way he had done so far with Barney Loomis and would continue to do throughout the day as events unfolded. This way, there'd be no surprises and no mistakes. After they picked up the cash, they'd deliver the girl tonight as promised, and waltz off with a bit more than $83,000 each, though Cal had already begun complaining that their share – Avery's and Kellie's, since they were a couple – would come to twice what he was getting for the same amount of work and risk.

Avery had explained to him, as patiently as he'd explained everything to the girl, that they'd have had to pay the same amount to whichever third party they'd engaged for the gig. So what difference did it make if Kellie was that person? Kellie knew how to handle a boat, and Avery had taught her how to use the assault rifle, more or less, though frankly she wasn't too sure how she felt about maybe having to shoot the girl if she raised any kind of fuss while they were out there picking up the loot.

She was alone in the house with her now.

It was almost four-thirty. Kellie hadn't heard a peep from the bedroom since the boys had left the house. She hoped the girl was okay, they were supposed to drop her off tonight in the same condition as when they'd snatched her. She went to the bedroom door, knocked on it, and yelled, 'You okay, Tamar?' She felt sort of a thrill calling a rock star by her first name.

'I'm thirsty,' Tamar called from behind the locked door.

'Would you like some iced tea? There's some iced tea in the fridge.'

'Please,' Tamar said.

'No funny stuff when I unlock the door, right?'

'What funny stuff did you have in mind?' Tamar asked.

Kellie smiled.

'I'll bring you the tea,' she said to the door, and went down the hall and into the master bedroom. Cal had complained about this, too, the fact that the pair of them got to sleep in a big double bed in the big bedroom while he had to sleep on the living-room couch. Cal complained about a lot of things. She'd be glad when this gig — listen to me, she thought, it must be contagious.

The three masks were on a shelf in the closet. Avery had ordered them from the Internet at forty-five bucks a pop, for all three of them to wear on the job itself, and in the house whenever they were around the girl. Actually, Kellie thought it was idiotic to be wearing a mask after the girl had already seen her face, something like locking the barn door after the horse had run off.

This still bothered her.

The fact that the girl had taken a good long look at her face — well, just a short glimpse, really. Even so, she'd undoubtedly seen the red hair and the green eyes, Kellie's best features, actually, and maybe memorable, though she hated to sound conceited. Not to mention the freckles all over her Irish phiz, wouldn't Tamar remember those? Wouldn't she be able to describe her once they let her go free?

This really bothered her a lot.

Avery had chosen the Yasir Arafat mask for himself and the Saddam Hussein mask for Cal, probably because the two men were all over television these days — though not as often as Tamar Valparaiso. Kellie wished he'd ordered her at least a female mask, but certainly *any* mask other than the one he finally chose for her, which was a George W. Bush mask that bore an uncanny resemblance to Alfred E. Neumann. Which, come to think of it, so did the actual President.

Kellie took the rubber mask down from the shelf now, and pulled it over her head, covering her face and her short red hair. Maybe Tamar had forgotten what she looked like, after all. There'd been only that few seconds of exposure before she slammed the closet door shut again. Shrugging (but it still bothered her), Kellie went into the kitchen, took a bottle of Snapple from the shelf, unscrewed the lid, and poured most of the contents into a glass. She drank the rest of the tea herself, straight from the bottle. Then she picked up the glass she'd poured for Tamar, and lifted the AK-47 from where it was resting on the kitchen table.

With the glass of tea in one hand and the assault rifle in the other, she went down the hall again, and unlocked the door to the bedroom.

She sure hoped Tamar wouldn't try anything funny.

THEY'D BEEN PARKED in the drop-off area at the top of the ramp no longer than three minutes when the car phone rang again. This time, Loomis himself picked up.

'Hello,' he said.

'Mr. Loomis?'

'Yes?'

'Drive west on Hawkes,' Avery said. 'Make a right turn on Norman and proceed to the intersection of Norman and a Hun' Eighty-fifth. Park there. Repeat, please.'

'I'm driving to Norman and a Hundred Eighty-fifth,' Loomis said.

'More later,' Avery said, and hung up.

'The Wasteland,' Carella said.

THERE WERE SOME sections of this city that were completely forsaken, lost to rehabilitation, utterly resigned to rot and decay. The area that ran for some ten blocks west-to-east from 181st to 191st and another ten blocks north-to-south from Norman to Jewel was one such desolate location.

Appropriately nicknamed 'The Wasteland' long before its buildings were abandoned by landlords loath to spend another nickel keeping them in repair, the area was later renounced even by the squatters who had taken up residence in its empty dwellings. The city finally condemned everything within the square half-mile The Wasteland encompassed. Windows and doors were boarded over, once stately living quarters left to crumble into dust.

Today, even in the waning daylight hours, the area resembled nothing more than a war zone. Rats had chewed away the wooden barriers on windows and doors; they now scampered freely from building to building, foraging in the garbage residents from neighboring areas came here to dump whenever the Department of Sanitation neglected its scheduled pickups. Like eyeless sockets in forgotten faces, The Wasteland's empty windows stared out at only rubble-strewn lots.

Occasionally a patrol car from the Nine-Six swept through these potholed streets.

Occasionally, a dead body was discovered here before the rats left nothing but clean, picked-over bones.

When Carella was a college student, he used to call girls he was trying to impress and read to them passages from T. S. Eliot's collected poems. He read mostly from 'Prufrock,' which impressed nineteen-year-old co-eds with how deeply romantic and sensitive and experienced he was, especially when he came to the line 'And I have known the eyes already.'

But he also read from *The Waste Land* – well not much of it, just the very beginning of the first poem, before it got so morbid and preoccupied with burying the dead. He would say into the phone, 'I was just reading this poem a few minutes ago, and I thought, "Gee, I'll bet Margie (or Alice or Mary or Jeannie) would love to hear it, so I hope you don't mind my calling you,"' such baloney, such a line, but he was only twenty years old. He would then read the section beginning with the words 'April is the cruellest month,' and keep reading through the stuff about being surprised by a sudden summer shower, and drinking coffee and talking in an outdoor German garden, it must have been, or perhaps Austrian because there was a cousin who was an archduke. Carella would pause dramatically before reading the line 'I read, much of the night, and go south in the winter,' which was before the poem turned so serious, and which always evoked a sigh from Margie (or Alice or Mary or Jeannie).

He was so young then.

Handsome, too, he guessed.

Or maybe not.

He had graduated from high school at the age of seventeen, had attended college for a year before he was drafted to fight in one of America's far too many wars. Transported to a foreign land, he saw for the first time in his life (and grew old all at once) a wasteland that was a far cry from Eliot's poignant mix of memory and desire. Wounded in battle and shipped back to America when he was still only nineteen, he'd returned to college for a year and a half, and then, abruptly, decided to join the police force.

The Wasteland through which he and Barney Loomis drove on this fading May afternoon was not very much different from that devastated landscape in which Carella had fought all those years ago. Not so very different at all.

'Christ, what *is* this place?' Loomis asked, appalled, and parked on the corner of Norman and 185th.

'**PULL NOTHING** funny now,' Kellie said, and hefted the rifle onto her hip to show she meant business.

Tamar pulled a face. Her left hand was handcuffed to the radiator, what the hell could she try to pull?

Kellie set the glass of tea on the floor, within reach of Tamar's right hand. She picked up the glass and took a sip of tea.

'Who are you supposed to be?' she asked.

'President Bush.'

'After next year, that mask may be dated.'

'What do you mean?'

'He might not be elected again.'

'Who cares?' Kellie said, and shrugged.

'You wear that mask, people will ask who you're supposed to be.'

'You *already* asked that. Anyway, I won't have to wear it after tonight.'

'Why? What happens tonight?'

'We drop you off. Goodbye, Tamar Valparaiso.'

'You mean that?'

'That's the plan.'

'Whose plan?'

'Ours. Me and the guys.'

'Arafat and Hussein?'

'Yeah,' Kellie said, and grinned behind her own mask. 'Those are good masks, ain't they?'

'Very good.'

'Better than this one. I wanted Queen Elizabeth. Or Hillary Clinton. Instead, he gets me *this* jackass.'

'How do you know that's the plan?'

''Cause we're partners, the three of us. They're out right this minute, picking up the ransom money.'

'How much are you supposed to get?'

'None of your business.'

'I hope it's a lot of money.'

'Oh, it's plenty all right.'

'How much?'

'Never mind.'

'I just want to know how much you guys think I'm worth.'

'You're worth plenty, honey. Especially now.'

'Why now?'

'You've been all over television. You don't sell ten million copies of 'Bandersnatch,' I'll *eat* this friggin mask!'

'So how much did you ask for?'

'How's the tea?'

'Fine. Did you make it?'

'No, it's Snapple.'

'Who's paying the ransom?'

'Barney Loomis, who do you think? You know him, right?'

'Of course I know him.'

'You know everybody in the business, I'll bet.'

'No, but he's the CEO of my label.'

'You know Mariah Carey?'

'Never met her. How much ransom is Loomis paying for me?'

'Enough to make it worth our while. J. Lo? Do you know her?'

'How much is that?'

'How much do you *think* you're worth?'

'Ten million records, you said? How about a million bucks?'

'Oh, sure, he's just about to pay a million.'

'How much *is* he about to pay?'

'Enough.'

'How much is enough?'

'A quarter of a mil, okay?'

'Nice payday,' Tamar said, and drained her glass.

Kellie looked at her watch.

'In fact,' she said, 'they should be picking it up just about now.'

LOOMIS picked up the ringing telephone.

'Hello?'

'Mr. Loomis?'

'Yes.'

'I want you to make a right turn on a Hun' Eighty-fifth. Drive south for five and a half blocks. On the left-hand side of the street, you'll see a wrecked automobile in front of a red-brick building with no address numbers on it. Park behind that car. We'll be watching you from that minute on. We're in telephone contact with our partner. Any tricks and the girl dies. Repeat.'

'Five and a half blocks south on a Hundred Eighty-fifth. Park behind the wrecked car on the left.'

'And about tricks?'

'Tamar dies.'

'I think you've got it. By George, he's got it!' Avery said playfully, and hung up.

'You heard,' Loomis told Carella.

'I heard. I should be giving all this to our people. You're making a mistake here, Mr. Loo . . .'

'Then you *didn't* hear. Any tricks, and she dies. You want that on *your* head, Detective Carella?'

Carella guessed he didn't want that on his head.

'**WRECKED CAR**' had to be a euphemism for the rusted automobile skeleton that had been stripped, torched, and then abandoned in front of a building whose probably brass address numerals had been similarly desecrated. Only the ghostly images of an 8, a 3, and a 7 remained on the wall to the right of the entrance door, brighter in absence than the surrounding soot-covered bricks. Carella was thinking he could have phoned in an address. 837 South 185th. Get the Feds to throw a net over the surrounding five blocks. Follow whoever picked up the cash. But no.

Loomis parked the limo behind the skeletal wreck. The black Lincoln basked in bright sunshine like a sleek black cat. In front of it, the rusted Whatever-It-Once-Had-Been crouched like a starving hyena, its ribs showing. The two men sat in silence, waiting. The caller had told them they'd be watched from this moment on. Carella scoped the area. Any one of five deserted tenements could be a sniper's observation post. A rifleman could be kneeling behind any one of a hundred windows that looked down at the street.

'Why here, for God's sake?' Loomis asked.

'Deserted area, number one,' Carella said. 'Clear sight lines. From any one of these buildings, they can see for blocks around.'

The car phone rang.

He reached for it at once, but Loomis said, 'I'll take it,' and lifted the receiver.

'Hello?'

'Mr. Loomis?'

'Yes?'

'Put Steve on, could you please?'

'He wants you,' Loomis said, and handed him the phone.

'Carella,' he said.

'Are you armed, Steve?'

'I am.'

'What kind of weapon?'

'A Glock nine.'

'Do you have the money?'

'Yes.'

'Is it in a dispatch case?'

'Yes.'

'Step out of the car, Steve. Just you. Tell Mr. Loomis to stay in the car. Take the case with you. The phone, too. Don't forget the phone, Steve. Wouldn't want to lose touch, now would we? When you're out of the car, talk to me, Steve. We're not through here yet.'

Carella reached over for the dispatch case on the back seat. 'He wants you to stay in the car,' he told Loomis.

'Why?'

Carella gave him a look, and then opened the door on his side, and stepped out onto the curb, the dispatch case in his left hand, the phone in his right. He closed the door behind him. He brought the phone to his mouth.

'I'm out,' he said.

'Go to the back of the car,' Avery said.

Carella went around to the back of the car.

'Look at the license plate.'

'I'm looking.'

'I want you to believe we've got binocs on you right this minute,' Avery said. 'Is the license plate number BR-2100?'

'It is,' Carella said.

'Do something with your hands.'

'What do you mean?'

'Perform some sort of action.'

Carella put the dispatch case flat on the roof of the car, and then raised his left hand over his head.

'You put the dispatch case on the roof and raised your left hand, is that correct?' Avery asked.

'Yes,' Carella said.

'And the case is black, is that also correct?'

'Yes, it's black.'

'I want you to believe that we can see you and that a rifle with a telescopic sight is trained on your head. Do you believe that?'

'I believe it.'

'Good. Ask Mr. Loomis to come out of the car, please.'

Carella went around to the driver's side of the limo, rapped on the glass there. The window slid down.

'They want you to get out of the car,' Carella said.

'Why?' Loomis asked again.

Carella looked at him.

Loomis got out and slammed the door behind him.

'We see him,' Avery said. 'Give him the dispatch case.'

Carella handed it to him.

'Tell him we've got rifles trained on both of you.'

'They've got us covered from somewhere around here,' Carella told Loomis, looking up at the surrounding buildings. 'Rifles with telescopic sights.'

'Okay,' Loomis said, and looked up, too, and nodded.

'Steve?'

'Yes?'

'Here's what I want you to do, Steve. Unholster your weapon. Remember, we're watching you.'

Carella transferred the phone to his left hand. He

reached down into his holster, yanked the Glock up and into his hand.

'It's out,' he said.

'This is a bad neighborhood,' Avery said. 'I guess you noticed that.'

'I noticed it.'

'We don't want anything to happen to that money. Keep the piece in your hand, Steve. Make sure it's visible in case any stray squatters get any brilliant ideas.'

'Okay.'

'Now I want you and Mr. Loomis to walk that money right into the red-brick building there. Remember, we're watching you.'

'He wants us to go inside that building,' Carella told Loomis.

'Why?' Loomis asked, and again Carella looked at him.

Together the men walked toward the building where the absent 8-3-7 numerals left stark reminders on the entrance wall. The barricade was gone from the front door, fragments of wood still clinging to the door frame where the boards had been torn free. Carella walked into the building first, gun hand leading him. He heard a frenzied scurrying and squealing up ahead, and stopped dead in his tracks.

He did not appreciate rats.

When he and Teddy had been living in their Riverhead house for just a week, he'd opened the basement door and was heading downstairs when he spotted a rat the size of an alley cat sitting on the steps, staring up at him with his beady little eyes and twitching whiskers. He'd slammed the door shut at once, whirled on Teddy, and frantically signed, *We're selling the house!*

He definitely did not appreciate rats.

'What the hell is *that?*' Loomis asked behind him,

and then saw one of the rats and let out a short sharp shriek.

Into the phone, Carella said, 'The place is overrun with rats. Tell me what you want us to do, okay?'

'Go up to the first floor. Apartment 14. The numerals are still on the door.'

'Are you walking us into a trap?' Carella asked.

'You've got a gun in your hand,' Avery reminded him.

They started up the steps, Carella in the lead. The hand railing was gone. They braced themselves against the opposite wall. The building stank of garbage and human waste. Loomis covered his nose with a handkerchief. Carella felt like wretching. A single unboarded window on the first-floor landing cast uncertain light into the hallway. Apartment 14 was the fourth door down the hall.

'We're here,' Carella said into the phone.

'Go inside.'

They went into the apartment. They were standing in the middle of a small kitchen. There were still boards on the only window in the room. In the semi-darkness, they heard the scurrying of more rats.

A dead Golden Retriever lay on the floor in front of a gas range that had been disconnected and overturned.

It looked as if the dog's throat had been recently slit.

Flies were still buzzing around the open wound.

'Do you see the dog?' Avery asked.

'Yes?'

'That's what we'll do to the girl if there are any tricks.'

Carella said nothing.

'See the refrigerator?' Avery asked.

'Yes?'

'Open the door, Steve.'

Carella opened the door.

'The fridge doesn't work, Steve,' Avery said. 'No electricity in the building. I hope you didn't bring us hot money.'

He sounded almost jovial now. Big joke here, the son of a bitch. Slits a dog's throat, rats running all over the place, he jokes about hot money.

'What do you want me to do here?' Carella asked.

'You sound peeved, Steve.'

Carella said nothing.

'You didn't answer my question.'

'What did you ask?'

'Is the money hot?'

'No.'

'I certainly hope it's not marked or anything.'

'It's not marked.'

'Because I wouldn't want anything to happen to the girl.'

'It's not marked. Just tell me what you want me to do, okay?'

'What's he saying?' Loomis asked.

Carella shook his head.

'Put the dispatch case on one of the shelves, Steve.'

Carella slid the case onto the shelf under the ice cube compartment.

'Now close the door and hang up. When you're outside the building, I'll call again.'

Carella closed the refrigerator door, and hit the END button.

'Let's go,' he told Loomis.

They stepped out into the hallway again. Everywhere around them, there was the sound of chittering little creatures in the near-dark, glittering little eyes suddenly disappearing as the rats turned and ran off. He remembered being a rookie, remembered other cops telling him about babies in their cribs getting their faces chewed to ribbons by rats. Moving slowly and cautiously, he scraped his feet along the floor, feeling his way toward the stairwell.

'Here it is,' he told Loomis.

With his right hand, he felt for the wall again. With his left foot, he reached out for the first stair tread, afraid he would step on a rat. Behind him, Loomis said, 'He's gone too far. Why'd he kill that dog?'

'To show us he's serious,' Carella said.

'That wasn't the deal.'

'He wanted me along to bear witness. So I'd go back and tell the others he's serious about killing the girl.'

'We already knew that. He already *told* us that.'

'Show is better than tell, Mr. Loomis.'

'That wasn't the deal,' Loomis said again, sounding very much like a petulant child. 'Nobody gets hurt, that was the deal. He didn't have to kill the goddamn dog.'

They came down the stairs and out of the building. Both men blinked against the sunlight.

'Do you think they're holding her in one of these buildings?' Loomis asked.

'I hope not,' Carella said.

The phone rang immediately.

'Hello?' Carella said.

'This is what I want you and Mr. Loomis to do,' Avery said. 'Are you listening?'

'I'm listening.'

'Walk back to the car. Put the phone to your ear again when you get there.'

The two men walked back to the limo. Carella put the phone to his ear again.

'We're here,' he said.

'I see you,' Avery said. 'Just stand right where you are. I'll call you again when we have the case. You can hang up now.'

Carella hit the END button.

THEY CAME DOWN from the seventh floor of the building at 5107 Ambrose, from which they'd been watching the action across the street at 837 South 185th. Hidden by the building itself, they crossed the empty lot behind it, and entered 837 through the rear door. They were both carrying the AK-47s they'd used on the boat gig two nights ago, but this time Cal's rifle was fitted with a scope. On the first floor of the building, he told Avery he felt like shooting himself some rats. Avery told him to resist the urge.

They found the black dispatch case in the refrigerator, right where Carella had left it. Cal threw the beam of a flashlight on it, and Avery unclasped it. There was no time to count the money right now, but those looked like a whole lot of nice brand-new hundred-dollar bills in there.

They went downstairs and out the back door again. This time, they crossed the lot to where they'd parked the stolen Montana behind a twelve-story building on Lasser. Carella and Loomis may have heard them starting the car, but it wouldn't matter, anyway. The girl was their insurance. Nobody was going to do anything stupid while they had the girl.

They didn't call again until almost an hour later. By that time, they'd dumped all the cell phones they'd used since three this afternoon. It was now close to five-thirty, and Avery was using yet another stolen phone when he called from the house out on Sands Spit.

Barney Loomis answered on the second ring.

'Hello?' he said.

'You can go back to your office now,' Avery said. 'We'll call you again after we've counted the money. If it's all here, you'll get the girl back tonight. I promise.'

'Where will you . . . ?' Loomis started, but Avery had already hung up.

10.

TAMAR GUESSED she should have felt honored.

This was just like a summit meeting.

Yasir Arafat was smiling. So were Saddam Hussein and George W. Bush. All three of them were smiling – or at least their eyes were – but only Arafat was talking. Tamar figured he was the leader of the gang, the one who'd told her his eyes were brown. She could still see that his smiling eyes were brown. He was the same dude, all right.

'We have the money,' he told her. 'Everything went off without a hitch.'

No wonder he was smiling.

The other two nodded in agreement. They were still smiling. George Bush had nice tits; Tamar wondered which one she was sleeping with.

'I'm telling you all this,' Arafat said, 'because I want to warn you again not to do anything stupid.'

Do anything stupid! She was still handcuffed to the radiator!

'We're going to count the money now. If it's all here, we'll drop you off someplace, and you'll be home before you can spell your last name,' he said, and she wondered if that was an ethnic slur.

'Okay, fine,' she said. 'Thank you,' she added.

For nothing, she thought.

'So be a good girl, honey,' Hussein said, smiling, and all three jackasses went out of the room.

She heard the lock clicking shut behind them.

*

217

OLLIE STOPPED for a snack after he was relieved at a quarter to five, and then walked crosstown to his piano teacher's apartment, right here in the Eight-Eight. He had called her early Sunday morning to ask if she could get him the sheet music to Al Martino's 'Spanish Eyes' . . .

'Not the one the Backstreet Boys did,' he cautioned.

. . . and she had promised she would try. Now, at seven minutes to six on this Monday night, the fifth of May, Ollie climbed the steps to the fifth floor and rapped on the door to apartment 53. He was glad he couldn't hear the sound of a piano inside. This meant her previous student had already left. Helen Hobson's apartment was tiny, and if she was still giving a lesson when he arrived, he had to wait outside in the hall.

She was smiling when she opened the door for him. A woman in her late fifties, rail thin and wearing her habitual green cardigan sweater over a brown woolen skirt, she said, 'Well, Detective Weeks, you're right on time this evening.'

'Always a pleasure to come here,' Ollie said, which was the truth.

'Come in, come in,' Helen said, and stepped aside to let him by.

The grand piano always came as a surprise in this small apartment. Walking toward it behind his teacher, Ollie always felt as if he was being led onstage at Clarendon Hall. Sitting beside her on the piano bench, he always felt as if he was about to begin playing a duet with Arthur Rubenstein or Glenn Gould or one of those guys.

'Well, I got it,' Helen said, turning to him and beaming.

For a moment, Ollie was puzzled. Then he realized . . .

'"Spanish *Eyes*"?' he asked, his own eyes brightening.

'Yes, indeed. I tried half a dozen different stores before

I found it at Lenny's Music, all the way downtown. I was about ready to give up, Mr. Weeks, I must tell you.'

'I'm glad you didn't,' Ollie said.

'Oh, so am I. It's a lovely song.'

'You played it?'

'The moment I came home. It's truly lovely. And *so* romantic,' she said. 'What made you decide to learn this particular song?'

'Well, like you say, it's very romantic . . .'

'Oh yes.'

'And uh truly lovely,' he said.

'Indeed. So what shall we do first? Would you like to play what you've been practicing, or would you like to bust your chops on the new one, as they say?'

'Why don't we just bust my chops?' Ollie said, grinning.

'Very well,' Helen said, and turned to the piano.

'Spanish Eyes' had a picture of Al Martino on its glossy front cover. With a flourish, Helen threw the cover back to reveal the actual sheet music.

Ollie was looking at a whole hell of a lot of notes.

'Gee,' he said, 'I dunno.'

'Oh come now,' Helen said. 'Is this the man who mastered "Night and Day"?'

'Yeah, but . . .'

'Put your hands on the keyboard, Mr. Weeks,' she suggested. 'Please note that this is written in the key of . . .'

THEY LEFT THE masks on because being Arafat and Hussein and Bush made them feel like big shots. Sitting at the kitchen table, the television set going in the other room, they kept reaching for banded bundles of money in the dispatch case, counting each bundle and writing down their separate tallies. Each bundle had twenty hundred-dollar bills in it. That came to $2,000 a bundle. Altogether, there were a hundred and twenty-five packets in that dispatch case. That didn't seem like very much, but that's what $250,000 in hundred-dollar bills looked like.

While they counted, they started talking about what they were going to do with all that money, even though it didn't seem like all that much now that it was actually here in front of them.

Yasir Arafat said he was going to use his $83,333 dollars to hire 833 suicide bombers at a hundred bucks a pop to go blow up restaurants and school busses and dance halls and the like all over Israel. Avery thought he was merely speaking in character, but Kellie figured he was probably anti-Semitic.

Saddam Hussein picked up the cue and said he was going to use his share of the money to purchase intercontinental ballistic missiles to shoot at 'your father,' he told Kellie, 'get the job done right this time.'

George W. Bush said she would spend her share of the money on a pair of strappy Prada pumps.

'That's not in character,' Avery told her.

'They'll be in character if I wear them with an Armani dress,' she said.

'You're supposed to be Bush,' he said.

'Whoever,' she said, and shrugged airily. All this money was making her a bit light-headed. Though, to tell the truth, it didn't look like so very much, fitting in the dispatch case that way.

They kept counting it.

In the other room, the six o'clock news was coming on.

The lead story was about Tamar Valparaiso's kidnapping. This immediately caught their complete attention. They got up from the kitchen table at once and en masse. Leaving all that money behind – though now that they were used to it, it didn't seem like all that much, really – they went into the living room and plopped down on the sofa as if they'd just got home from school, three kids who bore unfortunate resemblances to Bush, Arafat, and Hussein. The real Bush, Arafat, and Hussein were probably watching CNN themselves at that very same moment, though probably not wearing masks. And they probably were not as interested in Tamar Valparaiso.

The anchorman was saying there were no clues as yet to the whereabouts of the kidnapped rock star.

When they heard the word 'star,' all three world leaders turned to look at each other, each of them realizing that Tamar hadn't been a star before they'd kidnapped her.

The anchor was saying that neither the police nor the FBI would ascertain whether or not a ransom demand had yet been made.

'Good,' Arafat said.

This was Avery Hanes, in case Kellie or Cal had forgotten.

The anchorman said, 'Meanwhile, Billboard 200 reports that *Bandersnatch,* the diva's controversial album . . .'

'*Diva,*' did you hear that?' Hussein said.

'Shhhh,' Bush warned.

'. . . the number-one position, having sold 750,000 copies since its debut this past Friday. This places it higher on the charts than Avril Lavigne's new album at number four, the Dixie Chicks at number six, and Xzibit in the number-eight slot.'

The anchorman took a breath.

'In Israel this morning, another suicide bomber . . .'

Avery got up to turn off the television set. He pulled

off his mask in the next instant. Kellie and Cal, taking this as their cue, removed their masks as well. They all looked very serious all at once.

'She's a fuckin star,' Cal said.

'I told her ten million,' Kellie said.

'What?' Cal asked, looking at her as if he wished she would speak English every now and then.

'I told her it would sell ten million copies,' Kellie explained. 'Her album.'

'Well, it only sold 750,000,' Cal said, still looking angry.

'Only enough for number one,' Avery said.

'She told me we should've asked for a million bucks,' Kellie said.

The men looked at her.

'But that was when I said she'd sell ten million.'

The men were still looking at her.

WHEN THE TELEPHONE in Barney Loomis' office rang at six-fifteen that night, Special Agent Jones was down the hall taking a pee. Endicott put on his ear phones, said to Carella, 'Wanna give a listen?' and waited while Carella put on the phones Jones had left behind. Endicott nodded to Loomis. Loomis picked up.

'Hello?' he said.

'Mr. Loomis?'

'Yes?'

'Mr. Loomis,' Avery said, 'we've counted all the money . . .'

'Yes, when can we pick up . . .'

'. . . and aside from the question of whether they're marked or not . . .'

'They're not marked. I promise you they're . . .'

'. . . there's the minor matter of the count being short.'

222

'First tower on it.'

'Short?'

'Yes, Mr. Loomis.'

'You said . . .'

'I said a million dollars, Mr. Loomis. You're short by . . .'

'No, you said . . .'

'. . . seven hundred and fifty large. Now I don't know what you're . . .'

'Just a minute, you never said . . .'

'. . . trying to pull here, but I thought the girl's safety was paramount.'

'Second tower's got him.'

'You never said a million dollars!' Loomis yelled into the phone. 'You told me two-fifty, and that's what I . . .'

'What*ever* I told you, it's a million now!' Avery said, yelling himself now. 'Get the rest of it by three tomorrow afternoon. I'll call again then. Have a nice night,' he said, and hung up.

'Listen . . .' Loomis started, but he was gone.

He looked blankly at the phone receiver, put it back on its cradle, looked at the detectives and the FBI agents and said almost plaintively, 'We had a deal. We agreed it would be two-fifty. He knew that. This isn't fair.'

'Should've let us do it our way,' Corcoran said.

'Here's the printout,' Feingold said.

'Another stolen phone, I'll bet,' Endicott said.

Feingold read off the name and address. The Voice-Stream subscriber was right here in the heart of the city.

'Roll on it,' Corcoran ordered. 'Just two of you. Waste of time, anyway.'

Jones came back into the room.

He saw their faces.

'What?' he asked.

'You're heading out again,' Corcoran said. 'Zip up your fly.'

'Lieutenant,' Carella said, 'can I have a word with you?'

'Why, certainly, Steve. What is it?'

Big grin on his face. Cut off a man's legs and then smile right into his face.

Carella took him aside.

'If nobody minds, I think I'll just mosey on home,' he said, sounding like John Wayne, and feeling like Roberto Benigni.

'Why's that?' Corcoran asked.

Carella looked him dead in the eye.

'I have nothing to do here,' he said.

'Your help was requested, Steve.'

'You should have refused it.'

'We're always open to suggestion.'

'Bullshit,' he said. 'Lieutenant,' he added.

'I beg your . . .'

'So long, Corky. Have fun.'

'Just a second here.'

Carella did not give him even a millisecond. He turned his back and headed for the door. Loomis caught up with him in the corridor outside.

'I'm sorry as hell about this,' he said.

'I had no right being here in the first place,' Carella said.

'I asked for you.'

'You shouldn't have.'

'They're just smelling blood,' Loomis said. 'They still haven't caught whoever sent those anthrax letters, probably never will. They keep sending out alerts to protect their own asses should someone blow up the nearest nuclear plant or television station. So now they think they're going to make headlines when they catch these

224

sons of bitches who've got Tamar, even though they can't even trace a fucking phone call. What they don't understand is that I don't *care* if we catch these people. All I want is Tamar back.'

'Well, I can't help you accomplish that, Mr. Loomis. They won't even give me a shot at that. Look, you're in good hands here. I wouldn't worry too much if I were you.'

'What is this, some sort of club here? They kick you in the teeth, and you're still defending them?'

'They know what they're doing.'

'So do you.'

'I told you. The last kidnapping case I investigated . . .'

'Did you get the victim back?'

'Yes, but . . .'

'That's all I want here.' He put his hand on Carella's shoulder. 'Stay,' he said. 'Please stay, Steve.'

'No, I can't do that. Too many other crimes out there screaming for my specific talents.'

'Sarcasm doesn't become you.'

'Neither does humiliation,' Carella said. 'Good luck, Mr. Loomis. I hope this works out for you.'

'Thank you.'

There was nothing left to say. Loomis extended his hand. Carella shook it briefly, and then walked toward the elevators.

He felt oddly elated.

THIS TIME he came into the room alone.

He was wearing the Arafat mask again.

He said, 'There's been a slight hitch.'

She looked at him.

'The count was short.'

She kept looking at him.

225

She hoped he realized she didn't believe him.

'We've asked Mr. Loomis to get the rest of the money by tomorrow morning.'

'Short by how much?' she asked.

'A lot.'

'Well, how much?' she insisted.

She was already thinking she had to escape somehow. She was already thinking these dudes were full of shit. They would take the money, however much money they were now expecting, and then they would kill her. It was as simple as that. She would have to get out of here somehow.

'I'm telling you all this . . .' he said.

'Yeah, yeah,' she said.

'. . . so you'll know it's not our fault.'

'Then whose fault is it?' she asked. 'Who was it came onto that launch . . .'

'This is nothing personal,' Avery said.

'Oh, fuck you,' she said. 'Of *course* it's personal. *I'm* a person, *you're* a person, this is *very* personal!'

'I can assure you . . .'

'What'd you do?' she asked. 'Tell Barney one thing, and then change your mind when you saw all the attention I was getting?'

She could see only the brown eyes behind the Arafat mask, but she knew she was right on target.

'Isn't that right?' she said. 'I'm all over television, isn't that it? I'm hotter than that fucking D.C. sniper was!'

He said nothing. The brown eyes were saying it all. The brown eyes were clicking like windows on a Vegas slot machine. Maybe she'd gone too far. But she knew they were going to kill her, anyway, so fuck it. Go all the way, she thought.

'That's it, isn't it?' she said. 'You saw what was happening, so you raised the ante?'

'The ransom was always the same,' he said. 'Your boss gave us a short count.'

'He's not my boss,' she said. 'In fact, *he* works for *me.*'

She didn't mention that whatever the ransom was now, it had been two-fifty a couple of hours ago. President Bush with the big tits and the red hair and the green eyes and the freckles had told her so, and if you couldn't take President Bush's word, who *could* you trust in this rotten world? She didn't mention this because she didn't want the girl to get in any trouble. She had the feeling that the girl . . .

'I'll keep you informed,' Arafat said, and went to the door. Before he went out, he said, for the umpteenth time, 'Don't do anything stupid.'

And was gone.

She listened for the click of the lock again.

Waited . . .

Waited.

There.

A heavy dull click.

She guessed that doing something stupid would be trying to open the handcuff with a bobby pin she didn't happen to possess. Or doing something stupid would be trying to cut a deal with Ol' Brown Eyes Arafat, who was obviously the mastermind here, the arch criminal, the genius behind this hare-brained little kidnap scheme. But he had already double-crossed Barney, so what chance would *she* have with him? Besides, suppose he had a partner higher up someplace who was calling all the shots, which was a distinct possibility, and something she didn't even want to *think* about.

She knew she could not deal with Saddam Hussein. She remembered him hitting poor Jonah with the rifle stock and then slapping her so hard she'd almost lost consciousness. No, Hussein was not the one to approach here.

The girl, in fact, was the only one with whom she felt she might stand the slightest chance.

The girl wasn't stupid, but she was vulnerable.

Yes, she would have to work on the girl.

HAWES KNEW that Honey Blair reported to work at six each evening, and didn't leave the studio till sometimes two or three in the morning, which was even worse than working the Graveyard Shift. He called her office at a quarter to seven, hoping she wasn't already out roaming the city on assignment.

She picked up on the third ring.

'Honey Blair,' she said.

'Hi,' he said. 'This is Cotton Hawes.'

There was that telltale moment of silence that told him she didn't know who the hell on earth Cotton Hawes was.

'The detective,' he said.

Another silence.

'The Valparaiso case. We watched the video . . .'

'Oh yes.'

'. . . together.'

'Yes, I remember now,' she said. 'How are you?'

'Fine, thanks. And you?'

'Busy,' she said.

There was a silence on the line.

'Did you catch them yet?' she asked.

'Well, no. Not yet.'

'I thought that's why you might be calling.'

'Well, no,' he said.

'Ah,' she said, and fell silent again.

He hesitated. Hang up, he thought. She hasn't the

228

faintest idea why you're on the phone. She's not expecting . . .

'Uh, Honey,' he said, 'I was wondering . . .'

Silence.

'I don't know what time you might be free tonight . . .'

The silence persisted.

'But I just got sprung here myself, and I don't have to be back till tomorrow morning, so I was wondering . . .'

'I've got to talk to a Russian dancer in Calm's Point,' she said.

'Oh,' he said.

'At the Academy of Music,' she said. 'I should be through before eight.'

He waited.

'I can meet you after that,' she said.

'Well, good,' he said. And then, not to sound too eager, he immediately asked, 'Where?'

SHE WAS STILL wearing the on-camera outfit she'd worn while interviewing the dancer at the Calm's Point Academy of Music. An olive-green woolen skirt, the same boots she'd worn on the night of the kidnapping, and a brown turtleneck with a collar as thick as chain mail. Tonight was the opening of the Kirov Ballet, she explained. Her interview with the prima ballerina would be shown on tonight's Eleven O'Clock News.

'So,' she said, 'do you get over to Calm's Point often?'

'Every now and then,' he said.

They had walked over to a very good steak joint she knew near the Academy. Neither of them had had dinner yet, and it was now only eight-fifteen on a slow Monday, so they had the place almost all to themselves. The maître d' recognized Honey when she came in, and led them to a choice table near a stained-glass window artificially lighted from behind. Hawes was thinking if he'd been here on his own, they'd have seated him either near the men's room or the telephone booths. He was wondering how much a steak would cost in this place. White linen tablecloths and all.

Honey ordered a Beefeater martini, straight up and very dry, with a couple of olives. Hawes ordered a Johnny Black on the rocks. She made the toast.

'To your case,' she said.

'To your interview,' he said, and they clinked glasses and drank.

'Mmm,' she said.

'Indeed,' he said.

'I'm famished,' she said. 'Do you think we could see menus right away?'

Hawes signaled to the waiter.

Honey ordered the filet mignon with a salad and a baked potato. Hawes ordered a sirloin with fries and a side of steamed spinach.

'So where'd you get the white streak?' she asked.

He reached up to touch his temple. They always asked about the white streak. They always told him the white streak was attractive.

'I was investigating a burglary,' he said. 'The vic was telling me what happened when all of a sudden she got hysterical and began screaming. The super ran upstairs with a knife in his hand . . .'

'Uh-oh,' Honey said.

'Yeah,' Hawes said, 'and mistook *me* for a burglar or something.' He took another sip of his scotch. 'Bottom line, he came at me with the knife and put a gash in my left temple.'

'Ouch,' Honey said, and plucked an olive from her martini and popped it into her mouth.

'Yeah. The doctors shaved the hair off so they could stitch the cut. The hair grew back white.'

'It's attractive,' she said, studying it.

He was beginning to believe it.

'You think so?' he said.

'Yes,' she said, 'I actually do,' and sipped again at her martini.

'So what'd you learn tonight?' he asked.

'From the dancer?'

'Prima ballerina, my my.'

'Who couldn't speak a word of English,' Honey said, and pulled a face. 'One of my crew finally translated. His mother was Russian. Stood off camera while I fumbled my way through. Great interview, right?'

'His *mother* stood off camera?'

'Sure, his mother,' Honey said, grinning.

'But you know,' Hawes said, returning the grin, 'that might come off kind of cute.'

'You think so?' she said.

'Yes,' he said, 'I actually do,' and sipped again at his scotch.

'Come to think of it,' she said, '*Tamar's* mother is Russian, isn't she?'

'Russian mother, Mexican father,' Hawes said, nodding.

'They did an interview together on ABC last night. Split screen, him in Mexico, her in Paris. Their five minutes of fame. Did you see them?'

'No.'

'They both speak perfect English. All they did was bitch about how everyone was paying so much attention to everything but the fact that their daughter was still missing.'

'Well, there may be some truth to that,' Hawes said.

'All this stuff about racism, and homosexuality . . .'

'Hasn't hurt the album any. It's already number one on all the charts.'

'That's just the point. With all the hype, people tend to forget there's a *victim* out there.'

'I'll bet you haven't forgotten, though, have you?'

'Ahh, here're the steaks,' Hawes said. 'Would you like a beer?'

'I'd love a beer.'

'Heineken okay?'

'Heineken's good,' Honey said.

She ate like a truck driver.

It must've been at least five full minutes before she uttered another word.

'Where'd you learn to eat that way?' he asked.

'With a knife and fork you mean?'

'That, too. But I meant so heartily.'

'In Iowa, when we're hungry, we go out back and kill a cow.'

'Is that where you're from?'

'Sioux City, Iowa, yep.'

'There's no such place.'

'Wanna bet?'

'How'd you end up here?'

'I was a roving reporter for KTIV, the local television channel. Ran around covering murders hither and yon. Believe it or not, we've got murders in Sioux City, too. Bottom line, I got spotted by Channel Four here, and they invited me east. Better pay, big bad city, how could a girl refuse?'

'I'm glad you didn't,' Hawes said.

'I'm kind of glad, too,' she said. 'Now,' she added.

For an instant, their eyes met over the table.

She went back to her filet mignon.

He went back to his sirloin.

They ate in silence.

'Good steak,' he said at last.

'My favorite joint in the entire city,' she said. 'I cover a lot of events at CP-AM. I always come here afterwards.'

'We'll have to come here again,' he ventured.

'Whenever,' she said.

Their eyes met again.

'So . . . uh . . . what is this?' she asked.

'What is what?'

'You know. This.'

'I'm afraid to tell you.'

'Big brave policeman who got stabbed in the head?'

'Yeah, well, not *that* brave.'

'Tell me.'

'How'd you like to marry me?' he said.

'Okay,' she said. 'When?'

'I may be serious.'

'Okay, so where's the ring?'

'Honey . . .' he said.

'Yes, Cotton?' she said, and put both elbows on the table, and cupped her chin in her hands.

'You are perhaps the most beautiful woman I've ever met in my life.'

'Perhaps?'

'You are in *fact* . . .'

'Too late to apologize,' she said.

Her eyes were dancing.

He said nothing for a moment.

She raised her eyebrows.

Yes? her eyebrows asked. Her eyes asked.

'If I were to offer you dessert . . .' he said.

'Yes?' she said.

'. . . would you accept?'

'Or?'

'Or would you rather we went home and watched you on television?'

'Offer me and see,' she said.

'Honey . . .'

'Yes, Cotton?'

'Would you care for dessert?'

'No, I would like you to take me home,' she said, and smiled as if she were still on camera. 'Would *you* care for dessert?' she asked.

11.

SEEMED like old times.

A bright morning in the merry month of May, and the detectives of the Eight-Seven were gathered in the Loot's office for a Tuesday morning confab. The lieutenant was late. Arthur Brown was telling a drunk-driver joke.

'Motorcycle cop's been hiding in the bushes all day, hoping to catch a speeder, he finally pulls over this dude doing eighty miles an hour in a convertible Jag. Grinning from ear to ear, the cop leans into the Jag and says, "I've been waiting for you all day long, pal." The dude in the Jag has three sheets to the wind. He says, "Well, offisher, I got here as fast as I could."'

Brown burst out laughing.

So did the other detectives in the room.

Seven of them altogether. Six men and one woman, typical of most squadrooms in this city. Andy Parker couldn't resist trying to embarrass Eileen Burke.

'Another motorcycle cop pulls over the same drunk,' he said. 'This time the cop's a female. She tells him, "Sir, you have the right to remain silent. Anything you say will be held against you." The drunk says, "Tits."'

Which Eileen guessed was better than breaking into her locker and pissing in her shoes. In fact, she thought the joke was pretty funny. After the meeting this morning, she was scheduled to interview a woman who'd been snorting cocaine since she was fifteen years old, but who was now ready to take a stand against the gang that was terrorizing her building in the projects. It was tough enough trying to quit the powder crowd. Protecting your kids against the people hoping to hook them was something else again. The woman was twenty-seven years old. She had a son of eleven who'd already been approached. Enough was enough.

'There's this guy gets stopped by a cop for speeding?' Richard Genero said tentatively. As the newest detective on the squad, he was still not too sure of himself at these weekly meetings. But the lieutenant wasn't here yet, and everyone seemed to be in a receptive mood this morning, so he was ready to venture a joke. 'The cop wants to know where he's going in such a hurry, and the guy says, "I have to do a show in New Haven." The cop asks, "What kind of show?" The speeder says, "I'm a juggler." The cop is skeptical. "Oh yeah?" he says. "Let's see you juggle something." The speeder says, "I'd be happy to, but all my equipment is at the theater." Well, the cop leads him around to the back of his cruiser, and he opens the trunk and takes out three flares, which he lights and hands to the speeder. "Here," he says. "Juggle these!" It so happens the guy really *is* a juggler, so he throws the flares into the air and is doing his little act when who should come speeding down the highway but that same drunk in the Jag! He takes one look, jams on the brakes, walks over to the cop, and says, "Take me to jail right now, offisher. I'll never be able to pass *that* test."'

Everyone was still laughing when Byrnes walked into the room. Gray-haired and bullet-headed, he walked behind his desk, said a gruff 'Good morning,' and then asked, 'What's so funny?'

Genero said they were telling drunk-driver jokes.

'This drunk comes out of a liquor store,' Byrnes said, 'sees a motorcycle cop at the curb, writing a parking ticket. He staggers over to the cop, says, "Come on, pal, give a guy a break." The cop keeps writing the ticket. "Come on," the drunk says, "don't be such a friggin Nazi." So the cop writes a second ticket for the car having bald tires. The drunk calls him an asshole, and the cop writes a third ticket for worn windshield wipers. This goes on for ten minutes, the drunk hurling abuse, the cop writing ticket after ticket. Finally, the cop closes his book, and says, "You satisfied now?" The drunk says, "I really don't give a damn, offisher. *My* car's parked aroun' the corner."'

The detectives laughed harder than perhaps they should have.

'Have some bagels and coffee,' Byrnes said, and turned to where Carella was standing over by the bookcases with all the legal tomes in them. 'What happened last night?' he asked. Carella told him everything that had happened to him down at One Fed Square and beyond.

'And?' Byrnes said.

'I walked,' Carella said.

'Why?'

'I was there through sufferance.'

'Sufferance, huh? Well, my beamish boy, what if I told you the Commish wants us to stick with it?'

Carella looked at him.

'This is all politics,' Byrnes said. 'We caught the squeal. If the Feebs crack the case, we look inept. If we're the ones who nab these guys, we come off smelling of roses.'

'The Feebs don't have anything yet. And neither do I,' Carella said.

'That's why we're here today, ain't it?' Byrnes said, and turned away and said, 'You ready to listen, men?' And immediately added, 'Eileen?'

'Good save, Loot,' Eileen said, and everyone laughed.

Score one for the frails, she thought, and crossed her splendid legs for emphasis.

Cotton Hawes thought of Honey Blair crossing her legs last night.

'Here's what we've got,' Byrnes said. 'You all know we caught this friggin kidnapping Saturday night . . .'

'Actually, I'm the one who caught it,' Andy Parker said.

'Bravo, you want a medal?' Byrnes asked. 'The Joint Task Force moved in and the vic asked for Carella to . . .'

'Not the vic,' Carella corrected.

'Right, the CEO of the company that *records* the vic, you've seen her all over television. He asked for Carella on the case because he has some sort of rapport with him . . .'

'Must be the smile,' Meyer said.

'Must be,' Carella said, and flashed a toothy grin.

'Anyway, they get him down there and treat him like a country cousin, except when the CEO demands he go along on the ransom drop. Am I getting this right, Steve?'

'More or less,' Carella said.

'So last night, when they diss him yet again, he walks. Told Corky Corcoran . . . any of you know him?'

'A prick,' Brown said. ''Scuse me, Eileen.'

'Why?' Eileen said. 'He *is* a prick.'

'Anyway, Steve told him to shove his job.'

'Good for you,' Meyer said.

'Only trouble is,' Byrnes said, 'I got a call from the Commish last night, soon as he heard what happened.'

'How'd he hear?' Genero asked.

'Corcoran called him. Filed a complaint.'

'The prick,' Eileen said.

'The Commish agrees. He wants Carella — he wants *us* — to stay on it. In fact, he would like nothing better than for us to crack it. Before The Squad does.'

'Fat Chance Department,' Parker said. 'They've got technology pouring out of their wahzoo.'

'Didn't help them locate the perps,' Carella said.

'What'd you learn down there, Steve?' Brown asked.

He told them about all the equipment the Feebs had set up, told them about the perps leading him and Loomis out to The Wasteland, told them about the dead Golden Retriever . . .

'Sons of bitches,' Parker said.

'So we'd know they're ready to kill the girl,' Carella said.

'Could've made their point another way.'

'That's what Loomis thought. He still thinks these guys are *honorable,* you know. That they'll make a deal and stick to it. They asked for two-fifty large the first time around, and when we delivered it, they came back asking for a mil. But he still seems to think . . .'

'A mil *more?*' Kling asked.

'No, altogether.'

'The girl's worth it,' Hawes said. 'Did you see that tape of the kidnapping? I saw it on a large screen down at Channel Four,' he said, and grinned sort of goofily.

'We got the MCU report, by the way,' Carella said. 'The guy was limping.'

'What guy?'

'One of the perps. The left-handed one.'

'Well, *there's* something,' Parker said.

'We already put out a medical alert,' Hawes said.

'Anything?' Eileen asked.

'Not so far.'

'I mean, how many limping left-handed guys *are* there in this city?' Parker asked reasonably.

'Who's an experienced thief,' Carella said, nodding.

'How so?' Genero asked.

'Stole the Explorer he used on the night of the snatch. Also has a barrel full of stolen cell phones. So at least one of them's a thief.'

'Means a record, maybe,' Hawes said.

'Maybe for the left-handed one.'

'Who limps, don't forget.'

'Any of you guys remember a movie called *The Fallen Sparrow?*' Byrnes asked.

They all looked at him.

'The bad guy limps. Drags his foot. Scariest scene in the movie is John Garfield waiting for him, his face all covered with sweat, and all we hear is that foot dragging down the hall, coming closer and closer.'

'Who's John Garfield?' Genero asked.

'That was *suspense,*' Byrnes said. 'Nowadays, they put a lot of bullshit technology on the screen, the directors think that's suspense.'

'Think we should put out a second med alert?' Eileen asked.

'Couldn't hurt,' Brown said. 'All these doctors are too busy to pay attention the first time around.'

'Too busy making money,' Hawes said.

'Too busy robbing Medicare,' Kling said.

'Come on, my uncle's a doctor,' Genero said.

'Am I the only one going to have a second bagel?' Parker asked, and pulled himself out of the only easy chair in the room and went over to the table near the windows.

'So is this ours or is it theirs, or what?' Carella asked.

'My guess?' Byrnes said.

'Good as mine, that's for sure.'

'My guess is it's ours *and* theirs.'

'A fuckin horse race,' Parker said, pouring himself another cup of coffee.

240

'So let's win it,' Byrnes said.

BACK IN THE good old days, every Monday through Thursday morning at nine o'clock, detectives from all over this fair city pulled what was known as 'Lineup Duty.' This meant that instead of reporting to work at their respective offices, two detectives from each of the city's squads trotted downtown or uptown or crosstown or across the rivers to the Headquarters building on High Street, where the Chief of Detectives presided over a parade of all the felony offenders who'd been arrested in the city the day before.

The purpose of these lineups was identification.

The Chief brought out the perps one by one, named the crimes for which they'd been arrested, recited a brief pedigree on each, and then conducted an interrogation for the next ten minutes or so. Most of these people were experienced thieves; the Chief didn't expect to get from them any information that would convict them in later trials. What he was doing was simply familiarizing his detectives with the people who were making mischief in this city. On a rotating basis, every Monday through Thursday, his detectives were able to get a good long look at troublemakers past and present, with the idea that they'd be able to recognize them in the future and prevent them from making yet more trouble.

Once a thief, always a thief.

Today, the police still had lineups (or 'showups' as they were sometimes called) but their purpose was identification of another sort. Nowadays, in a room at your own precinct, you placed a suspect on a stage in a row of detectives or officers in street clothes, and you asked the vic to pick out which one of them had raped her or stabbed her or poked out her eye on the night of January fifth. Back in the old days, the headquarters gym was packed with maybe a hundred detectives from all over the city. Today, sitting behind a protective one-way glass, you had the vic, and the arresting detectives, and the lieutenant, and maybe somebody from the D.A.'s Office if you were that close to making a case. Small potatoes when you thought back to the grand old days, eh, Gertie?

But nowadays, you had computers to tell you who the bad guys were. You didn't have to eyeball all those evil-doers from a hard bench in an austere gym. You sat in your own comfy swivel chair at your own cluttered desk, and you popped the question to the computer, and hoped it came up with something good.

By that Tuesday morning, not a single one of the myriad doctors in this city had responded to the precinct's medical alert for a man who might have sustained a recent injury to the right leg. While Eileen sent out a second alert, sounding a bit more urgent this time, Carella turned to the second supposition in Detective Oswald Hooper's report on the footprints the MCU had recovered aboard the *River Princess;* he considered the possibility that the injury to the right leg had occurred sometime in the *past.*

The men and sole woman on the squad were now working on the premise that the men who'd kidnapped Tamar Valparaiso were no amateurs. In many respects, this assumption was a throwback to the days of the old Monday-to-Thursday lineups. See those guys on the stage there? Yesterday they committed murder, armed robbery, burglary, rape, auto theft, whatever, and it seems like they all have records of felony convictions as long as my arm here, so look at their faces and remember them well because tomorrow these same people will be committing the same felonies or different felonies all over again.

Once a thief, always a thief, right?

In America, kidnapping was rarely a crime anyone committed more than once. It was fashionable among certain criminal types in remoter parts of the world to capture businessmen and hold them for ransom, but that was there and this was here. It was fashionable in some countries to eat raw crocodile eyes, too. Nobody on the Eight-Seven had ever heard of a serial kidnapper. You either kidnapped somebody and got away with it, in which case you flew to Rio and danced the samba till dawn, or you got caught and spent the rest of your life behind bars. Either way, it was usually a one-shot crime.

So when Carella went to the computer that Tuesday morning, he accessed the state's prison records by typing in first his name and then his password, but once he was cleared, he did not type in the key word KIDNAP because he didn't think that would bear any fruit. In fact, he didn't specify any crime at all. What he was looking for was a left-handed con who limped. In fact, what he was looking for was a left-handed con who'd limped his way out of jail and straight onto the deck of the *River Princess* this past Saturday night.

He called for a statewide search, but he limited it to just the past five years, otherwise he'd be here for the *next* five years. He went straight for the jugular. As his key word, he typed INJURY.

Got a menu asking him to choose among HEAD, TRUNK, or EXTREMITIES.

Hit EXTREMITIES.

Was asked to choose between ARMS or LEGS.

Hit LEGS.

Knew what he was going to be asked before it popped up on the screen, and was not surprised.

He hit RIGHT.

Got a list as long as a prison night.

He'd be here all next week looking through all these records, maybe five or six hundred of them. Who'd have dreamt there were so many cons with injuries to the right leg, and how in hell was he supposed to find the man among them who'd . . .

Wait a minute, he was looking in the wrong place.

In this state, a term of post-release supervision was mandatory for every determinate sentence. For example, a Class B felony was punishable by an incarceration period of five to twenty-five years. If you were paroled, you had to be supervised on the outside for a period of from two and a half to five years. On the other hand, for a Class E felony, you could be sent up for a term of a year and a half to four years, but after parole, you had to report to your parole officer for at least a year and a half or as long as three years. The message was the same one it had always been: If you can't do the time, don't do the crime.

Carella logged off the prison system, clicked on DIVISION OF PAROLE, was asked for his online name and password, gave them STEPHEN L. CARELLA and then his shield number, 714-5632, and waited for clearance. When he was online, he asked for a search going back five years.

When prompted for the NAME of the parolee, he typed UNKNOWN.

OFFENSE?

He typed UNKNOWN.

SCARS, TATTOOS, OTHER DISTINGUISHING MARKS?

He typed LEFT-HANDED.

DISABILITIES OR INFIRMITIES?

He typed INJURY TO RIGHT LEG, and got INVALID ANSWER and the same question again: DIS-

ABILITIES OR INFIRMITIES?

This time he typed LIMP, and hit the jackpot.

There were currently seven left-handed cons on parole from various prisons around the state, all of them with leg injuries. Four of these were injuries to the left leg. The remaining three were injuries to the right leg.

One of these injuries was sustained in the machine shop at Castleview State Penitentiary, when the heavy metal die for manufacturing license plates fell on the inmate's foot, fracturing his ankle bone. The inmate had subsequently sued the state, Carella noticed. And lost, by the way. He'd been released from prison two years ago, and had since got hit by a bus that fractured his skull and caused his untimely demise. Carella figured some guys were just born losers.

The other two men were still alive.

Carella hit the PRINT button.

SHE ACTUALLY heard the key being inserted in the lock.

Heard the tiny click of the key being turned.

Heard some fumbling outside the door, and then the door opened and standing in the door frame was Saddam Hussein.

Carrying the big rifle.

None of them came into the room without a weapon. Must have thought she was extremely dangerous, hand-cuffed to the radiator this way. Maybe they'd caught a glimpse of 'Bandersnatch' before they came down the stairs all macho-men, 'Don't nobody fucking *move!*' Weapons of mass destruction in their hands. Same as now. Maybe they'd seen her reach for the invisible vorpal sword and beat the shit out of the frumious beast.

Hussein closed the door behind him, came limping across the floor towards her, dragging his right foot.

She could still remember him slapping her.

She almost flinched as he approached.

'Don't be afraid,' he whispered, and stopped just a few feet away from her.

She said nothing.

Realized she was cowering, tried to straighten her shoulders, realized this emphasized the thrust of her breasts, hunched over again. Behind the Hussein mask, his eyes were bright and blue. He held the AK-47 in his left hand.

'I wanted to tell you how sorry I am,' he said.

I'll bet, she thought.

'For hitting you the other night.'

'That's okay,' she said. 'Forget it.'

'No, really,' he said, and knelt beside her on the floor. 'I got a little excited, is all.'

He's sitting too close, she thought. Watch it, Tamar.

'What can I do for you? To make you more comfortable,' he said, and put his right hand on her exposed knee.

'No, don't,' she said, and turned her body away, into the radiator.

'*Sorr-eee*,' he said, and pulled back his hand as if he'd burned it. 'Just trying to be helpful.'

How about unlocking this handcuff? she thought.

Only way out of here is to get hold of the gun, she thought.

Any one of the guns.

They all have guns around here.

'My wrist hurts,' she said.

'Ahh,' he said. 'Want me to rub it for you?'

'Be better if you took off the handcuff,' she said.

'But I don't have a key,' he said, and put his hand on her knee again.

This time, she did not tell him to stop.

'Why don't you go get the key?' she asked. 'It's very uncomfortable this way.'

'Avery has the key,' he said.

Avery, she thought. A name.

He did not seem to realize he'd slipped.

'Go ask him for it,' she said.

His hand slid onto her thigh.

'No, don't,' she said. 'Not now. Go get the key first. Take off this damn handcuff,' she said, and smiled.

'How does it feel to be dancing in front of people half-naked that way?' he asked. His eyes were shining bright in the holes of the mask. His hand on her thigh was trembling.

'Go get the key,' she said. 'I'll dance for you.'

'I could fuck you without having to go for the key,' he said. His voice was trembling, too.

'Be better if I'm loose,' she whispered.

'You promise?' he said, and his hand tightened on her thigh.

'I promise,' she said, and licked her lips.

He rose abruptly. Almost scrambled to his feet.

'I'll be right back,' he said, and hurried to the door, the rifle in his left hand.

Don't forget to bring your gun, she thought.

The door closed behind him.

She heard the soft click of the lock again.

Now she was trembling, too.

ONE CERTAIN AXIOM of this city is that you will never find a homeless shelter, a rehab center, or a parole office in a good neighborhood. If you're apartment-hunting, and you ask the real estate agent about the nearest location of any of these places, and she replies, 'Why, right around the corner, dearie!' then what you do is hike up your skirts and run for the hills because the onliest place you don't wish to live is right here, honey.

Early that Tuesday afternoon, Carella and Hawes visited a parole office in a downtown neighborhood that they could best describe as 'indifferent to law enforcement,' but perhaps this was a hasty judgment premised on the presence of hookers and drug dealers on every street corner. By one P.M., they had driven across the river and into the trees of a delightful Calm's Point enclave known as Sunrise Shores because once upon a time it had indeed been an elegant waterfront community that faced the sun coming up over a bend in the River Dix.

The neighborhood had long ago been overrun by street gangs who'd once been content to rumble among themselves for the sheer joy of claiming worthless turf or second-hand virgins, but who had since graduated into selling dope on a large scale, and were now killing each other and innocent bystanders in drive-by shootings that made it dangerous to go to the corner grocery store for a pack of cigarettes.

The Sunrise Shores parole office was above one such grocery store, outside which a huddle of teenagers who should have known better were smoking their brains out – and don't write me letters, Carella thought. There were two ways you walked in a neighborhood like this one, even if you were a cop. You either pretended you were invisible, or you pretended you had dynamite strapped to your waist under your jacket. Shoulders back, heads erect, both detectives strutted like walking bombs to the narrow doorway alongside the grocery store. The guys smoking outside figured these dudes were ex-cons here to make their scheduled visits, so they left them alone. So much for Actors Studio exercises, Carella thought, and went up a stairway stinking of piss,

Hawes sniffing along haughtily behind him. On the second floor, they found a wooden door with a frosted glass panel lettered with the words:

DIVISION OF PAROLE
MANAGER, KIRBY STRAUSS

The office was small and perhaps even shabbier-looking than the Eight-Seven's squadroom. Six metal desks were spaced around the room, two of them flanking a curtainless window with a torn shade. A straight-backed wooden chair sat empty alongside each desk. Early afternoon sunlight tinted the shade yellow. Dark green metal filing cabinets lined one windowless wall, and an open door revealed a toilet bowl and a sink beside it. An ancient copying machine was on the wall alongside the bathroom. A wooden coat rack was in one corner of the room. There were several topcoats on it, but only one hat.

Two men sat in swivel chairs behind the choice window desks.

They both turned to look at the detectives as they walked in.

Carella wondered if the hat belonged to one of them.

'Mr. Strauss?' he asked.

'Yes?'

He was a man in his fifties, Carella guessed, wearing brown trousers and a brown cardigan sweater, a shirt and tie under it. He was sitting at the desk on the right. Bald and a trifle overweight, he looked like someone you might find selling stamps at your local post office. Carella figured the hat was his.

'I called earlier,' he said. 'Detective Carella, the Eight-Seven. My partner, Detective Hawes.'

'Oh, yes,' Strauss said, rising and extending his hand. 'This is Officer Latham,' he said, and gestured with his left hand toward the man sitting at the other desk. Latham nodded. Strauss briefly shook hands with both detectives, and then said, 'Have a seat. You're here about Wilkins, right? Let me get his file.'

The detectives took chairs alongside Strauss' desk. Strauss went to the filing cabinets, opened one of them, began rummaging.

'Is it going to rain out there?' Latham asked.

'I don't think so,' Hawes said. 'Why? Who said it was going to rain?'

'Feel it in my bones,' Latham said, and shook his head mournfully.

He did, in fact, look a bit arthritic, a tall thin man wearing blue corduroy trousers and a gray sports jacket, a dingy white shirt with a worn collar, and a dark blue knit tie to match the trousers. A cardboard Starbucks container was on his desk, alongside his computer.

'Here we go,' Strauss said, and sat behind his desk again, and placed a manila folder between himself and the detectives. 'I could do this on the computer, but it's easier to look at hard copy,' he said, and opened the folder. 'Calvin Robert Wilkins,' he said, 'twenty-seven years old, took a fall for armed robbery when he was twenty. What happened was he went into this bank alone, must've been desperate, don't you think? Stuck a gun in a teller's face, ran off with whatever she had in the cash drawer, something like three thousand dollars, can you imagine? Gambles three thousand bucks against twenty-five in the slammer? He's driving away from the bank when he gets a flat tire, finally climbs out of the car and starts running. The cops chasing him get out of their car, and one of them fires a shot that catches him in the leg . . .'

'The right leg,' Carella said, nodding.

'Well, let me check,' Strauss said, and looked at the

report. 'Yes, the right leg. Knocked him ass over teacups, ended his Bonnie and Clyde career. He was convicted of Rob One, a B-felony . . . well, you know that. Caught a bleeding-heart judge who sentenced him to a mere twenty because it was a first offense and all that jazz.'

'When was he paroled?'

'Six months ago. Just before Thanksgiving. Lot to be thankful for, that kid.'

'How so?'

'Got sprung his first appearance before the Board. Served only seven of the twenty. I call that stepping in shit.'

'You said it was a first offense . . .'

'Well, first time he got *caught,* let's say. With these guys . . .'

'Any problems since he's been out?'

'Yeah. Violating parole, for one.'

'What'd he do?'

'First year of parole, he's supposed to be under what we call "Intensive Supervision." This is like a readjustment period for him, you know? He comes here to the office every week, and somebody from here – we've got six guys in this office, it's a fairly small one – visits him at home once every two weeks, once a month, whatever. It's an intensive period, that's what it's called, Intensive Supervision. This is supposed to continue for at least twelve months, after which we place him on what we call *Regular* Supervision, which means fewer home visits, and fewer visits to the office here.

'Well, he got out of Miramar just before Thanksgiving, that's a state lockup even worse than Castleview . . . well, you know that. And he started coming here like clockwork once a week. He was living in a decent furnished room, and he had a job washing dishes in a deli over on Carpenter. I'll tell you the truth, I figured he was a prime candidate for early discharge, which would've been three years instead of his maximum five. Then, all of a sudden, he doesn't show up the week after Christmas, which I figured the holidays and all, am I right? But then he misses the first two weeks in January, and I figure shit the man's absconded. Which is what it turned out to be. Failure to report here, changing address without permission, for all I know even leaving the fuckin' state. A classic case of absconding. I issued a warrant for his arrest. If we catch him again, he'll be doing his maximum-five behind bars. Some guys never learn.'

'Can we have that last known?' Hawes asked.

'Sure, but it won't do you any good. He's gone, man. And it's a big bad city out there.'

Strauss got up nonetheless, and carried the file on Wilkins over to the copying machine. Seeing the open bathroom door, he closed it as if sight of a toilet bowl might be offensive to his visitors from across the river. 'Why do you want him?' he asked.

'He may be involved in a kidnapping.'

'Graduation Day, huh? Some guys never learn,' he said again.

'How bad is that limp, by the way?' Hawes asked.

'Well, he's not a cripple or anything, if that's what you're thinking. He just sort of drags the right foot a little, you know?'

'Can you show me what you mean?' Carella asked.

'Charlie, show him how Wilkins walks, will you?' Strauss said.

Latham got up from behind his desk.

Like an actor preparing before he went onstage, he hesitated a moment, thinking, and then he started walking across the room. The limp he affected was a slight one. His impersonation captured perfectly the walk of the masked

252

man the detectives had seen on Honey Blair's tape.

'How's that?' Latham asked.

'Perfect,' Strauss said. 'Maybe we ought to send *you* up there to Miramar, finish out his term.'

'Yeah, yeah,' Latham said, but he seemed pleased he'd been such a big hit.

Strauss carried a sheaf of papers over from the copier. Stapling them together, he said, 'You might as well have *all* the vitals,' and handed the pages to Carella. 'If you find him, let me know,' he said. 'I really thought he was a candidate for early, the jackass. Goes to show, don't it?'

He actually looked sad.

CALVIN ROBERT WILKINS was still wearing the Saddam Hussein mask.

He had the rifle in his left hand.

Nothing in his right hand.

No key, no nothing.

He closed the door behind him.

Came limping across the room to her.

'He wouldn't give me the key,' he said.

She could swear he was grinning behind the mask.

Standing not a foot away from her, he unzipped his fly.

THIS, NOW, was what it was really like.

There was no vorpal blade this time.

There was no slow striptease, no musical accompaniment, no claws catching at her garments to tear them tantalizingly to shreds. This was her top being violently ripped from her breasts, this was rough hands reaching under her already tattered skirt to tear her panties open over her crotch. There were no biting jaws, he did not bite her, he simply slapped her again and again, kept slapping her as she tried to pull her manacled hand free of the radiator, slapped her until her face was aching and bruised, her free hand flapping on the floor where he had rested the rifle, trying to find the rifle with blind seeking fingers while he kept slapping her till she felt dizzy and weak, murmuring 'No, please don't, please don't, please don't.'

But still he had not raped her.

Still he seemed to derive pleasure from the incessant slapping, his hand rhythmically hitting her, the back of his hand, the palm of his hand, the back of his hand again until she collapsed against the radiator, murmuring soundlessly no please don't, no please please don't.

This time, there was no vorpal blade to save her.

This was merely rape.

Viciously, he spread her legs and forcibly entered her, tearing tissue as he plunged inside her. She screamed at the forced penetration, screamed again when he slapped her again and told her to shut up, and then slapped her again and again and again. And then his hands were on her breasts, squeezing her nipples hard, thrusting his overpowering rigidity into her below, grunting, his hands seeming not to know where to hurt her next, her face, her breasts, her buttocks, squeezing, slapping, punching her now, pinching her, punching her breasts, punching her face, blood suddenly bursting from her nose, until at last she screamed in agony, 'Please *stop!*' and he ejaculated in that instant, and the door flew open and Yasir Arafat came into the room and shouted, 'You stupid fuck!' and she lost consciousness.

12.

THE SQUAD was somewhat perturbed. One might even say they were quite blaxitomed! Special Agent in Charge Stanley Marshall Endicott had just learned from his superior at Division Headquarters that the Police Commissioner had ordered the 87th Squad to stay on the Valparaiso kidnapping case!

'A shitty little squad uptown,' he complained, visibly hummered.

The agents and detectives in the big conference room at Bison Records all shook their heads in solemn agreement. All except Lieutenant Charles Farley Corcoran, who was pacing the floor, quite red in the face, even for an Irishman.

'Dismissed my complaint,' he muttered, all visibly perscathed. 'Said Carella wasn't under my command and therefore could not have been insubordinate.'

'What do we do now?' Feingold asked. 'Whose case is it, anyway? Do we dismantle here, or what?'

'It's ours *and* theirs,' Endicott said.

'A horse race, you mean,' Feingold said sourly.

'I mean a horse race we'd better *win!*'

'Suppose a motorcycle cop on the fuckin *street* insulted me?' Corcoran asked the air, still fuming, still all dejebbeled. 'Would that be insubordination?'

'Damn right,' Jones agreed, kissing a little ass, not for nothing had he learned to make his way in the white man's police department.

'Son of a bitch said he'd call again at three,' Endicott said.

'The Commissioner?' Lonigan asked. He was none too bright, even though he'd been credited with smashing a big heroin ring in Majesta. But that was ten years ago.

'The perp, the perp,' Endicott said, getting more and more perplexed himself. 'This time we zero in,' he said, visibly afumitaxed. 'If Loomis can't keep him on the phone, I'll personally cut off his balls.'

'The perp's?' Lonigan asked.

Endicott merely looked at him.

THE TELEPHONE CALL came at precisely three P.M. The kidnapper was nothing if not punctual. Though she recognized the voice at once, Gloria Klein asked who was calling. When the kidnapper said, 'This is personal,' she asked him to hold one second, please, and then buzzed Loomis' inner office.

'Hello?' Loomis said.

'He's back,' she said.

'It's him,' Loomis told Endicott. He was already walking toward his isolation booth.

'Whenever you're ready,' Endicott said, putting on the ear phones. 'Keep him talking.'

Sitting in the booth, Loomis picked up the extension phone.

'Loomis,' he said.

'Have you got the money?'

'I'll have it by six tonight. I've had to sell . . .'

'Seven-fifty in new hundreds?'

'Yes.'

'Good. Put Carella on.'

'He's not here.'

There was a silence on the line.

'Where is he?'

'I don't know. I didn't realize you'd need him again.'

'I don't.'

'First tower's on him,' Jones said.

'Is there another detective there?'

Corcoran nodded.

'Yes,' Loomis said.

'Is he listening to this?'

Corcoran shook his head.

'No,' Loomis said.

'You're lying. Put him on.'

'Second tower's got him. He's in a moving vehicle,' Feingold said.

Corcoran picked up his extension.

'Hello?' he said.

'Who's this?'

'Detective-Lieutenant Charles Corcoran.'

'May I call you Charles?'

'Is the girl still alive?'

'I'll ask the fucking questions, Charles!'

Corcoran's mouth tightened. Endicott was scowling.

'Go down to the limo at seven P.M. sharp,' the caller said. 'You, Mr. Loomis, and the money. Get on the River Dix Drive and head east. Rush hour should be over by then. I'll call again at seven-fifteen. Any tricks and the girl dies. *This* phone is stolen, too,' he said, and laughed.

There was a click on the line.

'Son of a goddamn rotten son of a bitch bastard motherfucking *cock*sucker!' Jones yelled. 'He always gets off a second before we triangulate.'

'You want this printout?' Feingold asked.

'You heard him, it's stolen,' Endicott said.

'Will you have the money by then?' Corcoran asked Loomis.

'It should be here by six,' Loomis said.

'This time we play it our way,' Corcoran said.

THEY'D BEEN WAITING outside the building since a quarter past one, but the landlady didn't show up until almost three-thirty. She was dressed for Marrakech.

No burkah covered her from head to toe, but instead she wore a modest black abayah that billowed out like the sail on a Sumerian galley, covering everything but her face and her slender hands. She had extraordinary brown eyes, almost as black as the abayah. With all that protective clothing, neither of the detectives could tell her exact age, but they guessed she was somewhere in her mid-forties. They also guessed the eyes were a bit flirtatious.

The apartment building was in a Calm's Point neighborhood with a large Arab population, mostly Egyptians, Moroccans, and other immigrants from North Africa. The streets here were lined with Turkish coffee houses, shops selling hummus and baklava, katayif and kibbi, mjddara and tabbouleh. And although there were only twelve mosques in the entire city, one of them was located two blocks from the furnished room Calvin Robert Wilkins supposedly rented at the end of last year.

'We're looking for the man who was renting a furnished room here from just before Thanksgiving to shortly after Christmas,' Carella told the landlady.

The landlady nodded.

'Know who we mean?' Hawes asked.

'Yes, I know,' she said.

They followed her up to the third floor.

'Rent was coming due on January one,' she told them. 'Guess he was in a big hurry to leave, eh?'

Kirby Strauss the parole officer was right: The room Wilkins had been renting before he'd absconded was 'perfectly decent.' Small, neat, tidy, inexpensively appointed with thrift-shop furniture.

'When he rented it, did he say he'd be leaving in January?' Carella asked.

'No. Said he wanted it on a month-to-month basis,' the woman said. 'Which was okey-dokey with me.'

Showing off her American slang. Brown eyes flashing. Left hand on her hip. Big silver ring on the thumb of that hand. Some kind of bright green stone set in it. Not jade, something else. Not emerald either, not in a silver setting.

'When did he first tell you he'd be leaving?'

'Just after Christmas.'

'Did he say where he was going?'

'Sure. Jamaica.'

'No kidding? Jamaica, huh?'

'Sure. You know Jamaica? I asked was he going with his friends, he said no, just himself.'

'What friends?' Hawes asked at once.

'The two who came here all the time. Man and a woman.'

'When you say all the time . . . ?'

The woman shrugged under her voluminous garment. Ripples flowed down to her toes. He noticed she was barefoot. Ring on the big toe of her right foot, too. Red stone on this one.

'Three, four times. He had the room only a month, you know. Little more than a month.'

'Would you know their names? These friends of his?'

'I don't ask visitors' names. There's no trouble, I don't ask visitors' names.'

'What'd they look like?' Carella asked.

'The man was something like your height. Brown eyes like yours, curly black hair, very nice build,' she said, and rolled her eyes. 'The girl was a redhead. Not like your

259

red,' she said, turning to Hawes, 'more brown in color, yes? With green eyes and . . . what do you call them? When there are spots on the face?'

'Freckles?' Hawes suggested.

'English,' she said, shaking her head. 'Freckles, yes. I don't think they were married, those two, but I think they were close, eh?' she said, and winked.

'You mean, like engaged,' Hawes said, nodding.

'No, I mean like sleeping together,' she said, and winked again.

'So he was leaving for Jamaica, but he wasn't taking his friends with him, is that it?' Carella said.

'Well, not right that moment.'

'What do you mean?'

'He wasn't going to Jamaica that very moment when he left the room here.'

'Then when *was* he going to Jamaica?'

'He said in the spring.'

'When in the spring?'

'He only said the spring. "In the spring, I'll be on a beach in Jamaica." Was what he said.'

'So he might be in Jamaica right this minute, is that what you're saying?'

'This is the spring, yes,' she said. 'So he could be there now, yes. Who knows? I don't even know where Jamaica is. Do you know where Jamaica is?'

'Yes.'

'Have you ever been to Jamaica?'

'No, but I know where it is.'

'Where is it?'

'In the Caribbean.'

'Yes?'

'Yes.'

'Where's that, the Caribbean?'

260

'It's where Mr. Wilkins might be right this minute,' Hawes said.

'Mr. *Who?*' she asked.

'Wilkins. Calvin Wilkins.'

'That's not the name he gave me,' she said.

Hawes looked at her.

'He told me something else, not that.'

'What did he tell you?'

'I have to look,' she said.

They followed her downstairs to her apartment. There were beaded curtains and a double bed, and a calendar with Arabic lettering on it. She opened the top drawer of a small painted chest and took from it a ledger of some sort. She opened the book, trailed her forefinger down the page. Her fingernails were painted a green the color of the stone in the ring.

'Here,' she said, and tapped one of the names.

They looked at the page.

The name written there in a delicate feminine hand was:

Richard Martin

'Ricky, that's right,' the landlady said.

'Ricky Martin,' Hawes said.

'Yes. That's who his friends asked for, first time they came here.'

'Ricky Martin,' Hawes said again.

'Yes.'

'Ricky Martin is a singer.'

'This man was a *singer?*'

'No, this man was a thief. Ricky *Martin* is the singer.'

'He lived here more than a month, I never heard him sing,' the woman said, and shrugged again under the black garment.

'Did he say where he might be going? When he left here?'

'I told you. Jamaica.'

'I mean in January. When he moved out. Right then. Where was he going? Did he tell you?'

'Yes, he told me.'

'Where?'

'To stay with his friends. I think perhaps they had in mind a *ménage à trois,* eh? Perhaps that's why he was in such a big hurry.'

Hawes had once known a woman named Jeanette, or was it Annette, who'd called it a *'ménage de trois.'* For the longest time, he himself had called it that.

'Are you fellows in such a big hurry, too?' the landlady asked. 'Or shall I brew the three of us some nice jasmine tea?'

Laurette, Hawes guessed it was.

'Thanks,' he said, 'you've been very helpful.'

'You think it's because of the record store?' she asked.

Neither of the detectives knew what she meant.

'That he picked a singer's name?'

They still didn't know what she meant.

'Because he worked in a record store?' she said.

'Which one?' Carella asked at once.

'Laura something,' she said. 'In the city. Someplace downtown.'

SOMEPLACE downtown could have been anywhere.

In this city, when you crossed any of the bridges from the outlying sectors, you were heading into 'The City.' And once you got into the city, you invariably headed 'downtown' because that's where all the action was.

They started with the yellow pages for Isola, a literal translation of the Italian word *'isola,'* for 'island.' They

262

looked first under RECORDS, TAPES & COMPACT DISCS, and found a sub-heading that read *See Compact Discs, Tapes & Records – Retail*. They turned back to the Cs, and found a listing for exactly one hundred and twelve record shops. None of them were named Laura Something or Laura Anything. Under the L listings, they found seventeen. They called Wilkins' former land-lady at once.

'Do any of these names ring a bell?' they asked, and started reeling them off. 'L&M Records, Lane Books Music & Café . . .'

'No,' she said.

'Lark Music, Laurence's Records, Lewis Music & Video, Lexington Entertainment, Lion Heart Record Shop . . .'

'No, none of those.'

'Live Wire Compact Discs, Lone Star Records, Long John's Music, Lorelei Records, Lotus . . .'

'What was that Laura one?'

'Ma'am?'

'Laura *Lee*, was that it?'

'Lorelei Records? Is that what you mean?'

'That's it,' she said. 'Laura Lie.'

Lorelei Records was a chain of shops similar to Sam Goody's. There were six of them in Isola alone, but only two of them were located in what might have been con-sidered 'downtown,' one of them on St. John's Avenue in what was really 'midtown,' the other one in the financial district at the very tip of the island. They struck paydirt on the first call they made.

'I THOUGHT you said nothing fancy,' Patricia said.

'Nah, this is just a little Italian joint,' Ollie said, and held open the door for her to enter before him.

'This is fancy,' she said. 'We'll make it Dutch tonight.'

'No, no, I invited you.'

'Yeah, but I picked the movie.'

'Makes no difference. This is my treat. You want to take me out sometime, then you ask me.'

Patricia grinned.

'Okay,' she said, 'I'll do that.'

'Hey, Detective Weeks,' a man sitting at the bar said, and immediately rose with his hand extended. 'Long time no see, how you been?'

'Patricia,' Ollie said, 'this is Artie Di Domenico, owner and proprietor of this fine restaurant. Artie, meet Patricia Gomez, a fellow police officer.'

'Nice to meet you,' Di Domenico said, and took her hand and graciously kissed it. Patricia felt like the queen of England. 'Come,' he said, 'I have a nice table for you,' and led them across the room to a table near the windows. This was only five-thirty, the place was almost empty. They had walked here from the precinct, directly after the shift changed. It was not yet dark outside.

'Something to drink?' Di Domenico asked.

'Some wine, Patricia?'

'I really can't let you . . .'

'Tut tut, m'dear,' Ollie said. 'Artie, do you have any of that fine Simi chardonnay?'

'*Ma, certo,*' Di Domenico said, spreading his hands wide the way Patricia had seen Henry Armetta do in an old black-and-white movie on television. '*Subito,* Detective Weeks!'

'This is so nice of you, really,' Patricia said.

'But we can't eat too much,' Ollie said. 'Because zee clock, she is ticking.'

Patricia looked puzzled.

'The movie starts at seven-forty-five,' he explained.

'Ah,' she said. 'Well, I don't eat much, anyway.'

'Ah, but I do,' Ollie said. 'And this is very fine Italian food here.'

'I should have dressed more elegantly,' she said, looking around at the neat little tables with their white tablecloths and the candles burning everywhere and the posters of Italian villages on the walls.

'You are dressed to the nines,' Ollie said.

She was, in fact, wearing tailored brown slacks, and a pumpkin-colored cashmere sweater with a neat little tan jacket over it, and a string of pearls around her throat. Ollie thought she looked beautiful. He looked at his watch.

'Five-thirty-five,' he said.

'Zee clock, she is ticking,' Patricia said.

'I learned that from the smartest man I ever met,' Ollie said.

'Who's that?'

'Henry Daggert. Though, actually, I never met him in person.'

'Is he a cop?'

'No, he's an editor. Though maybe a spook, too.'

'A spy, you mean?'

'CIA, maybe,' Ollie said, nodding.

'Get out!'

'I'm serious. Being an editor might have been just a cover. But he certainly gave me some good advice. To use in my work.'

'On the job, you mean?'

'No. Writing books, I mean.'

'I sure hope you catch that guy.'

'Oh, me, too.'

''Cause if for no other reason, I'd love to read your book.'

'I'd love you to read it. It's called *Report to the*

Commissioner. This cross-dressing hooker named Emilio Herrera stole it, the little prick, excuse my French. I'll get him, though. What he don't realize is zee clock, she is ticking.'

'What's that supposed to mean, anyway?' Patricia asked. 'I mean, as it pertains to writing books?'

'What it means is that a vital element of all good suspense fiction is a ticking clock. Take a truly great master of literature like James Patterson, are you familiar with his uv?'

'His what?'

'His uv. That's French for 'body of work,' an *uv,* they call it.'

'I forgot you were learning languages.'

'Yes, I am.'

'That's so impressive, you have no idea.'

'Patterson always has a ticking clock in his books. If I may quote Henry Daggert, fiction editor and master spy for all I know, "You Must Introduce a Ticking Clock."'

'Introduce it to who?' Patricia asked.

'Introduce it into your story. "You must give your protagonist only a limited amount of time to solve his problem," quote unquote. And to quote once again, "The reader should be regularly reminded of the urgency via Countdown Cues," quote unquote.'

'Gee, I never realized it was so complicated,' Patricia said.

'Ah yes, there are many tricks of the trade,' Ollie assured her, and looked at his watch again. 'Five-forty-one,' he said. 'Shall I get menus?'

Patricia waggled her eyebrows.

'Zee clock, she is ticking,' she said.

A HUGE POSTER of Tamar Valparaiso standing spread-legged in her torn and tattered 'Bandersnatch' costume was in each front window of Lorelei Records on St. John's Avenue. The poster did not show the actual beast attacking her, but its frumious shadow fell over her body, the jaws and claws threatening by implication. Scattered everywhere around each of the framed posters were stacks of the jewel-boxed CDs containing the title song and the album itself.

The manager was a black man named Angus Held.

Tall and narrow, he was wearing black jeans, a black sports shirt, and a gray sweater with a shawl collar when he came out of his office at the back of the shop. He knew why they were there; they had called ahead.

'Is Cal in some kind of trouble?' he asked at once.

Same thing he'd asked on the phone.

Same thing they always asked.

This time, they played it straight.

'He's broken parole,' Carella said.

'Didn't even know he was *on* parole,' Held said, shaking his head.

'When's the last time you saw him?' Hawes asked.

'When he left the job. Middle of April, must've been. Right around Easter time.'

'Did he say he was going to Jamaica?'

'No. Is that where he went?'

'We don't know where he went,' Carella said. 'We're trying to find him.'

'How long did he work here?' Hawes asked.

'Started just before Christmas. Comes and goes with the holidays, seems like. What was he in jail for?'

'A bank holdup.'

'Whoo,' Held said.

'Did he give you any trouble while he was here?'

'None at all. You say he was on parole, huh?'

267

'That's right.'

'Can't understand why he broke it. Had himself a good job here.'

'What'd he do?'

'Worked in the stock room. This is a good location, we do lots of volume here. Wonder why he broke parole.'

Carella was wondering the same thing. Wilkins left a job as a dishwasher, got a better job here, you'd think he'd run to his parole officer and ask for a medal. Instead, he absconds. To do what? Kidnap Tamar Valparaiso? Whose picture was now in both front windows?

'Mind if we talk to some of the people in your stock room?' Hawes asked.

'I'll take you back,' Held said.

THERE WERE three people in the Lorelei stock room. One was Hispanic, one was Asian, one was black. Only the Asian guy had known Wilkins while he was still working here.

'Quiet type,' he said.

Which was what most of them said about people who'd committed crimes of violence.

'Kept mostly to himself.'

Which is what they also said.

'Can't imagine him doing anything wrong.'

Ho-hum, Carella thought.

'Did he mention why he was quitting the job?' Hawes asked.

'Said he had bigger plans.'

'Like what?'

'Said he was going to retire to Jamaica.'

Jamaica again.

'Did he say how he planned to do that?'

'Nossir, he did not.'

'Mention any get-rich-quick scheme?'

'Nossir. I told you. He kept mostly to himself.'

'Ever see him with a redheaded girl and a . . .'

'Nope.'

'. . . guy about my height?' Carella said. 'They might've been friends of his. Brown eyes, curly black hair, good build.'

'Sounds almost like Ave.'

'Ave? Who's Ave?'

'Avery, I guess was his complete name. Feller worked outside selling records. I saw them together a few times.'

'Avery *what?*' Hawes asked.

'**AVERY HANES,**' the manager told them. 'He used to work at The Wiz, selling computers and such. I hired him last year around this time.'

'We understand he was friends with Wilkins.'

'I guess maybe so. They'd talk music together all the time. Avery knew every record ever made. Always coming to me with ideas about how we could sell more records. Was him who suggested we put in the listening booths. I was about to give him a raise when he left. Come to think of it, they both left around the same time. Around Easter.'

'Maybe something bigger came along,' Carella suggested.

'Maybe so. He was opportunistic, that's for sure.'

'How do you mean?'

'Oh, alert to possibilities. I'd hear him talking with customers, not just the usual do you like jazz, do you dig hip-hop, are you a Tony Bennett fan? He'd inquire what line of work they were in, were they musicians, were they in advertising, were they in publishing? I had the feeling he was looking for a better job. Didn't want to sell records all his life, was all the time *trawling,* you know whut I mean, *trawling?*'

'Yes, sir,' Carella said. 'I know what you mean.'

'So maybe he hooked something,' Held said.

'Maybe he did,' Carella said.

'You wouldn't happen to have his address, would you?' Hawes asked.

IF CARELLA and Hawes had walked around the corner from Lorelei Records on St. John's Avenue at precisely five past seven that evening, they'd have seen first a black Lincoln Town car pulling out of the garage under the Rio Building, and next two unmarked Mercury sedans behind it. Barney Loomis was at the wheel of the limo. Corcoran was sitting beside him, a dispatch case with $750,000 in new hundred-dollar bills on his lap. Endicott and Lonigan were in the lead Mercury, the blue one. Feingold and Jones were in the white Mercury behind it. The rest of The Squad was back at Number One Fed, manning the computers. This time, they were playing it their way. This time, the Joint Task Force had every intention of winning the horse race the Commissioner had created.

Carella and Hawes did not walk around the corner to the building in which Bison Records had its offices. Nor did either of the men connect the proximity of Lorelei Records to the company not a hundred yards away on Monroe Street.

Instead, while the caravan made its way south through the last of the evening's rush-hour traffic, the detectives drove in the opposite direction toward 8412 Winston Road, which was the last address the manager of Lorelei Records had for Avery Hanes.

It was beginning to get dark.

13.

THE CELL PHONE in Barney Loomis' Lincoln Town car rang at precisely seven-fifteen P.M. By that time he and Corcoran were on the River Dix Drive heading downtown in thinning traffic. Loomis picked up at once.

'Hello?'

'Where are you?' Avery asked.

'On the Drive. Approaching the Headley Building. Exit 12.'

'Get off at Exit 5, park in the little parking area there. I'll call you again in ten minutes. Any tricks and the girl dies,' Avery said, and hung up.

'What?' Corcoran asked.

'Exit 5 parking area. He'll call again when we're there.'

Corcoran was on his own phone at once.

'He said any tricks . . .'

'Yeah, well, we have a few tricks of our own,' Corcoran said.

'Endicott.'

'He's taking us to Exit 5. The parking area there. Why don't one of you get there before us? Keep circling, low profile.'

'Will do,' Endicott said.

'He said he'd kill Tamar if we tried any tricks,' Loomis said.

'What he considers tricks is not what we consider tricks,' Corcoran said. 'Do you want the girl back, or don't you?'

'That's *all* I want.'

'Well, the only way to get her is to get these guys first.'

'That's not my view.'

'We tried your way already, Mr. Loomis. And you got double-crossed. Leave this to people who know what they're doing, okay?'

'Tamar is with a confederate, you know that. If we try anything funny . . .'

'Let me tell you something, Mr. Loomis, okay? Tamar Valparaiso . . .'

'I don't want to hear . . .'

'. . . may already be dead.'

'**OH JESUS,**' Kellie said.

She had just entered the room, and the first thing she saw was blood.

She closed the door behind her, went swiftly to where Tamar lay huddled near the radiator, her hand still cuffed to it, her wrist torn and caked with blood where she had tried to pull the hand free. Her nose was crusted with blood as well, her lips swollen, her eyes puffed and discolored. There was blood on her thighs and higher up on her legs.

'Oh, baby, what did he do to you?' Kellie asked, and put the rifle down on the floor, and took Tamar's free hand in her own.

'**YOU GONNA** not talk to me forever?' Cal asked.

'Just shut up, you freak,' Avery told him. 'Soon as we get this money, you're history.'

'She asked for it,' Cal said. 'Wasn't my fault what happened.'

'I said shut up. You jeopardized this whole deal. This whole deal was we send her back safe. You wrecked her looks, you fucked up the whole deal, you fuckin moron.'

'He'll bring the money, anyway. He don't know what she looks like, all he knows is we got her. He don't know nothin happened to her. He'll bring the seven-fifty, you'll see, and we're on our way.'

'Just keep quiet, I'm not interested in anything you have to say.'

Avery looked at his watch.

It was seventeen minutes past seven.

THE SUPERINTENDENT of the building at 8412 Winston Road told them his name was Ralph Hedrings. Hawes thought he'd said 'Ralph Headrinse.' That was okay because Hedrings thought Hawes had said 'Detective Horse.' When they got there at seven-twenty, the super was still at dinner. He didn't particularly enjoy being interrupted by a pair of detectives looking for someone who'd moved out last month. Particularly someone who Hedrings considered had a superior attitude. But he asked his wife to keep his 'supper' warm, was what he called it, and then stepped outside the building with them and lit a cigarette.

'She doesn't know I still smoke,' he explained, letting out a self-satisfied poisonous cloud. 'Her brother had his larynx removed last month, she thinks everybody in the world's gonna get throat cancer now. I been smoking since I was sixteen, I don't even cough. Why are you looking for Avery Hanes?'

'Few questions we need to ask him,' Carella said. 'Would you know where . . . ?'

'Him and his girlfriend were living here for almost a year. All of a sudden, he tells me he's moving when the lease expired.'

'When was that, Mr. Hedrings?'

'April one,' Hedrings said.

273

'Any idea where he went?'

'None at all.'

'And you say he was living here with his girlfriend?'

'Redheaded girl.'

'Would you know her name?'

'Kellie. With an *i.e.*'

'Kellie what?'

'Don't know. He was the one signed the lease.'

So now they had three names.

Or, more accurately, two and a half names.

JUST AS LOOMIS pulled the town car off Exit 5, he spotted the blue Mercury with Endicott and Lonigan in it driving past the parking lot as though looking for an address somewhere on the street, cruising slowly, stop-and-go-ing. He pulled the car into the lot, and sat there, looking out over the wheel at the headlights zipping by on the Drive. Sitting beside him, Corcoran said into his phone, 'We're here. See anything yet?'

'Nothing,' Endicott said.

The car's cell phone rang a moment later.

It was seven-twenty-six P.M. on the dashboard clock.

'WHERE are you?' Avery asked.

'Off Exit 5,' Loomis said.

'Take a left onto Fairlane. Drive downtown to the Grace Wagner School of Design on Cronley. Park in front of the statue there. No tricks.'

There was a click on the line.

'What'd he say?'

'The Wagner School of Design on Cronley. Wants us to park in front of the statue there.'

Corcoran tapped a button on the face of his cell phone.

'Endicott.'

274

'Heading downtown to Cronley, Wagner School of Design. He wants us to park there. Check out the building. Careful, they may be watching, same as before.'

'Moving,' Endicott said.

'He told me no tricks,' Loomis said.

Corcoran merely nodded.

'IS THIS PICTURE a mystery or something?' Ollie asked.

'No, not at all,' Patricia said. 'It's Shakespeare, I told you.'

'Because it's called *Looking for Richard,* you know,' Ollie said, 'which sounds like a sort of mystery, doesn't it?'

'Maybe so.'

'Like a missing person or something, you know?'

They were sitting watching commercials on the screen, eating popcorn and waiting for the movie to start. Ollie had bought two big cartons of popcorn with extra butter, and two Diet Pepsis because a person couldn't be too careful, and two big bars of Hershey's chocolate with almonds in case Patricia was still hungry after she finished her popcorn. It bothered him that he had to sit here and watch commercials for restaurants and clothing stores, as if he hadn't paid for the tickets and was getting something free.

It also bothered him that he didn't know *exactly* what this movie was about. If it was about a missing person, he'd had some experience along those lines, you know, and could relate to the movie more easily. But if it was about Shakespeare, the way Patricia said it was, then why had they named it *Looking for Richard,* which made it sound as if somebody had been kidnapped or something?

'Are you sure this is going to be Shakespeare?' he asked her.

'Oh yes,' she said. 'It's about doing *Richard the Third*.'

'Ah-*ha!*' he said. 'It *is* a mystery!'

'It is?'

'You just said it's about doing Richard the Third.'

'Oh. I didn't mean "doing" in that sense. I meant performing the play. Doing *Richard the Third*.'

'So why are they calling it *Looking for Richard* if there's no ticking clock?' he asked. Reminded, he looked at his watch. It was seven-forty-three and the movie was scheduled to start at seven-forty-five. So where was it? Why did they have to sit here watching a commercial for an antiques store, as if anyone would want to buy old used furniture and stuff?

'I'm really excited about seeing this again,' Patricia said, and suddenly reached over for his hand and squeezed it.

'Me, too,' Ollie said dubiously.

His hand was sticky with butter.

Which was okay because her hand was, too.

THE GRACE WAGNER School of Design had once been called William Howard Taft High School, after the twenty-seventh President of the United States. Back then, it was a so-called academic high school, which meant that its students took subjects to qualify them for college entrance. But that was the good old days.

Nowadays, it was a vocational high school for kids looking for easy entrée to the world of high fashion. If you could maintain a C-average and draw a straight line, you were admitted to Grace Wagner, which incidentally had been named after a woman who'd served on the Board of Education and played flute.

A bronze statue that looked like a huge bolt of lightning striking an oversized soccer ball stood on the patchy front lawn of the school. By the time Loomis pulled the Lincoln up in front of the statue, Endicott and Lonigan had already driven twice around the school's surrounding blocks. They had seen no one suspicious lurking about, but there was a light burning in one of the school's top-floor windows, and they thought they'd seen shadows moving past.

Endicott reported this to Corcoran now.

'May be using the same M.O. they did in The Wasteland,' Corcoran suggested. 'Take the high ground, cover the area through binocs.'

'I'll wait for the second car to show,' Endicott said. 'We'll go in the back way, try to surprise them up there.'

'Don't do anything to jeopardize the girl's safety,' Corcoran warned.

Loomis figured this was for his benefit.

Besides, his phone was ringing.

'HELLO?' he said.

'We see you,' Avery said. 'Get out of the car, both of you. Leave the money on the back seat. Leave the car unlocked with the keys in the ignition. Walk toward the school entrance. Now! Do it *now!*' he said, and hung up.

'He wants us to leave the money and get out of the car. He wants us to walk toward the school. Wants it unlocked with the keys in it.'

Corcoran stabbed at his cell phone.

'Endicott.'

'They're trying an end run,' he shouted. 'Get around to the front of the school! *Quick!*'

'What?' Endicott said.

The car phone rang again.

Loomis picked up.

'Yes?' he said.

'I said *now!*' Avery said, and hung up.

'Let's go!' Loomis said. *'Please!'*

Both men got out of the car. Corcoran looked up the street, to where he could see a green SUV moving swiftly toward the parked Lincoln.

'Here they come!' he said, and reached under his jacket into his shoulder holster.

'Don't!' Loomis shouted.

IT ALL HAPPENED so fast that later none of the agents or detectives could reconstruct it in proper sequence. It was rather like one of those movies directed by someone fresh out of film school, with jump cuts and flash forwards and four or five stories unreeling at the same time.

The first story was Barney Loomis wetting his pants the moment all those guns opened fire. Actually, there was only one gun at first, and it was in the right hand of Detective-Lieutenant Charles Farley Corcoran and he opened fire the moment the two men got out of what he now could see was a green Montana, and climbed into the black town car waiting at the curb in front of Grace Wagner. The Lincoln's engine roared into life an instant later, and the car pulled away from the curb just as its rear window slid down and a second gun opened up, a rifle this time spewing automatic fire, which is when Loomis wet his pants because he could actually hear bullets whizzing past his right ear.

The two Mercurys came around the corner at that very moment, Endicott and Lonigan in the lead car, Feingold and Jones in the second. Corcoran had sprinted to the curb by then, and was flagging down the blue Merc. Loomis had thrown himself flat to the ground the way he'd seen them do in better movies than this one, even though there were no bullets flying at the moment.

At the moment, in fact, and even before Corcoran

jumped into the blue Merc like somebody about to yell 'Follow that car!' the black Lincoln Town car had raced out of sight like the *Enterprise* zooming off into a star-filled void.

Where it was zooming off to was a spot a mile away, where they had parked the very last of the stolen cars.

THEY HAD LEFT 8412 Winston Road in Calm's Point at seven-thirty, had encountered heavy traffic coming over the bridge, and did not get back to the squadroom till a minute past eight. A minute after that, Carella was calling the number he had for telephone company Special Assistance.

The Joint Task Force's hi-tech triangulation had ended in something like strangulation, and their Trap-and-Trace routine had proved futile in the face of stolen and disposable cell phones. So it got down to a weary detective sitting behind a cigarette-scarred desk in a grimy squadroom making a good old-fashioned phone call. In many ways the good old telephone company was always reliable if not always courteous. Even dealing with a so-called Special Operator assigned to helping law enforcement agencies working so-called important cases, the civility level was barely acceptable.

'Here's what we're looking for,' Carella told a woman named Miss Young. She had no first name. Just Miss Young. 'We've got an Avery Hanes living at 8412 Winston Road in Calm's Point, for the year prior to this April first. And we've got . . .'

'Was that Winston as in Winston cigarettes?' Miss Young asked.

'As in Winston Churchill, yes,' Carella said. 'And we've got a man named Calvin Wilkins, living at 379 Parrish Place in Calm's Point, from just before

Thanksgiving to around the same time, April first. That's Parrish with a double-R.'

'And what is it you're seeking, Detective?'

'List of phone calls made from each of those numbers in March. I want phone numbers, names and addresses.'

'You'll need a court order for that.'

'That's not my understanding. We're not looking to put a pen register on those lines. In fact, the numbers are probably no longer in service. All I want is the numbers called and the names and addresses of the parties called. I'm sure you have those. If for billing purposes alone.'

'It's my understanding that a court order . . .'

'Miss, we're dealing with a kidnapping here. Any assistance you can give us . . .'

'One moment, please,' Miss Young said.

Carella waited.

'Miss Cole,' another voice said. 'How may I help you, sir?'

Carella told her how she might help him.

'We'll need a court order for that,' she said.

'There's a certain urgency here,' Carella said.

'I'm sorry, sir.'

'I'll get back to you,' he said, and hung up.

It was now five minutes past eight. It would take him forty minutes to get downtown and another forty minutes to shake a judge out of a tree at that hour. By then, Tamar Valparaiso might be dead. He picked up the phone and dialed the number he had for the Joint Task Force downtown.

'Task Force,' a voice said.

'This is Carella,' he said. 'Who's this?'

'Special Agent Jakes.'

'I need some help, Jakes.'

*

280

THEY PULLED THE Lincoln in alongside and slightly to the rear of the Grand Cherokee Laredo they'd parked there earlier today. Cal threw up the hood of the Jeep and jump-started the vehicle. They were on their way again in three minutes flat, leaving the Lincoln with the key in the ignition in a neighborhood where 'Your Money or Your Life' was a nursery rhyme. Avery figured if they had a little luck with traffic, they'd be at the beach house in half an hour or so. Then they'd return the girl and that was that.

End of story.

They never once considered the fact that an armed and dangerous person was in that house, and she was only twenty-four years old, and she had never in her life fired an AK-47.

'**DETECTIVE** Carella?'

'Yes?'

'This is Miss Cole again.'

Carella looked at the clock on the squadroom wall. The time was eight-fifteen.

'I just got a call from an FBI agent named Randall Jakes,' Miss Cole said. 'He faxed me a copy of a court order that would seem to cover the request you made. Do you have a fax machine there?'

He gave her the fax number.

Five minutes later, he had on his desk two separate lists of the calls Avery Hanes and Calvin Wilkins had made from their respective telephones during the month of March. Not surprisingly, many of the calls had been from Hanes to Wilkins or vice versa. From Wilkins' number, there were half a dozen calls to Air Jamaica and American Airlines. From Hanes' number there were a dozen or more calls to American, British Air, Virgin Atlantic, Delta, and Air France. There were calls to Capshaw Boats, the marina from which they'd rented the Rinker presumably used in the kidnapping. There were calls to a person named Benjamin Lu, whoever he might turn out to be. Almost every day in March, Hanes had called a party listed only as 'Unpublished.' An asterisk at the top of the page explained: 'AT THE CUSTOMER'S REQUEST, THIS NUMBER IS UNPUBLISHED.' In the month of March, Hanes had also made seven calls to a real estate agent in Russell County.

Carella pulled the phone to him and began dialing again.

BY EIGHT-TWENTY-SEVEN, he had dialed the number for Margaret Holmes Realty twice, on the off chance she'd been down the hall the first time. Concluding that she was closed for business at this hour, he dialed Information and told the operator he wanted a residential listing for a Margaret Holmes, as in Sherlock Holmes, in the town of South Beach, which was where the real estate office was located. The operator came back to say she had no listing under that name. He asked her to try all the towns in Russell County, and she said she couldn't do that, she needed a specific town. He told her he was a police officer investigating a kidnapping, and she asked him to wait while she put a supervisor on the line. The supervisor told him he had to have a specific town, did he know how many towns there were in Russell County? It was eighty-thirty-three when Carella once again dialed the number he had for Special Assistance and asked for Miss Cole.

'I already *faxed* you those numbers,' she said. 'Didn't you get them?'

'Yes, I got them, Miss Cole,' he said, 'and thank you so much for your assistance,' turning on the charm and wondering if he should read a little T. S. Eliot to her. 'Miss

282

Cole, I wonder if you can help me here again,' he said. 'I need a home number for a Margaret Holmes, as in Sherlock Holmes, somewhere in Russell County, I don't have a specific town, do you think you can help me? I would so appreciate it.'

'Hmm,' Miss Cole said.

But then she said, 'One moment, please.'

THE NUMBER Miss Cole gave him rang four times before someone picked up.

'Hello?' a woman said.

'Miss Holmes?'

'*Mrs.* Holmes, yes?'

'This is Detective Carella of the Eighty-seventh Squad? In the city?'

'Yes, Detective?'

'Are you the Margaret Holmes who runs Margaret Holmes Realty in South Beach?'

'I am,' she said.

'Mrs. Holmes, we have an Avery Hanes calling you some six times this past month. Is that name familiar to you?'

'It is.'

Carella took a deep breath.

'Did you rent or sell anything to him?' he asked.

'I rented him a house on the beach,' she said. 'Why? What's he done?'

THE PLAN WAS to drop the girl off just anyplace. Give her some change to make a phone call, let her find her own way home, she was a big girl now. That was the way Ave had explained the plan to her.

They'd drop the girl off just anywhere on their way to the airport. Cal was supposed to be going to Jamaica, but

283

they didn't care where he went, they didn't care if they ever saw him again as long as they lived. Ave was heading for London first, while Kellie herself flew to Paris where he would meet her later. It was a swell plan. Paris. Lah-dee-dah.

There was only one problem.

The girl had seen Kellie's face.

Tamar Valparaiso still didn't know who was behind those Saddam Hussein and Yasir Arafat masks, but she sure as hell knew that George W. Bush was a redheaded Irish girl with green eyes and freckles.

'You know,' Kellie confided now, 'we're supposed to set you free as soon as they get back.'

'Promises, promises,' Tamar said.

'No, really. That's the plan. We leave here and drop you off someplace.'

'That would be nice,' Tamar said.

'Well, that's the plan.'

'Good,' Tamar said.

She ached all over. Her face, her body, everywhere he'd hit her, but especially below, where he'd brutally entered her. Cal, she thought. His name is Cal. And the other one is Ave. You'll pay, boys.

'You saw my face,' Kellie said out of the blue.

Tamar looked at her.

'You know what's behind this mask.'

'Well, don't worry . . .'

'You know what I look like.'

'You don't have to worry about that,' Tamar said. 'Really, you've been good to me. I wouldn't do anything to hurt you.'

'Because I wouldn't want to lose all this, you know,' Kellie said reasonably.

'You don't have to worry, really.'

'We worked hard for this,' she said reasonably.

'I know you did. But, really, you don't have to . . .'

'You can describe me.'

'I hardly remember . . .'

'You know what I look like,' Kellie said again.

'Lots of girls look like . . .'

'Lots of girls didn't kidnap you,' Kellie said, and raised the AK-47 onto her hip.

'Don't . . . just be careful with that thing, okay?' Tamar said and reached out with her free hand.

Kellie backed away a pace.

The rifle was on single-shot. She fired three times. Two bullets entered Tamar's face just below the left eye, and the other took her just below the nose. The three shots blew off the back of her skull and splashed gristle and blood all over the radiator behind her.

Wow, Kellie thought.

14.

IT WAS eighty-forty-five on the squadroom clock.

'The address is 64 Beachside,' Carella told the detective in the South Beach Police Department. 'There may be a kidnap victim there, so proceed with extreme caution.'

Out there in Russell County, they used more paramilitary rank designations than they did here in the big bad city. Detective-Sergeant James Cody asked if there was likely to be anyone armed and dangerous in that house.

Carella said, 'Yes, that's likely.'

'We'll be careful then,' Cody said.

There was no need.

The only person in that house was a dead girl chained to a radiator.

Everyone else had driven off five minutes ago.

MISS COLE was getting used to phone calls from Detective Stephen Louis Carella.

'Yes, Detective?' she said almost cheerfully.

'Miss Cole, I'm sorry to bother you again . . .'

'Oh, it's no bother at all,' she said.

'On this list of calls made from those two addresses I gave you . . .'

'Yes, Detective?'

Almost cooing the words.

'There were almost daily calls listed to an unpublished number. Now, I know it's telephone company policy not to reveal . . .'

'Don't be ridiculous,' she said. 'This is a kidnapping. Just give me a minute.'

She came back in three.

'All those calls were made to the same party,' she said.

'And who was that, Miss Cole?'

'A man named Barney Loomis,' she said. 'At 583 South Thompson. Is that helpful to you, Detective?'

'**THEY HANDED US** a beaut,' Detective-Sergeant James Cody told the County Medical Examiner.

It was five minutes past nine that Tuesday night and the house at 64 Beachside was swarming with men wearing blue windbreakers, the word 'POLICE' lettered in yellow across their backs. The dead girl was in one of the bedrooms. Her wrist was still handcuffed to the radiator.

'Christ, look what they did to her,' the ME said.

Cody nodded. 'Can't find the key anyplace,' he said. 'We were waiting for you to get here, see do you want us to saw through the cuffs or what. I figure they got out of here in one hell of a hurry. Left her behind all chained up that way.'

There were three spent cartridge cases on the floor, presumably spewed from the murder weapon.

'Shot her in the face at close range,' Cody said.

'Looks like,' the ME said.

The equivalent of South Beach's Crime Scene Unit was busy dusting for prints and vacuuming for fibers and hair. One of the technicians glanced toward the dead girl and muttered, 'Fuckin animals.'

In one of the other bedrooms, they found three masks. Saddam Hussein, Yasir Arafat, and George W. Bush.

'Three of the world's great leaders,' Cody said dryly.

Just about then, Detectives Carella and Hawes were knocking on the door to Apartment 22C at 583 South Thompson.

AT NINE-FORTY-FIVE that night, just as Air France's flight #23 for Paris was about to take off, Ollie and Patricia came out of the movie theater into a fairly decent rain. He took off his jacket, and over her protests draped it over her shoulders.

'You'll get all *wet!*' she told him.

'Tut tut,' he said. 'Would you care to go for some pizza?'

Patricia said she wasn't hungry, but she'd be happy to join him.

Over his third slice, he told her he had learned a lot from that movie.

'Like what?' she asked.

'Like it ain't only about a ticking clock,' Ollie said.

CARELLA DID NOT learn that Tamar Valparaiso was dead until he and Hawes got back to the squadroom with Barney Loomis in tow. It was now ten o'clock. Flight #23 for Charles de Gaulle airport had been in the air for ten minutes already, and Avery Hanes was waiting in British Air's lounge to board flight #82 to London's Heathrow. Sergeant Murchison behind the muster desk told them that Mr. Loomis' attorney was waiting in the lieutenant's office.

'Also, you got a call from a Detective Cody out at South Beach,' he said, and handed Carella a folded message.

Carella glanced at it briefly.

'Want to take Mr. Loomis to his lawyer?' he asked Hawes, and then went to his own desk and immediately called the Joint Task Force, grateful when they put him through to Endicott rather than Corcoran.

'Stan,' he said, 'the girl is dead. I just heard from the

South Beach Police, she was being held in a house out there. All three of the perps are gone. I've got full names for two of them, and a given name for the third. They made calls to Air Jamaica, British Air, Air France, American, Virgin Atlantic, and Delta. You've got better ties to Homeland Security than we do, maybe you can flash their names on the airport computers here and across the river. I've got Barney Loomis in custody, I think he was an accomplice . . .'

'Wait a minute, *wait* a minute! Barney *Loomis?*'

'One of the perps called his home number every day in March.'

'You've been busy,' Endicott said dryly.

'Can you cover the airports?'

'What are those names you've got?' Endicott said.

BARNEY LOOMIS' attorney was a man named Roger Halliday. He'd been watching *The West Wing* on television when Loomis called from his apartment. Balding and a trifle portly, he'd come to the squadroom in a dark blue business suit and tie, looking more like a banker than any criminal lawyer the detectives knew. Actually, he was a skilled corporate attorney, and it never occurred to him that he might be out of his league here.

'Is my client being charged with something?' he asked.

'Not yet, Mr. Halliday,' Hawes said. 'We'd just like to ask him some questions.'

'He doesn't have to answer any questions, you know that.'

'Yes, we know that.'

'Has he been read his rights? The man's under arrest here, have you yet . . . ?'

'We read them to him in his apartment,' Carella said.

'Read them to him again now,' Halliday said.

Carella read Loomis his rights again.

Halliday looked bored.

'So what do you want to do?' he asked Loomis. 'You don't have to answer any questions if you don't want to. My advice is you ask them either to charge you or let you go. Even if they charge you, you don't have to answer any questions. This is America, don't forget.'

'Charge me with what?' Loomis asked. 'I haven't done anything.'

'Why don't you just satisfy our curiosity, Mr. Loomis?' Carella said. 'Answer a few questions for us, okay?'

'No, I don't think so,' Loomis said.

TWO HOMELAND SECURITY agents boarded British Air's flight #82 ten minutes before it was scheduled to take off for London. They found Avery Hanes in the first-class section, where he was already enjoying a scotch and soda, and they asked him if he would mind accompanying them off the aircraft. Since they were both armed, he said he wouldn't mind at all.

Fifteen minutes later, he ratted out Barney Loomis, and told them they could find Calvin Wilkins in American Airline's first-class lounge. He also told them that his girlfriend Kellie Morgan would be landing in Paris at eleven-fifteen tomorrow morning.

Wilkins' flight to Jamaica was not scheduled to leave until seven A.M. tomorrow morning. He was curled up asleep on one of the lounge's sofas when they shook him awake. Looking up into what appeared to be nine-millimeter weapons, he said, 'Oh shit.'

WHEN NELLIE BRAND got to the squadroom at close to eleven, she was still wearing the long green gown and green satin slippers she'd worn to the annual May Cotillion at the River Dix Yacht Club, to which she and her husband belonged. She was also wearing a mink stole, and a jade necklace her husband had given her this past Christmas, and she looked less like a District Attorney answering a rotation call than a stockbroker's wife who'd been drinking champagne not an hour and a half ago, which she was and which she had been.

Carella took her aside and told her what he had.

'That's purely circumstantial,' she said. 'Is that why you dragged me all the way up here?'

'I think it'll wash.'

'I don't. Guy could've called him for any one of a thousand reasons besides criminal chicanery.'

'How'd he happen to know him? How'd he get his home number?'

'How do I know? Having a person's home number doesn't add up to kidnapping.'

'The girl's dead, Nellie. This is now a death penalty case.'

'Where are these people with whom he allegedly conspired?'

'Flew the coop.'

'That's nice. And you say they left a dead girl behind?'

'Yes.'

'This singer I've been seeing all over television?'

'That's the one.'

'Very high profile, Steve. You'd better be right.'

'What can we lose?' Carella said. 'Let's give it a shot.'

'I must be out of my mind,' Nellie said.

THE Q AND A started at a quarter past eleven.

It had been a long Tuesday for everyone in that room. Well, everyone except maybe the police stenographer, who took down every word as Loomis was read his rights for the third time, and then advised that he did not have to answer any questions if he chose not to . . .

'I choose not to,' he said.

'In which case,' Nellie said, 'we'll be charging you with Conspiracy to Commit Kidnapping . . .'

'That's ridiculous,' Halliday said.

'. . . and Kidnapping itself, which is an A-1 Felony . . .'

'You truly can't be serious, young lady.'

'Oh but I am, Counselor. Under the laws of this state, your client acted in concert, and it doesn't matter whether he was a principal or an accomplice . . .'

'A Grand Jury will kick this out in five minutes!'

'We'll see, I guess,' Nellie said. 'You think they'll also kick out Felony Murder?'

'Murder?' Loomis said.

'Murder during a kidnapping,' Nellie said. 'The same thing as Murder One.'

'What do you mean *murder?*' Loomis asked. 'Did they *kill* Tamar? Are you saying they *killed* her?'

'She was shot in the face at close range with a high-powered rifle,' Carella said.

'That wasn't the *deal!*' Loomis shouted, and suddenly he was sobbing into his hands.

I LOVED THAT GIRL as if she was my own daughter, he told them. The deal was they'd hold her till the ransom was paid, and then they'd let her go. They weren't supposed to hurt her, they certainly weren't supposed to . . . to . . .

And here he buried his face in his hands and began sobbing again.

Halliday took this opportunity to remind him that he was not compelled to say anything.

Loomis kept sobbing into his hands.

'Mr. Loomis?' Nellie said.

He just kept sobbing.

'Would you like to tell us what happened?' she said softly.

She was skilled at such things.

Loomis nodded into his hands.

Halliday shook his head.

I MAKE A HABIT of stopping in record stores, checking on how our product is displayed, what kind of space we're getting, all that. I normally introduce myself to the manager, sometimes to the floor personnel, tell them I'm the CEO of Bison Records, explain how much this or that CD or album means to me, ask them to keep a personal eye on it. I love every record we put out. Every one of them. I love this business. I love music.

I knew Tamar was going to be a big star the minute I heard her for the first time. She could bang out a song like Cher, or hoot and holler like Steven Tyler. She could bend notes like the best blues and country singers, or break and yodel like Alanis Morissette. And sweet! Oh Jesus, what a *sweet* wonderful voice! She could break your heart with the simplest ballad. Like an angel. She sang like an angel.

Every store I went into, I told them to watch out for Tamar Valparaiso.

I told them Tamar Valparaiso was going to be the next big singing sensation.

THIS KID WORKED in the shop just around the corner from our office. I used to stop in there after lunch almost every day. Just before I went back upstairs. Lorelei Records. I checked out the product, the displays, told this kid what was hot for us this week . . .

Avery Hanes.

That's his name.

Told him what was coming down the pike, what he should be on the lookout for. Tamar Valparaiso, I told him. Coming in May. The album is called *Bandersnatch*. That's the title song, 'Bandersnatch.' Watch for it. We'll be doing a terrific video. Watch for it. Tamar Valparaiso.

One day . . .

Q: Is Avery Hanes the person who made the ransom calls?

A: Yes.

Q: Is Avery Hanes the person who actually kidnapped Tamar Valparaiso?

A: Well, not alone. He wasn't working alone. I gave him all the information about the launch, and he told me he thought he could do it with just three people. Himself and two other people.

Q: Who were these two other people?

A: I have no idea.

Q: Do the names . . . excuse me. Steve, what were those names again?

A: (from Detective Carella) Calvin Wilkins and Kellie Something, we don't have a last name for her.

Q: Do those names mean anything to you, Mr. Loomis?

A: Nothing at all.

Q: So the only person you dealt with was Avery Hanes.

A: Yes.

Q: Was the kidnapping his idea?

A: Well, it sort of evolved.

Q: How do you mean?

A: From talks we had. We discussed all sorts of approaches, he's really a quite brilliant young man. Primarily, I was concerned with how to make the debut album a success. I had such faith in Tamar, I wanted so much for her to make it in a big way . . .

Avery didn't care how he spent my money, of course, well, you know how young people are, nothing's impossible to them. All these big ideas about massive in-store promos, and TV ads, and subway posters, and ads on the sides of busses, ten cities, twenty cities, a hundred cities! He was talking about millions in advertising and promotion alone, a prohibitive approach, really, on top of everything else we'd be doing.

At first, we met in my office. He'd come up on his lunch hour, and we'd discuss his ideas. I like to encourage young people, I'm very good with young people. And he was so . . . *enthusiastic,* do you know? One day, he said something about five minutes of fame, fifteen minutes of fame, whatever it was, Andy Warhol's famous saying. He said if only we could do something that could give Tamar just those fifteen minutes of fame, was what it was, then the rest would follow. Like if she broke her leg onstage during a concert . . .

'But she won't be doing any concerts till after the album release,' I told him.

'Or got hit by a bus . . .' he said.

'Oh sure, hit by a bus.'

'Do you remember when this writer Ira Levin wrote a book called *A Kiss Before Dying,* where the last chapter is this girl gets pushed off the roof? Well, right after the book was published this girl in real life fell off a roof someplace in New York, and she had a copy of the god-damn *book* in her pocket! Something like that, you know?'

'Sure, we'll push Tamar off the roof.'

'Come on, Barney . . .'

He was calling me Barney by then.

'. . . I'm talking about something spectacular. Something that will make headlines.'

'Like what?'

'Like she gets smacked around by some goon in a disco . . .'

'No, no.'

'. . . or somebody's stalking her . . .'

'That won't make headlines.'

'. . . or she gets kidnapped or something,' Avery said, and we both looked at each other.

There's that moment, you know?

There's that moment when you realize this is it.

Avery suggested fifty thousand dollars as the ransom, but I said we'd never find anyone to do it for that kind of money, so he said, 'Okay a hundred, how does that sound?' and I said that still sounded too low, one minute he's talking about spending ten million dollars in as many cities, and now he's down to a hundred grand! I told him that would sound phony as hell, and besides, no one would risk a kidnapping for a lousy hundred thousand dollars! So we batted it back and forth until we hit on two-fifty, which was, after all, a quarter of a million dollars, a not unreasonable asking price for someone who was not yet a star.

I don't think he was playing me, do you think he was playing me? I mean, I don't think he knew all along that he was the one who'd be doing the actual kidnapping, I don't think he was bargaining for a higher fee. There was an innocence about Avery . . . well, he double-crossed me later on. But at the time, I think he genuinely was just so enthusiastic about the idea, just *into* it, you know, working with me to find what would sound like a reasonable ransom demand, not too low, not too high, two hundred and fifty thousand dollars had just the right *ring* to it, the way the whole idea seemed absolutely *right*.

But then we faced the reality.

Never mind the fifteen minutes of fame. Who were we going to find who'd risk getting caught doing something as serious as a kidnapping? And who could we trust to keep quiet *if* they got caught? Who could we trust not to say that Barney Loomis of Bison Records had engineered the kidnapping of his own young recording artist?

'You could trust *me,*' Avery said.

I looked at him.

'I'd do it,' he said.

Q: When did you hatch this brilliant scheme?

Little touch of sarcasm there, Carella thought. Be careful, Nellie. He'll spook and tell you to go to hell, no more questions.

Q: Mr. Loomis? When did you and Mr. Hanes decide that he would be the one to carry out the kidnapping scheme?

A: It must have been in March sometime. We set everything in motion in March. That was when he found the house at the beach . . .

Q: The house at the beach?

A: South Beach. He rented a house there. To take Tamar to. He had his team together by then, he told me they were both experienced people, it should go off without a hitch. As a matter of fact, it did. Though I have to tell you I could have killed whoever that was with him on the night of the launch, when he slapped Tamar . . .

Q: The name Calvin Wilkins still doesn't mean anything to you, is that correct?

A: I never heard of him.

Q: And the first name Kellie?

A: No. Whoever it was, the deal was nobody lays a finger on her, Avery knew that. Keep her for forty-eight hours, collect the ransom – which was really his fee for his role in all this – and then let her go safe and sound. That was the deal. He knew all the details of the launch party, I'd provided him with those, he even had a floor plan of the River Princess. It was frightening as hell when they came down those stairs, wasn't it? Did you see the Channel Four tape? It looked real as hell, didn't it?

Q: It was real, Mr. Loomis.

A: Well, certainly. To the observer, it looked real, especially when that idiot hit Tamar's partner with the rifle and then slapped her, I could've killed him. But it was all fake, you see, it was all a hoax, you see. We kept reminding ourselves of that all the time we were planning it. It's a hoax, stupid, it's a hoax.

Q: Yes, but it was real.

A: It only became real when he double-crossed me. Asked for a million instead of the two-fifty we'd agreed upon. Well, sure, he saw what was happening, I'm sure he was glued to that television screen day and night. Tamar had her fifteen minutes of fame, all right, in spades. It worked, you see! She was a diva overnight!

'A dead one,' Nellie said.

And Loomis buried his face in his hands and began sobbing again.

15.

BERT KLING felt uncomfortable because the comic was telling jokes about black people. Even holding hands with Sharyn Cooke, even sitting at a table with her and Artie Brown and his wife, Kling felt uncomfortable. Maybe that was because he was the only white man in the place.

This was a black comedy club uptown in Diamondback, highly recommended by Brown, seconded as a good idea by Sharyn, who now seemed to be enjoying the black comic's interpretation of an addict hitting on his mother for money.

'Like this is the first time the poor woman has heard this hard luck story, you know whut I'm sayin?' the comic asked. 'Mama, I just needs a li'l bread to tide me over till mornin, Mama, I'll pay you back then, I swear on Grandma's grave, may she rest in peace.'

Laughter.

Even from Artie Brown, who'd dealt with a few addicts in his lifetime.

'Same tale he tell her ever time he strung out,' the comic said. 'He Mama s'pose to believe it now. He goan take that money, friens, and shoot it in his arm or sniff it up his nose. He Mama know that! Y'know whut she should give him? A swiff kick in the *bee*-hine!'

Applause now.

'Now whut's all this fuss about this Tamar whutever her name is, some La-tino name? Ain't she never dance with a black man before? She got to know, you dance with a black man, he goan rape you. Now that's it, man. He just goan get all woody in his pants, and he goan rape you. How many of you ladies here has danced with a black man din't get all woody on you? Am I right? You know whut I'm sayin, ladies, don'choo?'

Everybody laughed again.

Kling was not laughing.

Sharyn looked at him.

'What?' she said.

'Nothing,' he said.

'No, what?' she asked again, and squeezed his hand.

He shook his head.

She looked into his eyes.

'Really,' he said. 'Nothing.'

But she knew him.

And it was something.

THEY HAD BEEN sitting in Ollie's car, listening to music and discussing the movie, which he couldn't get over.

'It was so helpful to an emerging artist like myself,' he told Patricia. 'Character,' he said. 'Who'd have thought a person had to worry about character? With all the other things that burden a writer?'

'I'm so glad you enjoyed it,' she said. 'I was so afraid you might not.'

'Hey, just being with you would have been enough,' he said.

They were both silent for a moment.

It was now almost midnight, and the rain had let up, so Patricia suggested that maybe they should call it a night. Ollie got out of the car, and came around to her side to let her out. The rain had driven all the neighborhood gangstas inside, so he didn't have to flash the Glock.

He took her inside her building, and they waited for the elevator together. They both had to report for work at a quarter to eight, but neither of them seemed aware of the late hour.

When the elevator came, Ollie put out his arm to hold the doors open for her.

'Goodnight, Oll,' she said, 'I had a wonderful time.'

'So did I, Patricia.'

'May I take you to dinner this Saturday night?' she asked.

He looked at her.

'Well, you said I should invite you.'

'Ah yes,' Ollie said, doing his world-famous W. C. Fields imitation. 'I would be delighted, m'little chick-adee.'

'Well good then,' she said, and raised herself on tip-toes and kissed him on the mouth.

Smiling, she stepped into the elevator.

She waggled her fingers at him as the doors closed.

She was still smiling.

In the softly falling drizzle, Ollie walked back to his car. Sitting behind the wheel, he closed the door against the rain, and put the key into the ignition.

Then, for some reason he could not quite understand, he put his head on the steering wheel and began weeping.

'I KNOW IT'S LATE,' Hawes said into the telephone.

'What time is it, anyway?'

He looked up at the squadroom clock.

'Almost twelve-thirty,' he said. 'But we just wrapped up here, and . . .'

'Anything I should know?'

'Well, I don't know who's going to release this, us or the Feebs.'

302

'You cracked it,' Honey said.

'Well . . .'

'Come on over,' she said. 'We'll discuss it here.'

'It's not too late?'

'I don't have to be in till six tomorrow night.'

'Me, neither,' Hawes said. 'Quarter to eight, in fact. Should I come over?'

'Sure,' she said. 'This might turn into a scoop.'

'It very well might.'

'"Boy Detective Cracks Kidnapping Case."'

He visualized her spreading her free hand on the air.

'So . . . uh . . . should I come over?' he asked.

'Must be an echo in this place,' she said.

'Are you hungry?'

'Are you?'

'Shall I bring some sandwiches?'

'If you like.'

'I'll see you soon.'

'I'm here,' she said, and hung up.

TEDDY WAS AWAKE when Carella got home at almost two in the morning. She turned on the bedside lamp, and then opened her arms to him, and he went to her and kissed her, and held her a moment longer before he began undressing. Looking at his face, she knew there was something. Everything this man felt showed on his face. She waited until he was in bed beside her, and then she signed *What is it?*

'He thought I was the weakest link,' Carella said. She was watching his lips. He saw on her face that she hadn't caught it all. Everything this woman felt showed on her face. This time, he signed it.

He thought I was the weakest link.

Who did? she signed.

303

'Barney Loomis,' he said, signing and speaking simultaneously.

I don't know what you mean.

'He asked for me on the case because he thought I'd never in a million years tip to what was going on. He couldn't trust The Squad to be fools . . .'

The Squad?

'The Joint Task Force. So he picked the weakest link. Me. Detective Steve Carella. His insurance policy. To make sure they got away clean.'

Does this mean you cracked it?

'It means we cracked it.'

Then Mr. Loomis made a mistake, didn't he?

'I guess he made a big mistake,' Carella said, and took her in his arms. 'Right from minute one.'

What time do you have to be in tomorrow? she signed.

All Orion/Phoenix titles are available at your local bookshop or from the following address:

Mail Order Department
Littlehampton Book Services
FREEPOST BR535
Worthing, West Sussex, BN13 3BR
telephone 01903 828503, *facsimile* 01903 828802
e-mail MailOrders@lbsltd.co.uk
(Please ensure that you include full postal address details)

Payment can be made either by credit/debit card (Visa, Mastercard, Access and Switch accepted) or by sending a £ Sterling cheque or postal order made payable to *Littlehampton Book Services*.
DO NOT SEND CASH OR CURRENCY.

Please add the following to cover postage and packing

UK and BFPO
£1.50 for the first book, and 50p for each additional book to a maximum of £3.50

Overseas and Eire
£2.50 for the first book plus £1.00 for the second book and 50p for each additional book ordered

BLOCK CAPITALS PLEASE

name of cardholder _____   *delivery address*
                     _____   *(if different from cardholder)*

address of cardholder _____

_____

_____

        postcode _____   *postcode* _____

☐ I enclose my remittance for £ _____

☐ please debit my Mastercard/Visa/Access/Switch (delete as appropriate)

card number [ ][ ][ ][ ][ ][ ][ ][ ][ ][ ][ ][ ][ ][ ][ ][ ]

expiry date [ ][ ][ ][ ]   Switch issue no. [ ][ ]

signature _____

prices and availability are subject to change without notice